# A Canary Girl in Plotlands

Dawn Knox

© Copyright 2024 Dawn Knox

The right of Dawn Knox to be identified as the author of this work is asserted by her in accordance with the Copyright, Designs and Patents Act 1988

All rights reserved. No parts of this publication may be reproduced, stored in a retrieval system, or transmitted in any form or by any means, electronic, mechanical, photocopying, recording or otherwise without prior permission of the copyright owner.

A Record of this Publication is available from the British Library.

ISBN: 9798335085557

This edition is published by Affairs of the Heart

Cover © Fully Booked

Editing – Wendy Ogilvie Editorial Services

To Mum and Dad.
Thank you for believing in me.

# Also by Dawn Knox

**The Great War** – 100 Stories of 100 Words Honouring Those Who Lived and Died 100 Years Ago

**Historical Romance: 18$^{th}$ and 19$^{th}$ Century**

The Duchess of Sydney

The Finding of Eden

The Other Place

The Dolphin's Kiss

The Pearl of Aphrodite

The Wooden Tokens

**Historical Romance: 20$^{th}$ Century**

A Cottage in Plotlands

A Folly in Plotlands

A Canary Girl in Plotlands

A Reunion in Plotlands

**Humorous Quirky Stories:**

The Basilwade Chronicles

The Macaroon Chronicles

The Crispin Chronicles

The Post Box Topper Chronicles

# Chapter One

September 1940

Bethany Anderson kept an eye on Captain Hugh Barnes-Crosier while she carefully ladled vegetable soup into his bowl. His hands were lying in his lap, the fingers lightly laced.

Strong hands.

Capable hands.

Pilot's hands with long fingers that earlier had pinched her bottom as she'd taken his RAF uniform jacket.

She might only be a housemaid, but she would not put up with that sort of behaviour. If his hand should move now, she wondered if she was brave enough to slop hot soup into his lap to stop him.

No, of course, she wasn't.

His companion had frowned and whispered, "Hugh!" in shocked tones when he'd pinched her bottom.

But the captain had merely winked. "What's the matter, old boy? She doesn't mind."

Bethany had not dared tell him that she most definitely *did* mind. She'd set her jaw and narrowed her eyes to slits through which she'd glared at him. Completely unacceptable behaviour for a housemaid towards her employers' guest.

Not that the captain had noticed. He'd already turned his back on her and walked into the dining room. She'd been dismissed and forgotten. His friend had followed with an apologetic glance over his shoulder.

Bethany looked at her employers, Mr and Mrs Richardson, sitting on the opposite side of the table to their two guests. No, she could not – would not – disgrace them. They'd been so good to her. Especially the mistress.

If Mrs Richardson ever discovered what Captain Barnes-Crosier had done, Bethany was sure she'd be angry. Nevertheless, he was Mr Richardson's cousin and any rude behaviour on his part would be accepted because he was family.

Any rude behaviour on hers would not.

Thankfully, the captain's hands remained laced together in his lap, and Bethany served his soup as quickly as she dared, mercifully, without spilling a drop. She moved on to his friend, Dr Matthew Howard. Bethany would have no problem with him. He was very different from his friend. Yes, Dr Howard appeared to be a serious man, with his dark hair and dark eyes. He was definitely not at ease. But then he'd never been to Priory Hall before; neither had he met the Richardsons. That would be enough for him to feel slightly out of place. Although, if anything, he appeared to be more distracted than awkward.

But his state of mind was none of her business. She was certain each of the four people around the Richardsons' table had enough money to stimulate good cheer if they were downhearted. After serving everyone, she bobbed a curtsy and retreated to the kitchen.

"All right, love?" Cook looked up from dipping a spoon into the sauce and tasting the contents.

Bethany nodded. "Yes, thank you, Mrs Stewart."

"Him with the wandering hands didn't get adventurous again, then?"

"No, he behaved himself."

"Them RAF pilots, they're a law unto themselves." Mrs Stewart clicked her tongue in annoyance. She tasted the sauce for the next course and nodded in approval. "They think they're God's gift, they do. I know we owe them a lot. I mean, if they weren't doing such a good job against the Jerries at the moment, we'd be Heil Hitlering all over the place, I suppose. But some of them pilots need taking down a peg or two. And to think nice Mr Richardson is the captain's cousin. Oh well, you can't choose your family, I suppose…"

She poured the contents of the pan into the sauce boat. "Never mind, love, just a couple of hours and we'll be finished. By the way, don't forget Mrs Richardson wanted you to stay the night if it got late. And it will be late. I can promise you that. Them RAF blokes can drink a normal man under the table and back again. Yes, it'll be a late one. You mark my words."

The thought of finishing work that night did nothing to cheer Bethany. Despite Mrs Richardson's invitation to stay, she knew she'd have to go home.

Pa had gone to the pub earlier. He'd pawned her mother's ring. The one Ma had promised Bethany. The one Pa had sworn to Bethany he'd never part with after her mother's untimely death a few months before.

She swallowed down the bile that always rose to her throat when she remembered the night her mother died. Then – as now – her father had been in the *Coach and Horses*. He would undoubtedly be as drunk tonight as he had been the night Ma had gone into labour and had died along with Bethany's newborn baby brother. Bethany had been the only one there – even at that time – still believing her father had really gone for help as he'd promised. Still believing he'd be back in time.

But on his way for assistance, he'd passed the *Coach and Horses* and had dropped in for a fortifying drink. By the time he'd staggered home many hours later, Bethany had been alone sobbing next to the lifeless, bloody forms of her mother and baby brother.

"They'll be ready for this now, love." Mrs Stewart handed Bethany the tray and jerked her head in the direction of the dining room. "And if 'im with the wandering hands gives you any trouble, let me know." She raised a large saucepan menacingly and winked.

After the meal, Bethany served drinks to her employers and their guests in the drawing room then cleared away the dining table. She helped Cook wash and clean everything, leaving the kitchen tidy for the next day. Or more accurately for later that day, as it was past midnight.

"That's it, love, if you want to go now," said Cook. "And don't forget if you want to stay, there's a bed for you."

Bethany thanked Mrs Stewart and left. It was best she went back to her cottage and made sure her father had found his way there, too. As soon as she was home, she intended to rescue her mother's last remaining necklace from her jewellery box.

Bethany intended to hide it in her secret place under the floorboards, or eventually, like Ma's ring, the necklace would be too tempting for her father to resist. He'd pawn it and drink himself senseless with the proceeds. One day, he'd completely overdo it and drink himself to death.

When Pa found out she'd taken the necklace, he'd be furious. It was in the dressing table in his room, and he'd be angry she'd taken something from there without asking. However, he'd forced her hand. She was the only one who could save him from himself.

Her mother had promised the necklace to her, so she had every right to it. And realising she was dying, Ma had also begged Bethany to look after her father.

"Keep him safe, Bethany, love."

Bethany kept her promises, even if her father didn't.


Bethany walked down the gravel drive of Priory Hall to the road. She had a torch but despite the dark night knew she wouldn't need it until she turned off onto the unmade roads of Plotlands where she lived. Having worked for the Richardsons for years, she knew every twist and turn of the road.

But on Plotlands, the contours of the ground changed according to whether it had rained heavily, as well as the number of wheels that had churned up the resulting mud that day.

As she turned onto Second Avenue where she lived, she switched on the torch. The faint light that passed through the narrow slit of the blackout cover was watery weak but welcome. It had rained earlier that evening and the road was more rutted and furrowed than ever, so her progress was slow.

She shivered. The air was damp and filled with the distinctive smell of wet grass and mud.

To the west, she could see brilliant beams of light sweep the sky, criss-crossing each other, and the distant drone of aircraft. The deep thud of explosions and the rapid ack-ack-ack of anti-aircraft guns drifted towards her. She guessed enemy pilots were attacking the RAF base in Hornchurch – the station where that ghastly Captain Barnes-Crosier was based.

While she'd been serving him brandy earlier, he'd tried to engage her in conversation. She'd been polite but remote, as a maid should be. But really, it was none of his business what she did on her days off. Thankfully, Mrs Richardson had noticed. She'd cut in and diverted the captain's attention away from Bethany.

The other man, the doctor, had looked lost all evening. Bethany felt sorry for him. Perhaps he had good reason to be sad. It was a shame because he was a good-looking man when he smiled. His eyes were dark and brooding, yet they had a gentleness about them that made Bethany want to stare. Only once did his smile reach his eyes and light up his face. The captain was telling Mrs Richardson about a prank he and the doctor had got up to when they were at university. It was obviously a happy memory for Dr Howard.

By the time Bethany reached the broken gate of her cottage, her eyes were aching, gritty and hot. It felt as though she had a tight band around her head, squeezing her skull. Not surprising. She'd been up since dawn, and the last part of her journey home had required her to stare intently at the ground to pick out a route without tripping or turning an ankle.

Bethany had been tempted to take off the torch's blackout cover but didn't dare. Instead, she'd played the narrow beam of light over the uneven contours and hoped for the best.

It would be good to go to bed and rest her feet after such a long day. At least Mrs Richardson had paid her well – more than any other local family would have given to their maid. Bethany clutched her bag tightly. Before she went to bed that night, she'd put the extra she'd earned that day in the secret cocoa tin with her other savings. If she could find her mother's necklace, she'd add that, then hide the tin beneath the floorboards under her bed.

The cottage gate clung on by one hinge and she raised it, half-lifting, so it didn't scrape across the path. It was a miracle it had hung on for so long, but Pa didn't notice it, despite being a joiner who could easily have fixed it. Bethany had given up asking him to mend it.

Anyway, it was an early warning of his arrival home, should she be counting her money or looking at her shorthand books. Not that she had much time to do either of those things, but it was best she kept everything hidden from him.

Pa wouldn't have been able to resist if he'd know about her savings in the cocoa tin and he'd soon have taken everything to the *Coach and Horses* and spent the lot.

And as for the books, he didn't agree with 'book-learning'. He'd told Bethany she should accept her station in life and be satisfied. Hadn't he provided everything she needed? So why was she trying to do better than her father? That was arrogance.

It obviously upset his pride at the thought she wanted a better life, so who could guess what he'd do with the shorthand books Mrs Richardson had lent her?

Anyway, he didn't provide everything she needed. Bethany spent her wages on food for them both. True, Pa occasionally found work and contributed small amounts. But Bethany knew he kept most of his earnings back.

But then he didn't know she received extra for working when the Richardsons had guests for dinner. One day, she'd have enough to go to London and become a shorthand typist. Or at least to learn what she needed to know to become one. She wasn't clear about how to do that, but Mrs Richardson was helping her.

If Pa had thought about it, he'd have known she earned extra, but he wasn't a man who spent much time thinking. Probably with good reason. His memories of fighting in the trenches in the Great War always took over, so he drank to forget.

At night, he cried out, dreadful screams that had grown worse since

Ma had died, and Bethany could only assume he drank to stifle his dreams too.

She pushed the front door open. Only a little, so she could slip through without making the hinges squeal. Snores from Pa's bedroom surged and subsided like the tide. He was home. It was a relief he was safe but also a nuisance because she wanted to get Ma's necklace.

Should she creep in and look for it?

Bethany had never dared take anything from Pa's room before. She'd always respected his things. But he'd sworn he'd always keep Ma's jewellery and he hadn't kept that promise. She had to do something, or it would be too late.

Before she'd left that morning, he'd woken and staggered out of his bedroom. Through his tears, he'd told her he'd pawned Ma's ring. It had been a moment of madness, he'd said. Then, he'd held her to him and told her he loved her. Through his tears, he'd said he'd work that day and get the ring back. He'd meant it then. But once he'd had a drink? Would he have remembered?

Could she trust him?

Hope suddenly rose in her chest. Had she underestimated him? Perhaps he had got the ring back after all and had put it back in Ma's jewellery box. Dithering outside his door, she listened to the raucous snores. There was no doubt, he was deeply asleep. And anyway, she had no choice – she must find out if he'd kept his promise.


Bethany had successfully negotiated the creaking floorboards in Pa's bedroom and crept to the dressing table her father had once made for her mother. It was simple but skilfully constructed. A gift of love from her father to her mother before he'd gone off to fight in the Great War and returned a broken man.

Bethany closed her eyes and held her breath as she gently pulled open the top drawer. Pa spluttered in his sleep and, after a second's silence, began to snore again. She paused, the jewellery box in view. The drawer would have to be opened further before she could take it out.

Slowly, slowly, she pulled the handle towards her, timing her movements with each loud intake of Pa's breath. Finally, she had enough room to lift the jewellery box out and undo the clasp. She raised the lid, hoping.

Praying.

Hot tears pricked her eyes and she stifled a gasp. The box was empty. Pa had not replaced the ring and now the necklace had also gone.

"W... what are you doing?" Pa spoke from the bed, his voice slurred. He was obviously drunk but not so far gone he didn't know what she was doing. There was an edge to his words. Sharp and argumentative.

It was pointless lying.

"I'm looking for Ma's ring and necklace. You promised you'd get the ring back and you'd keep the necklace for me." Shock drove her to speak with more confidence than she felt.

Pa sat up and, swinging his legs to the floor, rose unsteadily to his feet. He swayed, then righted himself. "While you live under my roof, you live by my rules. If I want to do something, I don't need your permission."

Bethany was too outraged to take any notice of his angry words. "Have you pawned everything Ma left?" Bethany held out the empty box, her face showing disbelief.

"So what if I have? A man's got to live. You don't bring home enough to live on."

"Well, I might have been able to earn more if you'd let me keep up with my shorthand—" Oh, why had she said that? Such unwise words, guaranteed to anger Pa. But the bitter disappointment of finding Ma's belongings gone and her overwhelming tiredness had clouded her judgement.

"Why, you..." He lurched towards her, half-tripping on the rug, and grabbed her arm.

Seizing the jewellery box, he wrenched it from her hands.

"You've no right coming in my room, taking my things. Get out!" He threw her towards the door and, taken by surprise, she fell, knocking her cheek on the tiled hearth.

"Get out!" he yelled, throwing the box at her. It caught her on the chin and bounced off onto the rug.

Bethany lay there, looking up at her father, blinking. She wasn't badly hurt, just shocked. Pa had never treated her like that before. He'd never pushed her. Was he too drunk to know what he'd done?

"Get out of my house and don't come back." He picked up the box and stared into its empty depths as if he couldn't believe the jewellery was missing.

He couldn't mean it, surely? How would he cope without her wages? Without her?

"But Pa—"

"To think a girl of mine would come into my room and nick my things. You thieving wretch. How dare you? Who d'you think you are? Pauline warned me about you."

Pauline Cresswell? Bethany raised herself to her knees. The woman in the cottage opposite that was as dilapidated as Pa's? The woman who also drank too much?

Pa hung on to the foot of the bed, swaying and jabbing the air with a finger. "Pauline said she'd look after me. So, don't you worry your thieving little head. I've been helping her out a bit with a few jobs and she's keen to move in. Not while you're here, of course." His eyes narrowed. "That's taken the wind out o' yer sails, hasn't it, Miss Hoity-Toity? Putting on airs and graces just cos you've got a job in the Richardsons' house. You obviously don't think yer father's good enough, so if yer want a better life, go and get it."

He didn't know what he was saying. This wasn't her father. He'd clung to her sobbing that morning while he told her he loved her.

Bethany stood up, gripping the mantelpiece for support while her head stopped swimming. When she was steady, she walked out of her father's room. Her cheekbone was throbbing, and her eye had begun to close up. A thin trickle of blood ran down her neck from the cut on her chin and her teeth ached where her jaws had clacked together. He slammed the door behind her.

She stumbled back to her room, and after putting the chair beneath the doorknob, with shaking hands, she started to pack her things.

Pa was drunk. In the morning, would he remember what he'd said? Possibly not. He'd shouted at her before – many times. He'd threatened to give her a good thrashing if he thought she wasn't behaving but he'd never gone through with it, and he'd certainly never accidentally caused her harm before. And now, with the possibility of Pauline Cresswell moving in, Bethany had no choice. She must leave.

It wouldn't be forever. Perhaps one day Pa would come to his senses, and she could move back in. Pauline had been associated with a string of men. She'd soon tire of Pa. Perhaps once he realised how much he missed his daughter...

Bethany retrieved the cocoa tin containing her savings from under the floorboards and added that day's money. She didn't have many clothes or belongings, so it didn't take long to pack.

Pa's snores echoed around the cottage as she quietly removed the chair from beneath the door and avoiding the creaking floorboards, let herself out of her home. It was still dark as she retraced her steps to Priory Hall, tears streaming down her cheeks. She would wash and tidy herself when she got to Mrs Richardson's. Mrs Stewart would look after her.

# Chapter Two

♥

Dr Matthew Howard woke up at first light. For a second, he didn't know where he was. He hadn't pulled the blackout curtains the previous night because he'd undressed and got into bed in the dark. Now, steely grey light seeped in through the window, draining everything in the room of colour and substance.

Footsteps crunched on the gravel drive. A light touch, not a heavy man's tread. Getting out of bed, Matthew slipped on his dressing gown and looked out of the window to see who was arriving so early. It was the maid that Hugh had treated so outrageously the previous evening.

She was carrying a suitcase and a large bag. Her head lowered and her pace slowed, as if Priory Hall was the last place she wanted to be. Perhaps she hated her job. Certainly, Hugh hadn't made it any easier the previous evening, and he had been embarrassed when he'd seen how uncomfortable she'd been.

Hugh's personality had changed since he joined the RAF. Years ago, when they'd been at university together, he'd been different; kinder, more aware of other people's feelings. Matthew understood how Hugh's outlook would have altered. Since July, the aerial conflict over England had intensified as the RAF fought to prevent the

Luftwaffe from achieving air supremacy. Fighter pilots, such as Hugh, measured their life expectancy in weeks; Matthew couldn't imagine how it might feel to risk his life every time he went to work. No wonder Hugh had altered so much.

This dreadful war.

Matthew shook his head as if ridding himself of the threat of constant danger such as Hugh faced each time he took off in his Spitfire.

And yet, as Matthew looked out at the Essex landscape, it was almost possible to believe the country wasn't at war at all. All was calm. Timeless even, as if the countryside refused to be changed by mankind's foolishness. Several birds had started their song, and the hint of a rosy glow gleamed in the east. This view was so different from the one to which Matthew usually awoke.

He lived with his brother, Robert, and sister-in-law, Julia. Their magnificent home, Brent House, was in the middle of Elmford Mere, a few miles north of Chelmsford. Matthew's bedroom was at the front of the house, overlooking the High Road. Each morning, he awoke to the sounds of the market town coming to life with shop owners and market traders making their way to work. Horses clip-clopping and cartwheels rumbling over cobblestones. Drivers' distinctive cries as they urged their horses to set off or to stop while they made deliveries.

The area was low-lying – usually damp and often misty, and those who were out early often had to make their way to work through the early morning fog or rain.

The family factory, sited several miles from Elmford Mere, was also frequently shrouded in fog. For that reason, when it was assumed another war was imminent, Howard & Williams Engineering Co. had been chosen by the Ministry of Supply to be converted to a Royal Ordnance Factory.

Modifications had been made to the newly named ROF Elmford

Filling Factory and living quarters and other amenities were built for the vast number of workers required to manufacture armaments ready for the coming conflict.

Years before, Matthew's father, Thomas, and his business partner had set up Howard & Williams Engineering Co. which had produced electric and diesel motors as well as steam turbines. Thomas had taken over the running of the company when his partner had died a few years before.

When approached by men from the ministry, shrewd Thomas had been only too happy to comply with their request for a new armaments factory because with the war raging, bullets, mines and bombs were desperately needed by the armed services. The site at Elmford was still expanding – both the manufacturing facilities and the tiny new village that had sprung up next to it to accommodate many of the workers.

The heavy clouds and mist helped conceal the low, camouflaged buildings and the asphalt walkways apparently looked like water when viewed from above. Thankfully, so far, the precautions had worked as the factory and its accommodation had evaded enemy attack.

Even so, how such a development could exist without the enemy discovering it and bombing it to dust, astonished Matthew who was the medical doctor at the facility.

The new buildings and the roads leading into the site didn't appear on any official maps, and there was no mention anywhere of the railway line that extended from Elmford Mere Station into the factory. It was as if ROF Elmford and its living accommodation didn't exist.

Matthew checked his wristwatch. It was still early. He didn't need to get ready for the day yet, so he might as well enjoy the peaceful view. It didn't appear anyone else in the house had risen yet, although having seen the young maid arrive, presumably, she and the cook would have started work in the kitchen.

How lucky Ben and Joanna Richardson were to live here in the middle of the countryside. It was hard to believe Ben and Hugh were cousins;, they were so dissimilar. Ben and his wife, Joanna, were a lovely couple – devoted to each other. It was a joy to see two people who were so in tune. Certainly nothing like his brother and sister-in-law. Or, in fact, his parents.

Matthew closed his eyes and listened. Bird song. A cockerel crowing. Somewhere far off, cows lowing. And much closer – probably in the kitchen downstairs – the chink of china. It was like being on holiday.

He had a small room in the living quarters on the factory site where he sometimes stayed if he'd worked late rather than returning to his brother's house. When he woke in the morning, or if he woke at any time during the night, there was a constant low rumbling of working machinery that vibrated through his body. An unsettling, unnatural motion. But here in Priory Hall, he felt at peace.

In the factory, the reverberations never stopped. Twenty-four hours a day, people worked shifts, filling bullets and shells, assembling detonators and fuses which were carefully packed into crates. They were loaded onto the wagons of trains, which, after passing through Elmford Mere, were sent onwards to destinations both near and far.

It was all vital. But the constant hum and vibration was draining.

Matthew pulled his dressing gown tightly around him and opened the window slightly. He drew the fresh, cool Essex air into his lungs. It was sweet and clean – such a contrast to the air he breathed day in, day out, in the factory. The smell of oil, hot metal and a cocktail of chemicals that, to a greater or lesser extent, poisoned the people under his medical care.

He shivered and closed the window, wondering if it had been the cold or the thought that later that day, he'd be back in Elmford that had caused him to shudder.

The first few days of his leave had been spent with his parents in their large house. At the memory of his time in Suffolk, his body tensed and tried to control his breathing. It had been a miserable few days.

As usual, his father had treated him as a regretful disappointment. He'd wanted his sons to follow him into business and had never forgiven Matthew for deciding on a career in medicine. Father considered his eldest son, Robert, to be a war hero. If Father was to be believed, it was through Robert's single-handed efforts that the British Army, Navy and Air Force were supplied with all the armaments they required.

According to Father, his wayward younger son, took temperatures, prodded patients with his stethoscope and mopped brows. Matthew had tried to explain to his father that the time he'd spent in hospital when he'd been eight-years old had left a deep impression on him.

He'd been seriously ill with diphtheria and had been kept in isolation for two months. Not even his parents had been allowed to visit. The seemingly endless hours of monotony had been broken only by nurses and doctors. By the time Matthew had recovered, he'd made up his mind to study medicine and to try to pay back what the doctors had done for him.

But Father merely dismissed that as nonsense. Doctors were paid. That was their job. One didn't become a baker simply because one enjoyed a loaf of bread.

Matthew would never have revealed to their father Robert did very little other than visit his mistress several times a week and enjoy lavish lunches and dinners at his club in London. It would have been undignified to have disclosed such details about his brother. Father wouldn't have believed him anyway.

Neither would it ever have occurred to Father how the factory actually ran. Nameless, industrious people, like that maid he'd just watched walk up the drive, put their lives on the line each day for hours and hours of tedium, producing everything the country needed to wage war. And Matthew's job was to try to keep them as healthy as he could. Admittedly, he only played a small part in the process, but he was valuable nonetheless.

Father wasn't an idiot. Matthew was certain if he'd really thought about it, he must have known how the factory ran. But he also knew that if his father found the truth unpalatable, he simply made up his own reality and believed that.

Matthew let out such a long sigh, it misted the windowpane. He'd get ready and go downstairs. Perhaps he'd have a walk before breakfast and make the most of this time away from Elmford Mere.

If he had a chance, he'd have a word with Joanna Richardson. He hadn't been sparkling company the previous evening and he wanted to apologise. But there was so much on his mind.

At least, Matthew had now done his duty and wouldn't have to return to his parents' home for some time. Leave was precious, and he didn't intend to spend longer than was necessary being criticised and belittled by his father.

After washing and shaving, Matthew dressed and packed his bag. He'd agreed to accompany Hugh to Hornchurch before he returned to Elmford Mere. Not that Matthew would be allowed onto the airfield, but he'd be able to see the Spitfires and Hurricanes take off.

Matthew's heart plummeted. It was bad enough he would return to Elmford later that afternoon, but before that, he'd have to say farewell to Hugh – perhaps for the last time. Hugh's sense of living on borrowed time had deeply affected Matthew, even though he didn't believe in premonitions. However, the rule of probability suggested that each time Hugh took to the air, he was one step closer to disaster.

Matthew checked his watch. It was still early, so he crept downstairs following the distant sounds of rattling cutlery and a whistling kettle towards the kitchen.

He didn't intend to bother the cook, simply ask if he could make himself a cup of tea before his walk. Hugh wouldn't be up for hours. He'd drunk until he'd needed assistance to get upstairs to his bed the previous evening.

Matthew hadn't blamed him. Neither had their hosts, thankfully. Everyone understood Hugh and his fellow pilots were under terrific pressure.

Conversely, because of his job, Matthew drank sparingly. To be sociable, he sipped very slowly. A doctor needed a clear head and steady hands in case there was ever an emergency. He might be off duty, but accidents happened all the time, and how would he forgive himself if he'd been incapable of helping?

Matthew knocked at the kitchen door before entering and asked if he could make himself some tea. Cook threw up her hands in mock horror and, with a broad grin, told him it was her job. She poured him a mug of tea and made him a slice of toast to 'keep up his strength until breakfast'.

The maid he'd seen arrive earlier that morning glanced at him nervously, and he immediately saw why. One eye was livid purple and half-closed and her chin had a similar bruise with a cut in the middle.

She kept her eyes down and her head lowered. He suspected she wouldn't want him to make a fuss, but that was his job. He'd seen similar injuries during his time working in the London Hospital in Whitechapel. Many had been due to falls, but others had been inflicted by a bullying husband or father.

"Those are nasty bruises you've got there. Would you like me to look at them?" he asked, making sure to keep his tone pleasant and light.

She flushed scarlet. "Oh, no thank you, sir." Her voice was soft and polite, but it had caught in her throat as if she was close to tears.

"Have you lost consciousness since you got the bruises?"

"No, sir."

She looked like a rabbit who was ready to bolt but as a doctor, he had to take responsibility, even if she didn't welcome his professional attention.

"Do you feel sick or have a headache?"

She shook her head, her eyes wide with alarm. "No, nothing like that, sir. It looks worse than it is."

"I've cleaned the cut with iodine, thank you, sir," said the cook, inserting herself between him and the maid like a mother hen.

He nodded in approval. "Excellent. I can see you're in good hands. I'm assuming you fell?" he asked, trying to sound as if he were merely making conversation rather than probing.

"I tripped on the way home in the dark, sir."

"I see, well it's lucky you didn't knock yourself out. Presumably whoever was with you helped you up?"

"I was on my own, sir." She bobbed a curtsy and turned towards the pantry.

When she'd gone, Matthew said to the cook, "If she starts to feel dizzy or tired or has any other symptoms, please call her family doctor and explain what happened."

Cook nodded and quietly added, "I'll keep an eye on her, sir. And thank you."

After finishing his tea and toast, Matthew fetched his coat. He thanked Cook and let himself out of the back door. As he strolled across the garden – now given over entirely to growing vegetables – he couldn't get the young maid's face out of his mind. The previous evening, he'd been so taken with her he'd had to force himself not to stare.

She had a natural, fresh face. A mouth with full lips, and long-lashed, green eyes that had flashed like emeralds when Hugh had treated her so abominably. But today, one of those eyes was purple and puffy and he must speak to Joanna with urgency. She appeared to be a remarkably kind and sensible woman. He was certain she'd help if she could.

First, he'd find out a little more about the maid. The injuries to her head may or may not have been caused as she'd claimed. But Matthew had spotted other fresh injuries. More bruises on her arm, which he was certain were the result of having been grabbed by someone with strong hands. A husband? A father? Perhaps an unknown attacker? But whoever it had been, Joanna might know and would also have more idea if anything could be done about the situation. There was enough misery in the world with people dying needlessly without someone inflicting pain on another, especially someone large on such a small and fragile-looking girl.

# Chapter Three

Bethany could scarcely believe everything was happening so quickly. Was it only that morning she'd packed up her few belongings and left her father's home?

She'd intended to ask if she could stay at Priory Hall.

However, just after breakfast, Mrs Richardson had called her into the study. She said several of her husband's friends who worked in the government thought it most likely it wouldn't be long before unmarried women would be conscripted either into the services or into some sort of war work. If that was true, then eventually Bethany would have to leave Priory Hall.

Unsure where the conversation was leading, yet aware of her employer's serious mood, she heard the word 'leave' and gasped.

"Are you dismissing me, ma'am?" Bethany could scarcely breathe. Where would she go if she had to leave Priory Hall?

"Oh, no, Bethany. Of course not! I'd like nothing better than for you to stay here. However, it may not be up to me…"

She went on to say that many people now thought that if female conscription was introduced, young, single women might be moved anywhere in the country unless they found war work for themselves.

"Of course, it might not be true," she added, "but who knows what might happen with this dreadful war? If my husband's friends are correct, then you may not have a choice. Have you had any thoughts on what you'd prefer to do? Perhaps enlist in one of the women's services?"

Bethany shook her head. "No, ma'am. I don't want to join up. I... I don't know what I can do." Bethany looked at her employer aghast. What was she fit for? Nothing.

The day after she'd finished school, she'd started work in service in Priory Hall. She knew how to clean and keep house. Her mother had taught her to cook, but only simple food. It had been Mrs Stewart who'd shown her how to make special dishes such as might be served at a formal dinner.

Mrs Richardson had noticed Bethany's fascination with the books in the library and had allowed her to join in when she read to her own children. She'd also given Bethany time off to sit in the library and improve her reading. But still, she lacked confidence. Suppose she had to pass an exam to get into the services? She knew she'd fail.

Mrs Richardson smiled kindly. "Well, by chance, Dr Howard, who's currently our guest, works in a factory which is recruiting staff at the moment. He didn't explain exactly what the factory makes. I believe that's all rather hush-hush, but whatever they do, it's something to help the war effort. Dr Howard has written a letter of introduction, on my recommendation, for you. That is, if you think you'd like a factory job. It will mean moving to a place north of Chelmsford but there's accommodation on site and he said the wages are good and your fare will be reimbursed should you choose to take a job. Of course, it's completely up to you..."

Bethany's heart raced. A new job. A fresh start. Away from her father who'd thrown her out of the house and was likely to replace her with someone else.

But to leave Dunton... She felt torn in two. However, it appeared that, in the future, it was likely she'd be uprooted, anyway. She might be sent to the tip of Scotland or to Cornwall. At least if she was still in Essex, she could get home if she had to.

An unlikely prospect since her father didn't appear to need her, but nevertheless, she'd feel better if she wasn't too far away.

"I can see this has come as a shock, Bethany, and I'm not surprised. It's been very sudden. Would you like some time to think about it?" Mrs Richardson asked.

Go? Stay? Be sent away, anyway?

Bethany's stomach fluttered and quivered with fear and indecision. Better to take control while she still had some.

"I'd like to go, please, ma'am, if you don't mind." The words rushed out before her courage failed completely. It was a huge step, but what choice did she have?

To her surprise, Mrs Richardson suggested she leave that afternoon. She said she had some shopping to do in Chelmsford and that her husband was going to drive her there. They could give Bethany a lift to the station and lend her the fare. Dr Howard had said he'd repay them.

No, this was too fast. Bethany hadn't had a chance to think it through. As she felt the blood drain from her face, the word 'No' formed in her throat but failed to come out of her mouth.

But really, what was there to consider? Her life was about to change. She might not like it but that was too bad, she'd have to get used to it.


As Bethany waved Mr and Mrs Richardson goodbye at Chelmsford Station, the tears she'd tried to hide became a flood, gushing down her cheeks. She dabbed them away with a handkerchief, feeling foolish and very lost. Her employers had always been so kind to her. As their car drove along the road and turned the corner, Bethany's courage drained away.

She couldn't do this.

People bustled past her unheeding; some entering the station, some leaving. But everyone appeared to be intent on going somewhere. Everyone had a purpose. Bethany stood rooted to the spot.

*Come on...*

If she took a step, she feared her knees would buckle. A woman with a large basket over one arm and a crying baby in the other passed her and accidentally shoved her against the wall.

"Sorry, love," the woman said, still looking at the baby.

*Come on, Bethany. You're in people's way.*

She glanced along the road for the Richardson's car, wishing it would come back for her, but it had long gone.

*No one is going to help you now. You're on your own.*

Gulping air into her lungs, Bethany tried to reason with herself. One thing was certain: she couldn't stay where she was. She slowed her breathing and tried to concentrate. All she had to do was to buy a ticket, find the platform and get on the right train. It wasn't like she'd never travelled by rail before. She'd travelled to Southend-on-Sea with her mother on many occasions.

But she'd never travelled alone.

Then it was about time she learned how. This wasn't beyond her.

Find the ticket office and buy a ticket. That's what Mrs Richardson had told her to do when she gave her the money for her fare.

Bethany suspected Mrs Richardson hadn't really needed to drive to Chelmsford that afternoon. She knew Bethany had never been to Chelmsford alone, let alone further afield. But she believed Bethany could do it or she wouldn't have left her at the station on her own.

On unsteady legs, Bethany walked to the ticket office and joined the end of the queue, trying to steady her breathing. She began to feel lightheaded and was afraid of fainting. This was too much. Too fast.

*You can do this*, she told herself. *You must do this.*

There were two girls in front of her. One of them said, "Two singles to Elmford Mere, please."

They were going to the same place.

After Bethany had bought her ticket, she followed the girls. Usually, she would've been too shy to approach strangers, but if they were going to the same station, then perhaps they'd let her know where to get off.

One of the girls was obviously older than the other. Her blonde hair was pulled off her forehead and hung in curls to her shoulders. She was pretty and vivacious – full of confidence.

The younger girl appeared to be nervous. Her straight brown hair was almost shoulder length. It too, was pulled off her forehead, but whereas the style suited the older girl, it was too severe for her. There was a slight resemblance between the two girls, which suggested they were sisters, but otherwise, they were completely different.

After Bethany had nervously explained she was going to Elmford Mere and asked if they'd tell her where to get off, the elder girl insisted she accompany them.

Bethany felt giddy with relief.

"Alice Jenkins," she said, holding out her hand. "And this is my little sister Mavis. Are you going to ROF Elmford?"

Bethany nodded.

"D'you know anyone there?"

Bethany shook her head.

"I already work there," said Alice. "Mavis is just starting so you might work together."

This was a piece of luck.

Bethany finally found her voice. "What sort of work do you do?"

"Best not to say in public," Alice said with her finger over her lips. "Keep Mum. Careless talk costs lives." She laughed loudly, her eyes roving towards a group of soldiers sitting on their kitbags.

"So," said Alice, "who came off worse, you or the door?" She pointed at Bethany's face. "Nasty shiner you've got there. Who's the heavy-handed man in your life?"

"Oh no, nothing like that. I fell over. So clumsy of me." Bethany flushed. She didn't want strangers to know her father was a drunk who'd accidentally pushed her over. And he hadn't meant to hit her with the jewellery box. That had been an accident too.

Alice's eyebrows raised in disbelief. "Well, I hope you're not too clumsy or you won't last long. If you're that ham-fisted, you'll be likely to take the rest of the factory up too." She laughed, but her eyes hadn't smiled, and a shiver went through Bethany. Surely, she'd exaggerated. The factory couldn't be that dangerous.

Alice's mood lifted. "Well, at least you're pretty enough for those bruises not to have spoiled your looks. And they'll soon be gone. I expect you'll attract more men than bees to a honeypot."

Bethany stared at her. *Attract more men?* She hardly knew any men. Well, other than Mr Richardson, some of his farmhands and the local shop owners. She'd had no time for dances and trips to the pictures. No chances to meet anyone new.

"I don't know about you two, but I'm parched. It's time for a cuppa. Come on, there's a WVS van outside. Follow me," Alice said.

Bethany was thirsty, too. Before she'd left Priory Hall, Mrs Stewart had made her sandwiches and tea. Bethany had been so choked, she hadn't been able to eat them, and Mrs Stewart had wrapped them up and packed them in her bag. To Bethany's surprise, tears had run down the cook's chubby cheeks, and she'd wiped them away briskly with her apron.

After years of working together, it had been hard to part, and when Bethany had seen the older woman's tears, it had started her off. Before she'd had a chance to think, Mrs Richardson had called her. It was time to go. Everything was happening too quickly.

"Get along with you," Mrs Stewart had said, wiping away more tears. "You'll write now, won't you?"

Bethany had promised she would, and after grabbing her case and bag, she'd rushed to the front of Priory Hall where Mr and Mrs Richardson were waiting in the car.

Now, she realised she hadn't finished her tea. She swallowed back the tears at the memory of Mrs Stewart wiping her eyes.

Well, no point thinking about goodbyes now. She must look forwards. And thankfully, she'd found some friends.

"But look," Mavis said, pointing at the sign on the Women's Voluntary Service van. "It says they only serve people in uniform."

Alice laughed. "Oh, we don't take any notice of—" she broke off abruptly and her face lit up. She waved energetically, although her eyes appeared to be on a group of noisy soldiers, several of whom waved back.

A young woman pushed her way through the crowd and hugged Alice. They squealed their delight at seeing each other.

"This is Freda Bailey. My roommate at Elmford," Alice said excitedly, linking her arm through the new girl's. If Alice was pretty, Freda was stunning, and Bethany noticed she was wearing make-up.

"She looks just like Veronica Lake," Mavis whispered to Bethany with an approving, faraway look in her eye. Bethany didn't like to say she had no idea who Veronica Lake was. But it was plain from Mavis's reaction; whoever the woman was, she was someone to be admired.

"Call me, Freddie," Freda said, extending her hand to first Mavis then Bethany.

Freddie's hair was blonde and hung in elegant waves to her shoulders. Like a curtain, it draped over her forehead with an elaborate twisty roll on one side. But strangely, although her hair was blonde, just above her forehead a patch of hair was bright yellow.

Was this some new sort of fashion? Bethany had so much to learn.

"I've had such fun on leave. I'll tell you all about it later," Freddie said to Alice and winked. "Now back to work." She screwed up her face in distaste and Alice laughed.

"Come on, Freddie, I'm dying of thirst. Let's get a cuppa." Alice beckoned to Mavis and Bethany. "Follow us, girls. Keep close."

Arm in arm, they sauntered towards the WVS wagon, walking up to a group of soldiers, their hips swaying exaggeratedly. They stopped in front of the lads who whooped and whistled in delight. Then, pretending to see the soldiers for the first time, Freddie asked if they'd be so kind as to fetch four poor, thirsty girls, a cuppa.

She indicated a small badge on the lapel of her jacket, holding it forward, leaning further forward than was necessary towards one of the soldiers.

"ROF, Front Line Duty," he read, then looking up, he added, "you're one o' them canaries, ain't yer? My sister works in a munitions factory. She's got yellow bits on 'er hair like yours."

Then, as he straightened up, he brushed her cheek with his lips. The others clapped him on the back, laughing at his nerve.

Bethany expected Freddie and Alice to pull away, outraged, but to her surprise, Freddie put her fingers over the spot where the soldier had kissed her, and then put them to her lips. She blew him a kiss.

"Canaries, that's exactly what we are, boys. Now, who's going to be a gent, and get us a cuppa each?"

Several soldiers leapt up, stumbling over kit bags and feet as they rushed to fetch mugs of tea from the WVS ladies.

To Bethany's amazement, Mavis didn't appear to be surprised by Freddie's behaviour. She was more interested in Alice's badge.

Perhaps this was how Freddie and Alice always behaved. Bethany was shocked. Nobody she knew acted like that. It brought home to her how little she knew. In fact, how few people she knew. She recognised lots of neighbours in Laindon, but she didn't spend long enough with them to know what they were really like.

Alice held out the badge that was pinned to her coat so Bethany and Mavis could read it.

"We have a uniform, but we're not allowed to wear it outside the factory. The badge tells everyone we're doing war work too, but unfortunately the factories are kept so secret not many people realise who we are and what we do. That means the WVS ladies won't serve us. But they will serve the lads in khaki."

Four men returned with steaming mugs of tea and plied Freddie and Alice with questions. Were they spoken for? Where were they were going? When was their next leave?

Bethany listened closely, hoping to learn more about Elmford, but was surprised at how little Alice and Freddie gave away. Alice's earlier comment about Bethany's clumsiness taking the rest of the factory up had unnerved her. Surely she'd misunderstood. It had sounded as though she meant an explosion. But that wasn't possible. And what about Freddie's yellow streak? One of the soldiers had suggested it had something to do with the work.

"Nice cuppa?" one of the soldiers asked Bethany. There was something about his expression Bethany didn't like. He was looking at her in the way Captain Barnes-Crosier had done when he'd pinched her bottom. A look that suggested he was judging her. Or perhaps, was completely misjudging her.

"Yes, thank you," she mumbled, stepping away from him. He smelled of stale cigarettes and dirty clothes. He grinned, showing a missing front tooth and several blackened ones.

"Nasty shiner," he remarked. "Still, you're as pretty as a picture. It don't bother me none."

She stared at him. There'd been no sympathy from him, simply an estimate of the damage done to her looks and whether it bothered him.

"Are you girls all off to the same place?" he asked.

She nodded, backing away further.

"Are you anybody's budgie?" he asked with a sly grin.

She stared at him. "Budgie?"

"Yes, are you spoken for? Have you got a fella? If you haven't, you can write to me. My name's Bill, by the way. We're off up north training now, but when I come back, you could be my budgie if you like."

Bethany swallowed and recoiled. His girl? She could think of nothing worse.

"I'm sorry, Bill, I'm just starting at Elmford. I don't have an address yet."

Stupid, stupid. Why hadn't she said she had someone?

Well, too late now.

"Not to worry, darlin'. I'll give you my address. You can write and let me know." The soldier turned to one of his comrades and asked to borrow a pencil.

Bethany took the opportunity to slide away to the other side of Mavis who was standing like a rock in the middle of a river. Soldiers crowded around Alice and Freddie, jostling to be noticed, lighting cigarettes for them. Another soldier had slipped into Bill's position next to Bethany, but no one had spoken to Mavis who was staring fixedly at her shoes.

One of the soldiers had an arm around Freddie who looked up at him adoringly, and Alice had linked arms with two soldiers who were insulting each other, a cigarette dangling from her lips.

"Here," Bill said to Bethany, shouldering a man out of the way to get closer to her and thrusting a grimy piece of paper towards her.

"That's where I'll be up north. You'll write, won't you?" Before Bethany could react, he'd put his arm around her shoulders.

She froze.

How could she get out of this without hurting anyone's feelings or making a fool of herself? If this was accepted behaviour in the new world where she'd be living, should she join in?

She considered for a second, then decided that whatever the consequences, she simply couldn't allow that dreadful man anywhere near her.

"What shall I do with this?" she asked, holding out the empty mug and wriggling free. It was the first thing that had come into her mind.

The soldier next to Bill said, "I'll take it for you, love." His face lit up.

Bill shouldered him out of the way. "I'll do it." He took the mug and headed back to the WVS van. "Don't move," he said to Bethany. "I'll be right back." He glared at the other soldier as if warning him off.

Bethany looked at Mavis for guidance. Whatever she'd done had prevented her from unwelcome attention, but Mavis's face was impossible to read. Her thin lips were set in an even thinner line and a vein throbbed in her temple.

A sergeant strode towards the group of soldiers, chest puffed out and moustache twitching with outrage. He swore at them and loudly ordered them to board the train that was just about to arrive, threatening dreadful punishment to anyone who missed it.

Bill grabbed his kitbag and ran after the others before waving to Bethany. "Write, won't you?" he shouted over his shoulder.

"Will you write to him?" Mavis asked wistfully.

Bethany shook her head, her face twisted in distaste.

"I wish someone wanted to write to me," Mavis said, the corners of her thin mouth turning down. "You look like you've done ten rounds with a bus and the men are all after you. I wish I was beautiful."

Bethany wanted to reach out, to touch her arm to comfort her but didn't dare. How sad. Mavis craved the attention Bethany was reluctant to encourage.

"I've got a brother in the Navy," Bethany said. "Stevie. He's a couple of years older than me. I could ask him if he'd write to you." She wasn't sure he would, but she could ask. Letters had been infrequent from her brother since he'd enlisted. He hadn't been able to wait to get away from home and had joined up as soon as he'd been able. But it would be nice for Mavis if he'd write to her.

"Would you?" Mavis asked. She smiled and, for a second, she almost looked attractive.

# Chapter Four

Matthew checked his wristwatch as he joined the end of the queue in the ticket office in Chelmsford Station. Not long until his train. He'd timed it perfectly and would be back in Elmford Mere before dinner.

He'd passed an enjoyable morning in Hornchurch watching aeroplanes rumble along the runway and take off from the airfield. As one of the Spitfires had passed overhead, it had waggled its wings, and Matthew thought that might have been Hugh saying goodbye. He'd known where Matthew would be standing, and it was just the sort of gesture that would amuse Hugh.

After he'd gone, there'd been a dogfight. Matthew had seen two German planes shot from the sky, spiralling down, billowing thick black smoke punctuated by flames. Other Luftwaffe pilots who'd evaded the RAF lads had dropped bombs, and although they'd missed the airfield, Matthew could imagine the carnage. The wailing sirens rising and falling with the breeze made the hairs on the back of his neck stand up.

He'd briefly wondered whether to make his way to Harold Wood Hospital where the casualties – assuming the bombs had found targets – would be taken for treatment. Another pair of hands would undoubtedly be useful, but it would take him a while to get there. Perhaps he'd arrive too late to be useful. And besides, he was due back at Elmford Mere that evening. It was pointless trying to delay his return; he needed to be ready for work the next day. Dr Dawkins, who'd been standing in for him while he'd been away, would start his leave and the workers in the factory needed medical care.

Reluctantly, he'd made his way to Chelmsford.

After buying his ticket, he slipped it in his wallet and had been about to make his way to the platform when his attention had been drawn by some loud girls making fools of themselves. They'd been laughing raucously and flirting with a group of soldiers.

This war had certainly changed people's attitudes. Carpe diem. Seize the day. Plenty of people were doing that. And why not? No one knew when a well-aimed or even a stray bomb might pick them off. And spending his days in a filling station with so many workers – it only needed one accident for life-changing injuries or death to result.

He'd almost looked away from the loud women when he started with surprise. One of them bore an uncanny resemblance to the maid at Priory Hall. The one about whom he'd spoken to Mrs Richardson. No, it couldn't be. But as he drew closer, he saw the bruises on her face. Yes, there was no doubt it was her.

He slowly shook his head. At Priory Hall, she'd appeared to be vulnerable; small, delicate and defenceless, and he'd wanted to protect her. Two soldiers were vying for her attention. Well, she seemed to be able to take care of herself.

That's good, isn't it?

Yes, it was good, but at the same time, his efforts on her behalf now seemed wasted.

Surely not wasted?

No, not wasted exactly, but he'd wanted to feel he'd done something special for her. She'd piqued his interest, and she hadn't been far from his thoughts since he'd seen her injuries. He'd intended to check on her once she'd settled in at the factory. Just to be sure she was all right. Now, he needn't bother. She obviously had friends in the factory. One of them had a yellow streak in her hair – a sure sign she worked with explosives. Yes, although there were hundreds of women on the site, he definitely recognised the two blonde girls.

Matthew walked to the platform and found a space by the wall where he could wait. Men and women in uniform stood in groups waiting for the train, chattering excitedly.

If the train was on time, it was minutes away.

That was good news. But Matthew's heart sank. It would soon take him home and the truth was, he was dreading dinner.

When he'd left Brent House before his leave, Robert and his wife, Julia, had argued and weren't talking. Although Matthew didn't know the cause of that particular quarrel, it was unlikely they'd have made peace. If they had reconciled, it would be short-lived. Matthew was certain of that, after what Julia had confided in him just before he'd gone on leave.

Matthew had suspected for some time that Julia was having an affair, although he didn't know with whom. Perhaps since he'd been living in Brent House, she'd had several lovers. She was more discreet than Robert with the mistress who often accompanied him to clubs and restaurants in London.

Julia had come to Matthew in tears, begging to see him as a doctor, sobbing that she couldn't possibly see the family doctor.

Matthew had held his breath, waiting for the news he dreaded. She was pregnant.

"I'm desperate, Matthew," she'd said. "You must help me."

"Help you to do what exactly?" he'd asked, fearing he knew what she wanted him to do.

"Well, you're a doctor. Do something before Robert finds out. Surely you can see my predicament?"

He certainly could, but as he told her, there was nothing he could do other than to monitor the pregnancy.

She'd cried and thrown his paperweight at the wall, but he'd refused to be moved.

That had been one of the reasons Matthew had been keen to take leave. He certainly hadn't wanted to go and visit his parents.

So, what would have happened while he'd been away? Would Julia have confessed to Robert? He winced at the thought of the resulting tantrums.

He wondered if it might be wise to miss the next train and catch the following one, but when he checked the timetable, he discovered it would mean a wait of several hours. It might delay his return to Brent House but why should he have to stand on a draughty platform just because he dreaded returning home? No, best to get it over with.

A high-pitched whistle from further down the line announced the arrival of Matthew's train. And as the clickety-clack grew louder, the crowds on the platform began to jostle, picking up suitcases, kitbags and baggage. Men and women clung together – some sobbing – and others silent, resigned. Porters wheeling trolleys laden with boxes and cases wove between them towards the incoming train.

Matthew picked up his suitcase and threaded his way through the throng. As billowing clouds of steam shrouded the engine and filled the air with the smell of burning coal, the train squealed to a halt. Doors slammed and the hubbub rose as people shouted their goodbyes, their best wishes and promises to write.

Matthew kept an eye out for the girls from the factory. He didn't want to be anywhere near them. They'd made a spectacle of themselves, and he didn't relish spending the entire journey with them listening to their foolishness. And although he didn't want to admit it to himself, neither did he want to see the Richardsons' maid behave like her friends. It was too disappointing.

Stop it. You poked your nose into her business, she didn't ask for anything from you. She owes you nothing. She can behave as she likes.

And yet she'd looked so vulnerable and innocent. Well, as Matthew knew from his sister-in-law, appearances could be deceptive.

He climbed into the carriage, put his suitcase on the luggage rack and sat down next to the window. Immediately a large woman smelling of onions sat next to him, squashing him into the corner. But at least, he thought with satisfaction, the factory girls hadn't got into his carriage.

At Elmford Mere Station, he retrieved his case and got out of the carriage quickly making for the exit. He still had a walk of about twenty minutes through the middle of town to get to Brent House.

Not that he was in a rush. He peered in shop windows and realised the closer he got to his brother's home, the slower his pace.

Since his visit to his parents' house, Matthew had lost purpose and direction. How had his father done that? How could he have worn Matthew down in a matter of days?

Reminding himself he was in a far better position than many and that he should be content with life, he wondered why he rarely felt happy. One of the things that gave him pleasure was to help others. However, nowadays, although he helped the factory workers, he knew his job was to monitor them, knowing – as many of them did not – that the chemicals with which they worked were slowly – and sometimes not so slowly – poisoning them. He'd tried to help the housemaid, but it appeared she was perfectly capable of handling her own life.

Forget her.

But her elfin face with those two enormous bruises would not be banished.

It was enough he'd separated her from a bully and had given her an opportunity to make more per week than she'd earned in a month in service. He'd been able to do more for her than for many of the women he'd treated in the London Hospital when he'd worked there.

It had been his time in Whitechapel that had led him into gynaecology. Male doctors often focused on men's conditions, but Matthew had wanted to help each woman who was caught in a cycle of childbearing and childrearing for years until nature took over and stopped her fertility. Or perhaps she simply died of exhaustion. Those conditions didn't help anyone – not the woman herself, her children or her husband.

It had been Matthew's ambition to help treat women's complaints and to offer contraceptive advice, giving women choices and control over their lives.

Matthew had never told his father nor Robert of his special interest in gynaecology. His father hadn't understood his desire to help people. He certainly wouldn't have been able to grasp that Matthew wanted to help women and their complaints. How trivial he would have found that.

If either his father or brother had ever wondered what Matthew's role in the factory entailed, it was likely they have assumed his sole aim was to keep the employees fit to work.

Matthew saw it differently. He'd do his best to keep his patients healthy – whatever was wrong with them. If that involved giving contraceptive advice to the factory workers, then so be it. He was happy to do that as well as keep an eye out for rashes and other telltale signs of poisoning from the chemicals many of the women worked with.

If his father and brother had known, they'd probably have been most annoyed. Matthew could hear his father accuse him of time-wasting. But anything that helped his patients to achieve healthy lives could never be a waste of time.

Matthew crossed the road. Brent House was in sight and there was no point delaying further. Anyway, he was hungry. It was a long time since he'd eaten.

Almost home.

Well, not his home.

Almost at Robert's home.

A heaviness settled on him as he reached the house next door.

It began to drizzle.

Matthew wondered if he should move out of Brent House and live permanently in the room that was reserved for him in case he needed to stay overnight. But the constant noise and commotion bothered him. No account was taken of day or night; the machines worked without stopping. Once inside a bunker or workshop, it was impossible to determine the time. It was always artificially light. Permanent day for twenty-four hours. They were all the reasons he wouldn't like it, but perhaps it would be worth putting up with all those disadvantages to move out of Brent House. It was definitely worth considering.

With a sigh, he realised he'd arrived. He looked up at the impressive townhouse, steeled himself and walked slowly up the steps to the front door and knocked.

A red-cheeked maid opened the door, bobbed a curtsey, and let him in. He didn't recognise her. She was yet another young girl who'd come to work in this house with the ill-tempered master and mistress.

She'd hand in her notice shortly, no doubt, unable to put up with the constant arguments and fights. And if those didn't bother her, then as soon as she was of age, she'd be engaged to do war work – perhaps even in Robert's factory.

If only Matthew could shake off this gloom. He hadn't always been so miserable. He was getting on his own nerves. What on earth was wrong with him?

Matthew went up to his room and, after unpacking his belongings, he freshened up and dressed for dinner. While he was adjusting his tie, he caught sight of his face in the mirror. Such a miserable face. He forced himself to smile, but it was as though he was merely moving the corners of his mouth into a different position.

Enough was enough. His father didn't approve of his life choices. Well, that was too bad. Matthew was a doctor and proud of it. Why should he be defensive? And why should he have to watch what he said or did in front of his brother and sister-in-law for fear he'd spark an argument?

It was time to move out and be his own man. Perhaps he'd even remember how to smile.

Matthew went downstairs, wondering whether Julia had told his brother about her condition. However, all was calm over dinner. It certainly wasn't a pleasant meal because there was an underlying current of nastiness as each took the opportunity to snipe at the other. Nevertheless, at present, there appeared to be a truce.

Over his soup spoon, Matthew observed his flabby-jowled and portly brother. Robert enjoyed the good life, and despite the war and privations, he had enough money to ensure he maintained his standard of living. Matthew wondered if the rumours that as well as his mistress, he was now having an affair with an actress, were true. If so, his mistress would be furious.

And his wife? Well, Matthew had only known two women intimately, and that had been at university, so he was hardly an expert, but he was certain no woman wanted to be replaced in a man's affections, whatever the circumstances.

Perhaps that was why Julia had her own love affairs. Although he suspected not. She appeared to be the sort of woman who needed constant amusement and if it involved an element of risk, so much the better.

On several occasions, she'd propositioned him until he'd made it clear he'd never betray his brother. She'd been furious at being rejected, but Matthew had stood his ground and eventually she'd given up.

Julia was several years older than Matthew, still as beautiful as she'd been the first time Matthew had laid eyes on her at a ball. He'd been completely smitten with her. However, it rapidly became clear she had her sights set on the elder brother, the successful businessman, not the penniless doctor.

Matthew's heart had been broken, but eventually, when he'd realised the type of woman she really was, he'd been extremely grateful.

The maid removed the soup dishes, and another girl served the first course.

"You're very quiet, Matthew, darling," Julia said as she daintily cut a piece off her large steak and stabbed it with a fork. "Did you have a good time away? How were my dear in-laws? We really must take the time to go and visit them, Robert."

Robert grunted through a mouthful of potato. He swallowed.

"Too busy, my dear, as you well know. There's a war on, after all. But why don't you go? It might keep you out of mischief."

It was said as if a joke, but no one smiled.

"And how was that delightful RAF friend of yours, Matthew? Wasn't his name, Hugh? Robert said, shovelling more potato into his mouth. "You really must bring him here to stay again. The last time he came it was so diverting. I lost an absolute fortune to him on the cards, and I simply must have a chance to recover my losses.".

Matthew nodded, having no intentions of inviting Hugh again. He knew he ought to appreciate such a meal, especially during wartime rationing, but it tasted of nothing. He was too busy waiting for the inevitable fighting to start.

Matthew stared at Julia trying to spot any changes. Her waistline was covered in a large serviette, and she didn't look any different, although it was rather early for any changes to show. Perhaps she'd been mistaken when she'd thought she was pregnant. Perhaps there was no baby.

She intercepted his gaze and smiled knowingly. "I expect you want to know what's been going on here while you've been away, Matthew, darling," she smiled at him sweetly.

Matthew held his breath. Was this the point where she announced she was about to have a baby?

Please, no. Robert would be furious.

Julia smiled mischievously. "Well, I'm sorry to tell you, it's been very dull. So utterly tedious. Robert has spent most of his time in London and I've been here thoroughly bored. But now you're home..."

As soon as Matthew had finished eating, he claimed he was tired after his journey and went to his bedroom. He re-packed his bag.

In the morning, he'd thank Robert for his hospitality, then tell him he didn't intend to return to his room in Brent House. He'd claim he wanted to be close to the small hospital in the factory, so it would be better if he slept in his room at the hostel. He'd offer to return to Elmford Mere if Robert needed him there, but he doubted that would ever be the case. If Robert needed him for anything, he'd summon him to his office at work.

Being caught in the undercurrent of this household was uncomfortable, and for Matthew, it was completely unnecessary. He'd done nothing to create the problem; he didn't want to be one of those dragged under by it.

If Robert and Julia wanted to make each other miserable, they could leave him out of it.

# Chapter Five

Bethany turned on the tap, and with her finger under the streaming water, she waited until it was warm, then she put the plug in the sink. This simple act still made her want to clap her hands together like a child and laugh.

Even three weeks after she'd first been led into the bedroom she shared with Mavis, she couldn't get over the fact that she had – not only running water – but hot running water whenever she wanted it.

In Pa's cottage, she'd had to fetch water from a standpipe or collect rainwater. Priory Hall had plumbing, but it was old, and Mrs Stewart had preferred to boil water in the kettle or the large copper in the scullery.

However, here in Kestrel Block in the Elmford Factory living quarters, Bethany had hot and cold running water in her room. Along the corridor, there were showers and baths plumbed in. No need to fetch the metal tub from its nail outside the backdoor. No need to boil kettles of water to fill that tub once it had been placed in front of the fire. And she no longer had to go to the bottom of the garden for the earth closet – there were toilets in the washing room. It was luxurious indeed.

Not posh, like Priory Hall with its expensive furniture and curtains, its priceless paintings and vases. Everything in Kestrel Block was plain. But so modern and comfortable.

She and Mavis had a bed each, their own chest of drawers and a locker. Alice and Freddie had said when it got really cold, there was central heating. Central heating? Bethany could scarcely believe it.

If it hadn't been for the long, gruelling hours and difficult working conditions, it would almost have been like a holiday.

Bethany picked up the soap and looked down at her hands already stained yellow. It had soon become evident why Freddie's hair had a yellow streak at the front, like many of the other women in the factory. Bethany glanced in the mirror. Probably she would have yellow patches in her hair soon too.

"Come on, sleepyhead. It's time to get up," Bethany said, but Mavis pulled the covers over her head and groaned.

"Miss Mason'll be in to drag you out of bed again, if you don't get up on your own," Bethany added.

Kestrel Block's supervisor was a large, well-muscled woman with a booming voice who nobody dared disobey – not even Freddie and Alice, who were two doors along in the same block.

Mavis groaned and sat up, rubbing the sleep from her eyes.

"Come on, Maeve. Just one shift to get through and then we've got that dance in town. It'll be fun." Bethany flicked a few drops of water at her roommate.

"Well, you've changed your tune," Mavis said, throwing the covers back. "You were quieter than me when we first arrived here."

"I know, but I had no idea there could be so many things to do in this world." Bethany twirled on the spot, raising her soapy hands in the air. "I'd never danced before."

When Alice had heard Bethany didn't know how to dance, she'd squealed in dismay and insisted on teaching her at least a few steps in the communal sitting area of the block. Freddie had grabbed Mavis and made her practice too.

The first time Bethany had attended a dance, she'd expected to simply watch. However, she hadn't sat down all evening. It had been so much fun, and she'd been relieved that Mavis had been asked to dance too. The girls had been so excited, they'd discussed the dance long after it had finished, only to wake up the next day ready for the blue shift, exhausted.

Bethany had nearly nodded off at work and it had only been that someone had started singing that she'd woken up. If the supervisor had caught her, she'd have been in trouble. It wouldn't happen again. She must be more careful.

Bethany wiped her face dry and thought about the coming day. Until the beginning of this week, she'd been making bullets. She'd started as a first filler, working behind a protective screen. Her job had been to fill a tray with bullet shells, then added gunpowder to each. When they'd all been filled, she lowered a machine which pressed the powder.

When she'd first been shown, she'd wondered what she'd do to the bullets next. Would she be able to remember it all? Then, she discovered that was all she had to do. The tray of bullets she'd filled went off to the second filler and Bethany began again with another tray and more empty bullet shells.

And that was it – hour after hour doing the same thing. It was mind-numbingly boring, but she cheered herself up with the thought that any of her bullets might find their way onto Stevie's ship, HMS *Groundbreaker*. As far as she knew, it was in the middle of the Atlantic Ocean protecting merchant ships and would need all the armaments that factories like ROF Elmford could make.

She knew it was unlikely 'her' bullets would find their way to Stevie, but even so, each one of them would help their boys win this senseless war.

And so what if it was boring? As far as Bethany could see, everyone's job in that production line was as dull as hers.

Twice daily during the week, music boomed through loudspeakers as the BBC programme Music While You Work was broadcast, and often the women sang along. The sound of everyone singing as loudly as they could made Bethany's skin rise in goosebumps.

As if it had been created by one voice, the song rose to the rafters, almost drowning the din of the machinery. A song of defiance. A song of triumph to come. Surely the words would rise up into the air to any Luftwaffe pilots – perhaps even soar across the sea to Germany to tell the Jerries exactly what the women of Elmford thought of them.

Silly thoughts, but at least they kept her going during the long days.

Bethany washed quickly and dressed. Later, after she'd finished her day's work, she'd have a shower before the dance, and try to clean off the nasty chemicals. There were various remedies the other women recommended from time to time to remove the yellow from their skin. None of them had worked so far, but Bethany had some ointment she was going to try that evening. Not that she held out much hope it would take away the yellow colouration, but it made her feel like she was doing something.

Outside, further along the corridor, Miss Mason's voice boomed, warning the women to get up.

"Come on, Mavis." Bethany tugged at her roommate's bedclothes. "You don't want to get caught by Miss Mason."

"All right, all right. I'm getting up."

Bethany brushed her hair and peered in the mirror, studying her hair. There were auburn highlights but so far, no yellow. She'd been very careful to cover her hair with the turban she was provided with each day. But even so, it appeared some women were affected more than others – however much care they took.

The first morning she'd been handed a white jacket, trousers and a blue belt to show she was on blue shift as well as special shoes and the dreaded turban.

"Don't turn yer nose up," the woman who'd handed her the garments had said. "Trust me. You'll be glad of that turban."

It wasn't until later Bethany had realised how right the woman had been.

Each morning before changing into their uniforms, the women who were about to start their shift had to go to a special hut and leave anything made of metal or that might cause a spark, such as jewellery, cigarettes, matches and metal hair clips. During the day, spot checks took place and anyone found with any banned items would be in serious trouble. Bethany had been told of someone who'd even been imprisoned for smoking on site.

So, instead of pinning her hair up with Kirby grips, she tucked it carefully inside the turban. Freddie and Alice moaned they had to leave their matches and cigarettes in the 'contraband' shed, but neither of them would have dared disobey the rule.

Bethany looked at the reflection of her eyes in the mirror. So far, the whites hadn't turned yellow, but then she'd only been in her new department for three days.

She was no longer working with Mavis but with Freddie who'd told her that at the end of the week she'd go to the doctor for her blood pressure and breathing to be checked.

"I only have to look at that delicious Dr Howard and my blood pressure goes up. And as for my breathing…" Freddie held the back of her hand to her forehead and pretended to sway.

"And when he stares into my eyes, I swear I could eat him up."

"It's worth working with the dangerous stuff to spend some time with him," Alice agreed.

Bethany thought back to the rather serious-looking man who'd stayed at Priory Hall. Yes, she supposed, he was rather handsome.

But so what?

He'd never take an interest in anyone like Alice, Freddie or her. He belonged to the Howard family, the owners of the factory.

Anyway, he was probably married or spoken for.

Her first thought, when she'd heard she'd be checked regularly by the doctor, was alarm – not how handsome he was. What would she be working with that meant she had to see a doctor? Were the chemicals really that dangerous?

Well, at least she would only work in that section for a week, then be sent elsewhere for a month before she went back. The pay was better than anything Bethany could have imagined. She was making more than six times what she'd earned in service.

That money would mount up and one day she'd be able to afford to live in London and learn how to be a shorthand typist – once the war was over, that is. Then, she'd do as she wanted, and she'd come and go as she pleased.

At the end of the month, she'd send a little money to Pa. He'd probably just drink it away, and if Pauline Cresswell had moved in, she would help him drink it, but at least Bethany's conscience would be clear. What more could she do for him? And there was always the chance he'd come to his senses and would use it to buy food.

"Come on, Maeve, hurry up with your shoes; I'm starving." Bethany was ready to leave for the canteen.

Finally, Mavis was ready, and after breakfast, they showed their security passes, surrendered their wristwatches in the contraband shed and changed into their uniforms.

Another boring day loomed, but at least they could look forward to the evening when they'd go out dancing in town.

For once, Mavis got ready quickly for the dance and she, Bethany, Alice and Freddie arrived at the church hall in Elmford Mere just as the band began to play.

Alice and Freddie recognised a group of soldiers and joined them, so Bethany suggested she and Mavis get some drinks. Once in the queue, someone tapped Bethany on the shoulder, and she turned to see a tall man with piercing blue eyes and short blond hair behind her.

"Would you delightful ladies allow me to buy you drinks?" He smiled, revealing perfect, white teeth in a chiselled face. "I'm new here and I'm afraid I don't know anyone."

Bethany had been about to say they'd prefer to buy their own drinks, but she knew what it was like to be alone and lonely. He looked so lost.

She looked at Mavis to judge her reaction, but she wasn't looking at the man. Mavis was staring at her feet. It was as if she'd decided he'd only be interested in Bethany.

"Thank you," Bethany said, "that's very kind." She was still unsure she was doing the right thing. Alice and Freddie would have immediately accepted. Perhaps that was the correct way to behave.

"Harry Carpenter," he said, holding out his hand, first to Mavis, then to Bethany.

At least he was well-mannered.

"Would you like to dance?" A soldier Bethany had danced with the previous week smiled at her nervously.

She agreed, and when she turned back to check on Mavis a few moments later, Bethany was pleased to see her friend dancing with Harry. And while Bethany danced with many partners, Mavis stayed in Harry's arms for the rest of the evening.

Later that night, after the women had returned to their room and got into bed, Mavis couldn't stop talking. Her voice was edged with excitement. Bethany yawned; she was ready for sleep, but Mavis was still wide awake, wanting to talk about Harry. How charming he was, how well he danced and what he'd said to her.

"D'you know the best thing about him, Bethany?" she whispered into the darkness. "I've never met anyone who took so much of an interest in me. He wanted to know all about me – where I grew up. What I wanted to do in the future. Which books I read. Which films I like. And he's such a gentleman."

Harry had asked Mavis out to the pictures in town on Saturday night and she had already asked to borrow Bethany's best dress.

"So, what does he do?" Bethany asked, aware he hadn't been in uniform.

"He works on his cousin's farm outside Elmford Mere. He said he wanted to join up, but his cousin is seriously ill and he relies on Harry to do everything."

Mavis suddenly sat up in bed. "Oh, Bethany! My hair. What can I do with my hair? It's such a fright and I want to look lovely for Saturday. It's so dry and I keep washing it to keep the yellow colour out but that makes it drier, and it goes all frizzy. I don't want to put Harry off."

There was a hairdresser's shop on site in the main block and Bethany suggested she make an appointment there. "But I shouldn't worry about it, Maeve. I'm sure it'll take more than dry hair to put Harry off. He didn't take his eyes off you all night."

Mavis sighed and lay down again. "Did I tell you Harry said I have beautiful hands? I tried to hide them from him, but he linked his fingers with mine. And, oh, Bethany, the feeling was just wonderful. His hand was so soft, with long fingers – like a pianist's. I asked him if he played the piano and he said he did."

Mavis paused, presumably reliving the moment they'd linked hands. For a second, Bethany was envious. No one had ever told her any part of her was beautiful – well, other than that dreadful RAF pilot at Priory Hall, but he'd been drunk.

And no one had ever held Bethany's hand.

But that's good, she told herself.

Probably.

After all, where did that sort of behaviour lead? Usually to the altar. And after that, well, it was often the woman whose life changed for the worse.

Look what had happened to her mother.

Her family had forbidden her to marry Pa, believing their well-educated daughter could do better than the penniless joiner she'd fallen in love with.

At some time during their years of marriage, Pa had come to resent Ma's education and her genteel ways, belittling her, telling her she had ideas above her station.

Ma had said his pride was hurting because he'd been too ill when he first came home from the war to hold down a proper job. She'd had to take in laundry and clean other people's houses to feed the family.

"It upset him terribly, Beth, love. He's a proud man," Ma had said.

But in the end, what had it mattered?

He'd had so little respect for his wife, he'd drunk his fill while she'd bled to death.

No, Bethany would not be sweet-talked into anything. She'd build her own life. She wouldn't allow anyone to tell her what to do. If the price she had to pay was that people didn't hold her hands and compliment them, then so be it.

During the next few weeks, Mavis changed beyond recognition. She'd done as Bethany had suggested and gone to the hairdressers. The dry ends had been cut away, and although her hair was slightly short at first, it was much sleeker. And whereas before the corners of her mouth had drooped and her eyes had beenlacklustre, now she smiled and sparkled.

Apparently, Harry liked the change. Mavis said he was attentive and generous, and she often returned from their dates with a flower or length of ribbon. Recently, he'd bought her a small brooch and a necklace.

"Oh, Bethany! Harry's so kind," she said. "And he's started talking about the future. He's hinting at marriage. Just think of that! If we marry, I'll be able to leave my job. Imagine me being a bride before Alice. I never thought I'd get married, let alone find anyone before her. She's got so many men interested in her. Oh, my goodness! I could be Harry's wife soon…"

Bethany's heart sank.

She didn't want to share the room with anyone else, Mavis was easy to get on with – even if, lately, the only topic of conversation was Harry and how marvellous he was.

But she could hardly fail to be pleased for her friend; no one would begrudge Mavis this happiness.

This was what Mavis had always wanted, and the more Bethany thought about it, the guiltier she felt at her initial reaction.

One night, however, Mavis was unusually quiet; the worry lines between her brows had returned and the corners of her mouth curved down.

Bethany braced herself. If she and Harry had broken up, Mavis would be distraught.

She'd been so certain Harry would ask her to marry him. Perhaps she'd been pressing him, and he hadn't been ready to commit to her. Had she pushed him away?

"Everything all right, Maeve?" Bethany asked as casually as she could.

There was silence for a few seconds. Mavis placed her knuckles over her mouth as if not sure whether she should speak. Finally, she said, "Can you keep a secret?"

"Of course. What's bothering you?"

"Well, Harry said he loves me so much he can't wait until we…" She paused, and looking down at her hands, she shrugged. "Until we… you know."

"Until you…?" Bethany asked, assuming she was going to say 'get married'.

Mavis drew in a breath. "Until we… do it together." Her voice had dropped to a whisper, and she stared at her hands.

Then, seeing Mavis's discomfort, Bethany suddenly realised what she meant, and her hand flew to her mouth. "No!" she gasped.

"Please don't be shocked, Beth." Mavis looked stricken. "We love each other. We're going to get married, but it's so hard to wait."

Bethany hadn't meant to sound so judgemental. She smiled, softening her expression. "I'm not shocked, Maeve. It took me by surprise, that's all."

Mavis's eyes filled with tears. "It's just that I'm scared. A few of Alice's friends back home got themselves in the… you know… the family way and have had all sorts of trouble, specially once they started to show. But Harry said you can't get caught the first time you do it. I just don't know. What would you do?"

Bethany shook her head. She knew very little about the subject. Her mother had never told her, and she'd never had a reason to find out. Was it likely what Harry had said was true? She simply didn't know.

"Perhaps if you ask, Alice?" she suggested.

"Yes, maybe," Mavis said glumly. "I'm just not sure. Alice might tell our mam. I'd die if she did that."

"Well, don't do anything until you're ready. You don't have to rush into anything. You've got the rest of your lives," Bethany said.

"I suppose you're right and, anyway, we haven't got anywhere to go. Harry said he couldn't possibly take me to his cousin's house, and he can't afford a hotel room. He asked if he could come here but I told him he'd need a pass."

"Well, that isn't going to happen. The site's security is so tight."

"I know," said Mavis. "It's impossible. I was hoping he'd ask me to marry him soon and then we wouldn't have to worry about finding anywhere or about me getting... you know... in the family way. I overheard Freddie say that nice Dr Howard gave out advice about how to stop having a baby, but I'd be too embarrassed to go and see him. It's so unfair. Soon I'll be married and then I won't mind seeing a doctor, but it's now I need help."

"Perhaps Harry will propose soon."

Mavis nodded without enthusiasm. "Yes, perhaps. But he said we have to do it properly. We've got to wait until we've saved enough for a nice house..."

# Chapter Six

At the end of the week, Bethany was due another check-up with Dr Howard. She'd completed her second week filling paper tubes with that dreadful yellow stuff. As yet, there was no evidence of yellow in her hair, although she was certain the whites of her eyes were changing colour.

And as for her hands, she might as well have dipped them in yellow dye.

The previous time she'd visited Dr Howard, he'd been polite yet remote, as if he hadn't remembered he'd suggested to Mrs Richardson she should find a job in his brother's company.

Of course, there was no reason why he should remember. He dealt with hundreds and hundreds of workers – most of whom were women. Why should he have remembered her?

And yet once he'd taken her blood pressure, checked her tongue, eyes and hair, then asked numerous questions about her breathing, he'd surprised her by asking how she was settling in.

He'd said he'd seen her about with some of the women who'd been working at the factory since it had opened and asked if she'd known them before she started. She'd explained she'd met them at the station, but that now, one of them, the new girl, was her firm friend, Mavis.

The other two were Mavis's sister and her roommate.

"So, you have one good friend?"

"Yes," Bethany had said. "Mavis and I are both quiet. But we get on well."

Dr Howard had nodded his head as if in approval.

At first, she'd assumed it was the sort of thing he asked everyone, to make sure they were happy in their job. However, he'd added that Mrs Richardson had contacted him to ensure Bethany was settled.

She'd been touched. How typical of Mrs Richardson. Bethany had only been a maid in Priory Hall, although she'd worked there for several years.

She thought back to the times when Mrs Richardson had been so patient with her and had allowed her to borrow books from the library. Bethany had admired her employer so much, she'd decided to try to be like her, deliberately copying her manners and trying to speak like her. Not that Mrs Richardson had a posh accent, but when she spoke, people listened. Bethany envied her that.

Once Mrs Richardson had told Bethany she'd been a shorthand typist working in Mr Richardson Senior's company when she'd fallen in love with her husband. Mr Richardson's parents had been appalled at the thought of their son marrying the lowly office girl.

It was a similar story to her own parents with a mismatch of social standing. However, unlike Bethany's Ma and Pa, her employers had a successful marriage. You could see they cared about each other, working as a team, not constantly pulling against each other.

Perhaps if Pa hadn't come back from the Great War so damaged, her parents' marriage might have been more successful. Ma had often talked about when she'd first met Pa and how much in love they'd been, and then her face had been radiant. But when she spoke about Pa's return from the trenches, her expression clouded over, and she stared into the distance with sad, unseeing eyes.

It hadn't been her father's fault, but their marriage hadn't stood a chance.

Mr Richardson was younger than Pa and hadn't fought in the Great War, so he hadn't experienced such suffering. If he had, might he be a different man? It was hard to imagine him being anything other than the loving, easy-going man Bethany had known.

Sometimes she'd wondered if a greater factor than hardship was how much money you had. If you had plenty, you could live happily. If you were poor, like many of Bethany's neighbours, marriage might prove harder.

"Excellent," Dr Howard had said once the examination was over. "I'll be certain to let Mrs Richardson know you're happy when I contact her again. She'll be very relieved. And she mentioned that Mrs Stewart sent her best wishes. I believe she is the cook?"

Bethany had smiled and nodded.

"Now, if you have any symptoms, like a rash, breathing problems or anything that worries you, please don't hesitate to come and find me, Miss Anderson. I'm living on site most of the time now."

He'd observed her over steepled fingers and his face had softened. For the first time she saw him smile as if he really meant it, and something had squeezed her heart. If only she'd been responsible for making him smile, but it couldn't have been her. It was such a shame, though. How lovely it would have been to know she'd been the cause of his happiness. Like Harry said Mavis made him feel.

As Bethany had got up to go, her heart had still been thudding.

She wondered what he'd have made of it if he'd been listening with his stethoscope.

That had been several weeks before, but later that morning, she'd have a second check-up with Dr Howard to ensure the week working with the yellow powder hadn't made her too ill.

It was something to look forward to. A break in the monotony of filling those tiny tubes with that dreadful powder. And if she was honest, a chance to feel special – just for a few minutes – while he asked her questions and looked for any unwanted symptoms.

She'd like to see him smile again. Not that she'd made him smile before – she'd just been there when he'd thought of something amusing, but it had felt as though there had been some closeness.

Ridiculous, of course.

Hopefully, he wouldn't smile before he listened to her heart. It was already beating faster at the thought of seeing him again.

Careful. He'll assume you're ill and stop you working. No work, no wages.

She must stop this stupidity. It was just the result of doing a mind-numbing task over and over; she didn't have anything to think about. It was so easy for Dr Howard's face to creep into her mind.

She'd distract herself by counting the tubes. She'd get to one hundred and then start again. One, two, three...

After she'd been working for an hour, a messenger came to tell her she was expected in the medical room. Bethany happily passed her place to the supervisor who would keep the production line going until Bethany returned, then she left the workshop.

Asphalt walkways criss-crossed the site, linking the various workshops and buildings. Bethany walked along one of them towards the main administrative block where Dr Howard's medical room was located. As she walked along, she glanced upwards. The clouds were heavy and low, as they often were. That was a blessing. It was unlikely German bombers would find the factory flying through that.

The special surface of the walkway was designed to prevent sparks as people walked, but during the frequent security talks, Bethany had learned that from above, it also looked like water amongst the many camouflaged buildings.

It was hard to imagine. From where she was, it was obviously asphalt. But despite the importance of the site, it hadn't, as yet, been targeted.

"Touch wood," she whispered to herself, and when she reached the building, she touched the door.

Arriving at the medical room, she knocked and went in. Dr Howard was seated at his desk and he smiled at her. Did he greet everyone like that? He hadn't appeared to be so friendly the last time she'd had an appointment.

It's nothing to do with you. He's probably having a good day.

He'd remembered her the last time, but now, so many weeks later, he wouldn't recall she was the maid from Priory Hall. Nevertheless, it would have been lovely if he had remembered her amongst all the hundreds of people on the site.

He indicated she should sit in the chair by his desk, and after writing on his notes, he began the check-up.

His hands were warm and gentle as he cupped Bethany's face, and with his thumb, he gently lowered each bottom eyelid in turn. He was so close; she could smell something deliciously spicy or perhaps citrusy – she wasn't sure. But despite being so faint, it cut through the smells of the workshop; the bitter chemicals; hot oil and metal, cleaning away the dreadful odours that usually filled her nostrils. She breathed in deeply, trying to hold the memory of it.

He froze. "Did I hurt you?"

"No, no," she said, feeling foolish. She hadn't realised he'd be aware of her deep breath. "No, not at all."

Bethany blushed, knowing she couldn't possibly explain she'd been breathing in his scent.

He finished his examination, and after filling in his notes, he looked at her over his steepled fingers. "So, is everything going well?"

"Yes, thank you, doctor." She reddened again under his gaze.

"I've heard from Mrs Richardson again. I wrote to tell her you were settling in well and she asked me to let you know that if you'd like to return to Laindon when you have leave, you're welcome to stay with her. Your room is ready for you. She understands it might be easier to stay there than…" He paused, then added, "return to your father's home."

"Oh, how kind. But I hadn't thought about leave."

"Well, you must. You're entitled to time off. And as your doctor, it's highly recommended." He smiled conspiratorially. "You do a hard, tiring job and you'll do it better if you have a break occasionally. Although perhaps you don't want to go home. Perhaps you'd rather do something with your friend?"

Bethany shook her head. "No, Mavis and I haven't talked about leave." And if they had, Mavis wouldn't have wanted to go with Bethany. She'd have wanted to spend the time with Harry.

But life had been so full at Elmford, she hadn't thought further than the day's work and whether her shift would allow her to take advantage of whatever leisure activities or entertainment was on offer that day.

"The Richardsons are a remarkable couple," Dr Howard said. "I must confess, I've been corresponding regularly with them since I first visited, and we've become good friends. I can see they were excellent employers." He frowned. "Do you regret leaving your work in Priory Hall? Only I feel responsible for you moving here, and I wouldn't like to think you regretted it."

His concerned expression was disarming.

Surely, he didn't mean it?

Why would a man of Dr Howard's standing care about someone like her?

So, this was how special Mavis felt when Harry took an interest in her.

Then, without thinking, she told him her increase in wages meant that one day, she'd be able to realise her dream of becoming a shorthand typist and living independently in London.

She'd expected him to listen politely for a few seconds, then to make it clear he had other patients.

But not only did Dr Howard listen without checking his watch, clearing his throat or fidgeting, he actually appeared to be interested. He asked questions about how much training she'd need, where in London she'd like to live. Things that showed he'd been listening. Other than Mrs Richardson, he was the first person to take her seriously – and it felt good.

Not that she needed his approval – and to be fair, he hadn't offered her any. But he'd met her on equal terms and had recognised her ambition. If anything, he'd given her even more determination to continue.

The following morning, Bethany found a letter in her pigeon hole in Kestrel Block. It was from Stevie. And as if fate had been listening to Dr Howard, suggesting she should consider taking leave, Stevie asked if she could possibly meet him the following week. He said he'd be in London for several days with friends before joining his company and setting sail again.

If she was able to meet him, he'd book her a room in the boarding house where he and his mates were staying. It had been so long since she'd seen him, and although the thought of travelling to London on her own was daunting, she decided to ask for time off.

The following day, she wrote back to tell him she'd been allowed two days' leave. She told him she was looking forward to meeting him after so long, and would he book her a room for one night, please?

In Stevie's letter, he said he'd been writing to Mavis and wondered if she could accompany Bethany to London so he could meet her in person. He said he hadn't received a letter from her for a while. Was she all right?

Bethany replied to say Mavis wouldn't be able to join them and explained about Harry.

The following week, blue shift would be working from 10pm to 6am and Bethany planned to leave as soon as she finished work. She'd leave the factory site with the workers who didn't live in the hostel and she'd get on the bus to Elmford Mere with them. Then she'd catch the train to London.

She'd asked Mavis if she wanted to accompany her, just in case, but as she'd expected, Mavis refused.

As the day approached, Mavis became preoccupied and distracted.

"Are you sure you don't want to change your mind and come with me, Maeve? Stevie was so looking forward to meeting you and you could always share my room in the boarding house. You seem tired. Perhaps you need a break from work. Dr Howard advised me to take some leave."

"No, no, I'm fine, but you're right. I am rather tired. I'll sleep when you've gone and I'll be refreshed when I meet Harry later. Don't you worry about me. You just make sure you have a lovely time."

The hours of Bethany's shift crept past so slowly she wondered if the clock had broken. It was hard to concentrate on such repetitive movements, but towards 4am, the inspection men came in to carry out a spot check and that was always enough to wake up all the workers.

Luckily, everything was in order, and as a bonus, it had broken the monotony.

Bethany finished her shift and ran to her room to pick up her bag. She'd already packed so she could get out as quickly as possible and catch the bus with the other workers. Mavis was waiting for her outside their block and said she'd accompanied Bethany to the guards' hut so she could wave goodbye. Typical Mavis, always so thoughtful. Always fussing over her.

At the security hut, Bethany suddenly remembered she'd put her pass on the bed while she'd checked her bag. Had she picked it up again? If not, she'd have to run back to her room. No one got in or out without showing it to the guards. She'd reached the head of the queue as she rummaged in her handbag, trying to keep her other bag over her shoulder, but there was no sign of it.

"Where's you pass?" the guard demanded. "Get a move on. Can't yer see there's a queue?"

His irritation made her more flustered and, in her haste, she dropped her handbag. The contents rolled behind the guard into the hut. People behind her in the queue groaned and tutted, but thankfully, the other guard stooped to help her retrieve her things.

"Looks like yer mirror's broken," he said, holding out her compact. "That's seven years of bad luck." He chuckled as he passed it to her.

But dropping her bag had been a stroke of good luck because she spotted the pass which had slipped into a hole in the lining, and she held it out to him with relief.

If she'd left it in her room, it would have taken her so long to fetch it, the bus would have left without her. Then she'd have missed her train...

Bethany got on the bus with the other workers and looked back to wave at Mavis, but she'd already gone.

Poor Mavis had been so tired. She'd been desperate for sleep, so she'd be fresh when she met Harry later. Bethany was sympathetic; she was exhausted. It was lucky the hard wooden seats of the bus were so uncomfortable, especially when they turned a corner because there was no chance Bethany would doze off and miss her stop.

The London-bound train chuffed into the station several minutes after Bethany had arrived on the platform. Despite the early hour, there were many passengers – the majority of them from ROF Elmford and most people were subdued after having completed the late-night shift.

Bethany climbed into the carriage and sat down next to the blacked-out window. It was still dark outside, although by the time they arrived in London, it would be light. Two city gentlemen dressed smartly in suits and hats with briefcases sat opposite her and a woman settled in the seat next to Bethany.

"Where are you off to, love?" The woman asked, then before Bethany could answer, she said excitedly, "I'm going to Bethnal Green to visit my daughter. She's expecting, you know. The baby's due any time now, and I'm going to look after her other nippers."

Bethany smiled politely at the woman's excitement and listened as she continued to chatter. Thankfully, as the train pulled out of the station, the woman fell silent, concentrating on her knitting.

Bethany realised she was nodding off. No bad thing. She was tired after her shift. The train gathered speed and she drifted off, waking at each station. But it didn't matter if she fell fast asleep. The train terminated at Fenchurch Street Station, and if by chance she didn't wake up, someone would give her a nudge.

At each station, it was hard to sleep through the commotion as brakes squealed, whistles blew, guards shouted and doors slammed. However, as soon as the train eased out of the station, it rocked her back to sleep. Was that two or three stations they'd passed? She'd lost count, but it shouldn't be long before they reached Chelmsford.

She wasn't sure what woke her first, the ear-splitting squeal of metal on metal or the realisation she was being hurled forward. Luggage tumbled down from the luggage racks and the woman next to her grabbed her wrist, and as Bethany turned towards her, the lights went out.

Further down the carriage someone screamed a high-pitched howl of terror. The woman next to Bethany gripped her more tightly, her fingernails biting into Bethany's wrist. "Lord save us. We're going to die," she moaned. "I want to see my grandchildren."

Momentarily, the lights flickered and then remained on, although they were dimmer than they had been. Bethany strained to hear something – anything that would explain what had happened.

"Do you think the Jerries have bombed us?" the woman asked. Bethany managed to pull her wrist free and placed her hands over the woman's – she was trembling and her knitting had fallen on the floor.

"No, I don't think we've been bombed, or we'd have felt it. I'm sure we're safe. A guard will come in a moment and tell us what's happened. It'll be all right. You'll be in London in no time, ready for the birth of your next grandchild."

"D'you really think so?" The woman's voice trembled.

"Oh, yes, I'm sure," Bethany said, trying to sound more certain than she felt.

Eventually, the train eased forward and after creeping along, it pulled into a station and halted. Whistles blew, doors slammed and guards shouted. "Everyone out! All change!"

A guard helped get everyone off the train, some dazed after having been thrown onto the floor. Apparently, several bombs had been dropped outside Chelmsford, earlier, and although the railway line was still intact, the driver had spotted debris that had been hurled into the cutting and onto the line and had braked sharply. However, there was a lot of damage to the rail further along the line and the train would not be able to proceed to London.

A guard said that men were working on clearing the line and if people wanted to remain in the carriages, the train would eventually go to London, but he had no idea when. Trees had been blown up, and it wasn't known if there was any damage to the rails. Once everything had been cleared, the rails would have to be inspected to ensure they were safe before the train was allowed to proceed. Bethany gathered up her neighbour's knitting and helped her off the train. The woman was still shaking and her teeth were chattering.

"I can't believe my bad luck," she said.

"But you can carry on by bus," Bethany pointed out. "It'll take longer but at least you'll get there eventually. That's what I'm going to do."

"You're right, love. I might just do that." She brightened up and took her bag from Bethany. "I'm not gonna let Jerry tell me what to do."

However, Bethany soon discovered that although there were several buses that were supposed to be heading towards Chelmsford, they wouldn't be running either because the bomb had also damaged the road.

"Well, that's that then," the woman said crossly. "I'm going home. I'll try again tomorrow."

Buses had been laid on to drop passengers off at the stations through which they'd already passed on the train and Bethany and the woman climbed into one in silence.

There would be no way for Bethany to let Stevie know she hadn't managed to get to London until she got back to the factory. Luckily, he'd given her the phone number of the boarding house and she'd be able to tell him once she got back.

He'd be frantic with worry, especially if he found out there'd been an explosion near the railway line, but there was nothing she could do.

Once she reached Elmford Mere, she had to walk from the station back to the factory because the buses wouldn't be ready to convey workers until the next shift was about to begin.

By the time the security hut and perimeter fence came into sight, she'd rubbed a blister on her heel and her shoulders ached from carrying her bag.

"Give us a smile then, love. Yer look like yer lost a pound and found a penny," the guard said as he checked her pass. "Did yer fella stand you up?"

"Something like that," she said, too tired and disappointed to explain. Would she be able to get to London before Stevie had to return to his ship? Oh, what bad luck. She hadn't seen her brother for so long.

Bethany hurried to Kestrel Block and after quietly entering, she made her way to her room. When she opened the door, she stood staring, not believing her eyes. Mavis was lying on the bed with a stocking tied around her mouth. Her hands were bound behind her back and her feet tied to the bedstead.

She wasn't moving.

# Chapter Seven

Bethany smothered a scream and rushed to Mavis. She was warm and still breathing, although she appeared to be asleep. Bethany untied the gag and shook her, but although Mavis struggled to open her eyes, they didn't appear to focus on Bethany, and they immediately slipped shut.

Bethany ran to Miss Mason's room but there was no reply. Should she wake Alice? Well, what could Alice do? No, Bethany needed medical help.

Heedless of her blisters, she ran to the main block and knocked at the medical room. The nurse frowned as she opened the door, but after Bethany had quickly explained, her face registered shock and she ran to fetch Dr Howard.

He came to the door, his coat half on and his case under his arm.

"Where's the patient?" he asked, his voice calm and reassuring.

As Bethany struggled to keep up with him, she quickly explained what she'd seen, and his brows drew together in disbelief.

"She's tied up?"

"Yes, her feet are tied to the bedstead and her hands are behind her back. I took the gag off. Perhaps I should've untied her hands and feet too, but she won't wake up." Bethany realised she was babbling.

When they arrived at her room, Mavis was still asleep.

Dr Howard took control immediately. He raised her eyelids gently and shone a torch in her eyes but as soon as he'd let the lids go, they slid back into place. He checked her pulse, then sniffed the air. His eyes narrowed.

"Chloroform. She's been chloroformed. Have you any idea how this happened?"

Bethany shook her head.

"Go and alert security," he said, his eyes wide in alarm then. "If someone on site has done this, we need to lockdown. And if it's an intruder..." He left the sentence hanging.

"An intruder?" she whispered and groaned softly. The hairs stood up on the back of her neck. Surely Mavis hadn't got Harry in here. No, that wasn't possible.

"Do you know anything, Miss Anderson?" Dr Howard asked.

"No... I don't know." She looked at him, her eyes wide in horror. But there was no point making accusations. "I'll go and get security," she said. She needed to think it through. Harry couldn't possibly have done this, surely? He adored Mavis.

Soldiers came running to the room by which time Mavis was sitting up in bed, dazed; she didn't even recognise Bethany She simply rocked back and forth, moaning, "Harry, Harry, Harry."

Was it possible Mavis had got him in somehow? Surely the security was too tight. And even if she had managed to sneak him in, why would he do this to her? He'd asked her to marry him. I didn't make sense. He'd been so keen on her, so interested in everything she did. He loved her.

Think think.

Mavis had said he'd often asked her about her work. He'd said he liked to imagine her when she wasn't with him and asked her to describe what her day was like in detail. She'd said she'd told him she did boring clerical work and had then changed the subject. Once, Mavis had said he'd noticed yellow on her hands and asked her what it was. She'd made up a story about trying to dye her sister's hair and having got chemicals over her hands. But that had been shortly after she'd met him. Suppose Mavis had since told him what she did? Or had he known what the yellow was and guessed what sort of work she was really involved in?

Why would he be so interested in her work unless he was a... Bethany's mind was reluctant to even form the word – spy.

No, impossible. Harry was so normal. So ordinary. Just a farm worker. He'd told Mavis he'd been disappointed he'd had to help his cousin on the farm rather than join up.

But that was what he'd said. There was no proof.

Then something else occurred to Bethany. Mavis had said Harry's hands were so soft like a pianist's hands. All the farm labourers Bethany knew had rough calloused hands, jagged nails; some were grimy with oil from working on tractors, or simply from the earth itself. Was it possible Harry had workers for the farm – perhaps Land Girls? In which case he might not have often got his hands dirty, but that was unlikely.

Everything he'd told Mavis was believable, and yet she'd never met his cousin or his family; she'd never seen anything as far as Bethany knew to back up his story. They'd always met in town. Something else came to Bethany – Harry had always had plenty of money to spend on her.

Bethany sat on her bed and buried her head in her hands.

"Are you all right, Miss Anderson?" Dr Howard touched her shoulder. "You must've had a dreadful shock."

Bethany began to cry – tiredness, hunger and dread that her suspicions might be correct weighed heavily.

"Is Mavis going to be all right?" she asked as two soldiers carried her out on a stretcher towards the medical room.

"She'll be fine. We'll look after her. Now I suggest you try to sleep; you look exhausted."

Bethany awoke later with a start. Dreams had tainted her fitful sleep which were accompanied by Mavis wailing, "Harry, Harry, Harry."

She blinked several times, trying to clear her vision, but her eyes were dry and sore. The hammering on her door continued and she realised what had woken her.

As she sat up, Miss Mason barged into her room and stood, hands on hips.

"What's the matter with you? I've been knocking for ages. You're needed by Mr Howard. You're to go to his office now." She tipped her head to one side. "Well? Did you hear me? Get going!"

"Dr Howard?" Bethany asked, still groggy with sleep. Surely, she meant Dr Howard.

"I said 'Mr' because that's what I meant. Mr Howard, the man in charge of the entire factory. The man who decides whether you stay or go. Get up now."

She slammed the door as she left, and Bethany could hear the echo of her footsteps as she stomped back to her room.

Bethany got out of bed. Her head pounded, and she saw with dismay her heels were bleeding where they'd blistered.

Why did Mr Howard want to see her?

Bethany had told Dr Howard everything she knew. She splashed cold water over her face, trying to wake up.

There must be news about Mavis. Yes, that was it. Although why someone as important as Mr Howard would want to see Bethany to tell her, she didn't know. She dressed quickly, avoiding her reflection in the mirror. Her eyes were sore, and her face felt puffy from crying. She must look a sight. But the sooner she saw Mr Howard, the sooner she could get back to bed. She was, after all, still on leave.

When she entered Mr Howard's office, Dr Howard was there along with an army officer – presumably the man in charge of security.

"Sit down, Miss Anderson," Mr Howard said.

Alice had told her he was Dr Howard's elder brother, but there was no evidence of family resemblance. Mr Howard was large and shapeless with a nasal voice. His double chins hung low, and he repeatedly slipped one of his short, fat fingers inside his collar to ease the pressure on his neck.

He remained standing, as did the other two men, while she sat in the chair he'd indicated before looking up at them.

Dr Howard's face was guarded. But the other two glared at her with open hostility. She began to wonder if they thought she was Mavis.

Mr Howard looked at his watch, then glared at her again. "So, Miss Anderson, please will you explain your part in this deplorable business."

"My p... part?" She frowned, not understanding.

"Yes, yes. Come along, Miss Anderson, you're wasting our precious time. What part did you play in allowing the intruder to gain access to the factory grounds?"

"No... nothing, sir. I'm not even supposed to be here. I'm supposed to be in London tonight, staying with my brother." Surely, they couldn't think she was involved. She glanced up at Dr Howard, but still his expression was unreadable.

Mr Howard laced his podgy fingers together as if praying. "And yet you are here," he said slowly.

"The train didn't get through, sir. There was an explosion this side of Chelmsford and the train stopped. I couldn't get to London. I had to come back here."

"You didn't think to continue your journey by bus?"

"Yes, sir, I was going to do that, but the road was damaged too."

"And so you came back?"

"Yes, sir."

"And then?" His eyebrows were arched as if he didn't believe a word she was saying.

"And then I found Mavis, sir." She swallowed, trying to keep her voice level and blinked to prevent hot tears from trickling down her cheeks.

"Did you see the person who tied Miss Jenkins up?"

"No, sir. Mavis was like that when I found her."

"Very convenient." Mr Howard sniffed. "So do you know who tied her up?"

"I... I..."

"Well, do you?" He slapped his hands down on the table and leaned forward. "If you know anything, Miss Anderson, you must tell us immediately. The safety of thousands of people could rest on what you say next."

Bethany gasped. She's been thinking of the situation from Mavis's point of view. How devastated she'd be if Harry had betrayed her. Now she saw that if it was Harry, he wasn't simply betraying Mavis, but everyone in the factory. Hundreds and hundreds of people.

"I... Well, I don't have any proof, sir, but I think it might have been the man Mavis has been seeing."

"His name?" The officer barked abruptly.

Bethany jumped and swung to face him. "Harry Carpenter, sir. But

I don't have any proof it was him."

"And yet you provided a distraction in the guard hut so Miss Jenkins could allow him access?"

"Distraction, sir?"

"Distraction, Miss Anderson. You know what a distraction is, do you not?"

"Yes, sir, but I didn't cause a distraction."

"Did you, or did you not drop your handbag?"

"Well, yes, sir. But that was an accident."

"So you say. Apparently, while one guard was checking passes and the guard was helping you pick up your belongings, Miss Jenkins slipped away unseen and guided an intruder in through a hole in the fence."

Bethany stared at him. How could he believe she'd been involved? "But I was looking for my pass and I dropped my bag. I smashed my compact mirror."

Mr Howard arched his eyebrows again. "You smashed your compact mirror? And what exactly does that prove, Miss Anderson?"

Her mouth opened and closed.

"And you tell us you were going to visit your brother and yet, you told the guard on your return a boyfriend had stood you up."

"No, sir, I..."

"Don't even try to deny it. The guard has given his statement."

"Truly, sir, I was going to visit my brother. The guard assumed I had been stood up. I was too tired to explain."

The security officer snorted in derision.

"So," Mr Howard said sharply, "this man, Harry Carpenter, what does he look like?"

Bethany's mouth had gone dry. Not only did it appear they believed her best friend had allowed a stranger into the grounds, but they also thought Bethany was guilty. She described Harry and told the men everything she could remember that Mavis had told her. Would they be satisfied, or would those details merely convince them she'd had a part in it?

When she'd finished, Dr Howard spoke for the first time, "Well, gentleman, I think it's obvious Miss Anderson is an innocent party here. Now, if you have sufficient details, I'd like to take her to the medical room."

Bethany's teeth were chattering. She wasn't cold, so she assumed it was fear, but her mind had gone numb. While she'd been describing Harry, the officer had fired questions at her faster than she could think, and inside, she was quaking.

Dr Howard stepped forward and gently took her arm. "I will monitor my patient carefully and be assured that if she thinks of anything else I will let you know. Let's hope this man is apprehended as speedily as possible."

The officer harrumphed, and Mr Howard glared at his brother and at Bethany.

"Very well, but if she remembers anything else she is to let you know immediately. Until this matter is sorted, Miss Anderson is suspended. I'm still not convinced she isn't involved in some way."

Bethany gasped as she heard this. Suspended? She might lose her job and be sent home in disgrace. She wanted to bury her face in her hands with shame.

"And let's hope the Jerries don't come back tonight and blow us all to bits," the officer said as they left.

"I'll give you something to sleep, Miss Anderson. You did well giving so many details," Dr Howard whispered as he gently led her towards the medical room.

Bethany's mind was too numb to care.

# Chapter Eight

♥

"Doctor?" the young girl in front of Matthew said. "T, U, H, V? Do you want me to read the next line down?"

Matthew stared at the reading chart on the wall. "Oh, yes. Yes, please, Miss er..." he said, bringing his thoughts back to the present. He looked down at his notes. "Miss Watson. Please read as far down the chart as you can."

He finished her check-up and looked at his list. Two more workers to examine and then he'd go back into the small room that served as a hospital.

Miss Anderson, the only patient in his hospital, had been in shock and his brother and that idiot who was in charge of security hadn't helped. It was obvious she'd had nothing to do with the intrusion.

Are you certain? Or is that what you want to believe?

Well, he was as sure as he could be in this strange war-torn world, where perfectly ordinary people betrayed their fellow humans. Miss Anderson's story was certainly plausible. On the other hand...

Whatever his thoughts on the matter, she was innocent until proven guilty, and if they ever caught the intruder, then the truth would surely be revealed.

They must catch him. If Robert was correct, and Harry Carpenter – or whoever he was – had entered the factory site shortly after Miss Anderson had left, then he'd gained access at about 6.15pm. Presumably, he'd gone directly to Kestrel Block with Miss Jenkins and, assuming he'd immediately tied her up in her room, that would have given him several hours to wander through the site before Miss Anderson raised the alarm.

Miss Jenkins's pass was missing, and if he'd taken it, he could have flashed that. Of course, if anyone had looked closely at the pass, they'd have noticed it wasn't his, but he might have managed to remain hidden for some time. He could have gathered plenty of sensitive information and then escaped through the hole in the fence where he'd entered.

Robert had interviewed Mavis Jenkins's sister, Alice, and discovered the spot where the fence had been cut had been where she'd previously met with a man and spoken to him through the wire to arrange assignations. He was married and afraid letters or telephone calls would be traced back to him. The place was hidden from view by a large bush, which Robert had immediately ordered to be removed and the fence fixed.

Both Jenkins sisters had been suspended, pending dismissal, as had another girl, Freda Bailey. And, unfortunately, thrown into the mix was Bethany Anderson, the girl Matthew believed was innocent.

But how much had she known? Had she simply turned a blind eye? His common sense said no; after all, unless she'd planned on escaping that evening, she was as much at risk of German bombs, as anyone. There was no doubt they'd have made the destruction of Elmsford's filling factory a priority. No one in their right mind would still be here if they knew the Germans had sufficient information to blow them to the skies.

There had, indeed, been explosions near the railway line outside

Chelmsford early that morning, causing major disruption on the trains – so that part of her story was true. Furthermore, she'd returned after her journey had been interrupted. She could have gone anywhere but she'd come back to Elmford and raised the alarm.

Money? That was a possibility. Hadn't she told him she was saving as much of her wages as she could so that she could start a new life in London? If Carpenter had paid her, she'd simply have fled. Not to London that night perhaps, but no one would have missed her for several days. She could have been anywhere in the country in that time, but she'd chosen to return. No, the more he thought about it, the more he believed she'd been inadvertently ensnared in the mess. She valued her job in the factory. Matthew was certain of that.

When he'd finished examining his last patient, he went into the hospital. Miss Anderson lay in bed, white-faced and wide-eyed, staring at the ceiling.

"She's barely eaten a spoonful, doctor," Nurse Evans whispered to him. "She says she feels sick."

"Thank you, nurse. I've left my notes on my desk. Please could you check over them and make sure they're legible? You know how dreadful my handwriting is. I'll deal with the patient now, thank you."

The nurse rose, her starched uniform crackling as she left the room. There were only six beds and thankfully only one was currently occupied. It had certainly been busier in the past when there had been accidents in the factory.

Matthew sat down next to the lone patient.

"Well, Miss Anderson, how are you feeling now?" His smile was gentle. If he could gain her confidence, perhaps she'd respond.

She turned her head and looked at him with dull eyes. There was no spark there at all. She was still in shock.

"Would you mind if I called you Bethany?"

She blinked as if to bring herself to the present and nodded. "Yes, doctor," she said in a flat voice.

"Nurse told me she's concerned you've barely eaten anything today. When did you last eat?"

She shook her head as if she couldn't remember. "Before last night's shift, I think."

"Well, Bethany, I really think now is the time, don't you?"

He plumped up her pillows. "Here, let me help you." He lifted the bowl of porridge and held it out to her. "Or I could feed you." He dipped the spoon into the porridge and raised it with a large mound on top.

"Hmm," he said, inspecting it. "Canteen special. Nice and thick. Guaranteed to fill you up. Unfortunately for you, I'm not as practised as Nurse Evans in feeding people. This could end up anywhere…" His hand wobbled and the porridge trembled.

She smiled.

That was a good sign.

"So, please take pity on me. If this is left any longer, it'll set off like concrete and then how will I wash up the dish? The ladies in the canteen won't be happy." He smiled at her mischievously.

She returned his smile and took the bowl from him, putting the tiniest amount in her mouth.

"See? It's delicious," he said with a grin, rising and busying himself at the nurse's desk. The last thing she needed was an audience while she ate, although he glanced at her every so often to check she was still eating.

"Have they found Harry, doctor?" she asked.

"I don't know. I haven't been told. But your description was very good. I'm sure they'll find him soon."

"And if they don't?"

He turned to face her and shook his head sadly. Without thinking, he looked upwards towards the ceiling as if imagining the German bombers flying overhead, dropping their deadly cargo. He saw she'd glanced upwards too, her thoughts in tandem with his.

"Do you know what's happened to Mavis?" she asked.

He nodded. "Your friend has gone to the local hospital. They've got more equipment there. There's no evidence that Carpenter hurt her, and she maintains he didn't. Yet she's not as well physically as we'd expected. There's been a suggestion she might have had an unusual reaction to the chloroform for her still to be so low. Anyway, she'll be looked after until this matter is sorted one way or the other," Matthew said.

Bethany lowered her gaze.

"Did she tell you something we need to know that would help us to make her better?"

Bethany shook her head. "No, but knowing Mavis, it'll be more what's going on inside her head that's the problem. Not her body. She adored Harry."

"I see." Matthew sighed. "A very sad situation."

"She won't be back to work, though, will she? Even if Harry is caught."

"No. She's in a spot of bother, I'm afraid."

Bethany began to cry. "I know what she did was wrong, but she only ever wanted to be loved. When I first met her, she'd given up on anyone ever wanting her. And then we met Harry at a dance, and he was immediately attracted to her. Or that's what he said. He made her so happy. But none of it was true, was it?" She groaned. "He targeted us. He targeted Mavis."

The bowl was tipping precariously as she relived moments from the past, so Matthew took it from her.

"I'm afraid that looks very likely," he said kindly.

"Oh, poor Mavis. He was just leading her on. How could he have been so cruel?" She buried her face in her hands.

"Someone who's willing to gather information that might result in the death of thousands of people and the destruction of a factory that provides armaments for the country's defences, is probably more than capable," Matthew said, and then regretted it as Bethany cried even harder.

He handed her the porridge. "Now, finish this. That's doctor's orders. I shall come back and check. And please know I'm aware of all the hiding places in this room so I'll know if you've hidden it somewhere." He smiled, and once again, was pleased to see a glimmer of a smile in return.

"Am I still under suspicion?" she asked in a small voice.

He hesitated for a second, but there was no point concealing the truth from her. "I don't know. You certainly shouldn't be, but it's not up to me." He checked his watch. "I'm just about to go for meeting with Mr Howard and I hope to find out more. I'll suggest Nurse Evans sits with you. She's a kind woman." Not only that but she was practical and gentle. The perfect nurse and she'd look after their patient.

"I know," said Bethany. "Nurse Evans has been marvellous."


Matthew left instructions with Nurse Evans to keep an eye on Bethany and the medical room while he was gone.

Then he hurried to Robert's office.

When he entered, his brother was on the telephone, and he waved his hand in an irritable gesture for Matthew to sit. From his words, it was clear he was speaking to someone important – his usual edge of boredom and condescension had been replaced by reverential respect.

"Yes, sir. Of course, sir, I'll get right on to it. You can rely on me."

He replaced the receiver in the cradle.

"Good news," he said to Matthew. "They've apprehended our intruder. Not Harry Carpenter, but Heinrich Zimmerman, a German agent. He took that stupid girl in, plying her with presents and promises of marriage, which she swallowed wholesale. The girl's sister had told her about the place where she used to speak to a man through the fence. We don't believe the sister was involved but I've dismissed her anyway. As well as her roommate. She knew all about it and didn't report it. It was a security breach, even if the fence was intact."

"So, where's Zimmerman now?"

"London. Apparently, he's talking freely. No point doing otherwise – he was caught with his camera and rolls of undeveloped film so there's no doubt about his guilt. He said the Jenkins girl told him where they could meet without being seen so they could talk through the fence. She was waiting when he got there and he used wire cutters to cut the fence. He said she wasn't happy about it, but once he'd done it, he persuaded her to take him to her room so they could talk about fixing the situation. Stupid girl. How on earth did she think it would help taking him to her room? But apparently, she was so afraid he'd get caught, she did as he said. As soon as they got to her room, he knocked her out and tied up. And that was it. He had her pass, access to the entire site and a camera concealed in a bag."

Matthew shook his head, his mind exploring what had happened and how the outcome could have been so different. "Do we know if he managed to get any information back to Germany?"

"Apparently, Zimmerman had a wireless transmitter in a rented room, but he was picked up before he could send any messages. His landlady said he hadn't been home for hours. So, it appears he was caught in time."

"And he just wandered about the premises without being challenged?"

"It seems so, although he'd smuggled in white clothes which he'd changed into in the girl's room. She'd told him what sort of uniform our workers wear and he'd made something up. They weren't quite the same but close enough for no one to notice. Anyway, he's no further threat to us now. And since he's so talkative, who knows what else he'll be able to tell the Security Services in London? Apparently, he's of German parentage but was born and raised in England. He's convincing and polished. It's unlikely this was his first assignment."

Matthew gasped. That had been close. Suppose he'd managed to get his films or a message out of the country?

"Thank goodness Miss Anderson's description of the man led to him being apprehended before any harm was done," he said, wanting to remind Robert about his patient and her obvious innocence.

Robert snorted, obviously not convinced. "Well, one thing's certain, heads will roll around here. Security's been stepped up."

"And Miss Anderson?" Matthew persisted. "There's no evidence she was involved."

"We'll see. She's suspended without pay for the next week and should think herself lucky. After that, I shall reassess. In a few days, we should have a full report from the Security Forces. Zimmerman hasn't mentioned her yet – he's being interrogated about past assignments – that's most important. As I understand it, the Anderson girl is in our hospital, so she's currently under surveillance."

Matthew bit his lower lip, holding back the words he longed to shout, telling his brother not to be so unfair. Robert had already said Zimmerman had been candid. There had been no mention of Bethany. But if he expressed an interest, it was likely Robert would be even more unreasonable.

Matthew recognised his brother's expression from their childhood. It was the one when Robert knew he had an excellent hand at cards, or he'd worked out the winning move in chess. Or even more likely when he'd cheated and knew he couldn't lose.

So Bethany had met some women at the station on her way to Elmford and had made friends. She'd been put in the same room as a girl who should have known better, but who'd been cruelly used by a German agent. And for that, she'd been caught up in this mess? Well, not if Matthew could help it.

He'd go to the finance department and ensure Bethany was secretly paid out of his money for the week. And after that? She would either be dismissed, in which case he'd never see her again, or she'd be allowed back to work. But first she had to get better.

"In that case, she might as well go home as soon as she's well enough and recuperate there," Matthew said, but Robert had lost interest and glanced up from scribbling in his book as if he'd forgotten Matthew was still there.

"You're the doctor," he said, his tone suggesting his position was of no account at all. "Do what you think best. Sort it out with Miss Grant." He waved his hand in a gesture of dismissal.

Matthew stood up quickly and went into Robert's secretary's room. Efficient Miss Grant had been working for Robert for years. He wondered how she put up with his rudeness.

"Certainly, doctor," Miss Grant said, "leave it with me. I'll get the paperwork ready immediately."

Matthew smiled as he left the secretary's office. He'd expected

Robert to insist the girl stayed on site under surveillance. Next, he'd arrange for her to go to Priory Hall, unless she preferred to go to her father's home instead. But he'd ensure she was off-site and able to relax without being under surveillance.

# Chapter Nine

"Consider it time off from work so you can fully recuperate," Dr Howard had said. But still the word 'suspended' overshadowed everything in Bethany's mind. He'd assured her as soon as a decision was made, he'd let her know, and he was so sure it would be in her favour, he said she'd be allowed back immediately.

"Would you prefer to go home or to take up Mrs Richardson's offer?" he'd asked.

She certainly didn't want to be a nuisance to the Richardsons, but wasn't sure there'd be a welcome for her at Pa's.

Dr Howard had telephoned Mrs Richardson and explained the situation, arranging for her to stay in her old room in the servants' quarters.

She'd left shortly after, and the journey back to Laindon had been uneventful.

Walking out of the station into the High Road, she experienced a rush of pleasure at the thought of seeing Mr and Mrs Richardson and their children, and, of course, Mrs Stewart.

Bethany would go to see her father while she was there. She'd heard nothing from him, although she'd written regularly and sent him money. She wondered what state his cottage would be in. Would

Pauline Cresswell have moved in?

The walk from Laindon Station was pleasant, and she savoured the smells of the countryside. The crisp autumn air that swept through her, blowing away the chemicals and stench of the factory. What a shame it couldn't clean away the thoughts that were hanging over her. What would happen if the investigation found she was guilty?

How that could happen, she had no idea, but Mr Howard had twisted everything, and the people from Whitehall would be more likely to believe him than her.

Thank goodness Dr Howard had spoken up for her. He'd been a better friend to her than anyone else had ever been. Even Mavis. Not that it had been her fault. She hadn't deliberately trapped Bethany in this nightmare. In fact, Dr Howard said she'd told the men who'd questioned her that Bethany knew nothing about her plans. Furthermore, there hadn't been any plans. She'd simply met Harry at the fence and before she'd been able to stop him, he'd cut it with wire cutters. He'd told her he simply couldn't spend more time away from her. And she'd believed him. She hadn't wanted to take him to their room, but once he'd cut the fence, he'd claimed he'd done it in a moment of madness because he was so desperate to be with her. If he was caught, he'd be in terrible trouble, so they needed to discuss what to do next. Mavis hadn't felt she had any choice. But despite Mavis having told everyone Bethany hadn't known anything, Mr Howard had chosen not to believe her.

Bethany hadn't heard from Mavis either, which was probably as well, since letters from her might have been used to suggest the girls had been working together with Harry. It was likely Mavis had gone home with Alice, although Bethany didn't have her address.

Poor Mavis. What must she be going through? Harry, or Heinrich, had been so convincing. His accent was English, and his story had been constructed in such a simple manner yet so cleverly done it was completely believable.

Only his hands might have given him away, but sadly, Bethany had thought no further than her friend's happiness. It was unlikely Mavis would have believed Bethany, anyway, if she'd asked why his hands were not those of a labourer. Indeed, there could've been many reasons. It certainly hadn't been proof of anything.

Bethany stopped at the brow of the hill and looked out over the softly undulating countryside – still so green, but with many of the trees showing their brilliant autumn colours. She shivered with pleasure. This week, she'd concentrate on what was good in her life. Nothing would get her down.

She walked up the gravel drive, taking in the welcome sight of Priory Hall. Nothing had changed. It was an anchor in her life. She crunched across the gravel and went around to the kitchen at the back, knocking on the door.

Mrs Stewart threw her hands up in delight when she saw her. "Oh, my dear, my dear! Come in." She opened the door wide, and Bethany stepped into the warmth of the fragrant kitchen. It smelled of spices and sugar and took Bethany back to days before the war when life had been simple.

"Well, how good it is to see you," Mrs Stewart said, wiping her eyes on her apron. "Take off your coat and sit down. I'll make you tea. Mr and Mrs Richardson and the children are out but they'll be back this evening, but in the meantime, tell me all that's been going on."


The following morning, Bethany got up early and helped Mrs Stewart make breakfast.

"You don't need to help, love. Mrs Richardson doesn't expect you to work."

Bethany knew that was true, but even so, she wanted to thank everyone for their kindness.

The previous evening, when the family had returned, the children had flown to Bethany when they'd seen her.

Eight-year-old Faye had hugged her tightly and even her younger brother, Mark, who was usually so shy, held on to her hand. The family had eaten with Bethany in the kitchen like they usually did when they didn't have guests. They included her as if she was a friend and that night when she went to bed, she realised she hadn't thought about being suspended all evening.

"What are you going to do today, love?" Mrs Stewart asked. Her brows were drawn together in a frown.

"I'm going to visit Pa."

"I thought that's what you might say," Mrs Stewart said with a sigh. "Well, you be careful."

Bethany hadn't told her what life had been like at Pa's nor that he'd pushed her and given her a black eye, but it wasn't a large town. Mrs Stewart had friends who lived in Plotlands, and she'd have known about Dave Anderson and his drinking problem. She'd also have seen his tumbledown cottage.

"I will," Bethany assured her. "Everything will be fine." She was far from certain that was the case, but she could hardly visit Laindon and not see her father.

Mrs Richardson lent Bethany a bicycle and she arrived outside Pa's cottage with glowing cheeks and cold hands. She leaned the bicycle against the overgrown hedge and walked up the path.

The gate had finally fallen off and now lay in the front garden with grass growing through it.

For a second, she wondered whether to turn around and cycle back to Priory Hall, but she had to check her father was all right.

In the past, she'd simply have opened the door and walked into the cottage, but now, she hesitated. Finally, she knocked. It wasn't her home anymore.

Pauline Cresswell opened the door. "Yes?" she said, then added, "Oh, it's you." She turned and called over her shoulder, "Dave, yer girl's here."

Pa shuffled out of the bedroom, unshaven and dressed in stained shirt and trousers.

He stared at her silently, nodding. "So, you've come back, have you?"

"Hello, Pa. I've come to see how you are." Bethany kept her voice upbeat, hiding her disappointment at his surly tone.

"You have, have you? Well, as you can see, I'm fine. No thanks to you walking out and leaving me without a word."

"I wrote and told you, Pa. I've got a job in a factory. I've got leave, so I thought I'd visit you. How have you been?" A sour smell of unwashed bodies and clothes hit her nostrils, and she was glad Pauline hadn't invited her in.

"How d'you think I was. Cut to the quick. My own daughter deserting me."

Bethany took a deep breath to steady herself. He obviously didn't remember the circumstances of her leaving.

"I didn't desert you, Pa. I got a job doing important war work. I'd have had to leave in the end. All women will have to join up or do war work soon. I found a job before I was forced to do something."

Pauline sniffed. "So, I've heard women are earning a fortune working in factories. It might've been nice if yer'd shared some of yer wages with yer poor old dad."

"I sent you money when I wrote, Pa. Didn't you get my letters?" Bethany asked, ignoring Pauline.

Pa looked unsure. He peered at Pauline, then back at Bethany. Perhaps he didn't remember getting her letters and money.

Still, Pauline stood in the way and Pa didn't tell her to invite his daughter in. He nudged Pauline's dog out of the way and sank into a chair. The wolf-like animal snarled, and with a start, Bethany saw the dog had been lying on the floor on her mother's prized patchwork quilt. She turned away, not wanting to notice anything else.

"Well, I can see you're well, Pa, so I'll be off," she said, half-hoping, half-fearing he'd call her back.

She hadn't reached the end of the path before Pauline had slammed the door.

"Oh, Ma," Bethany whispered, "how I miss you."

She felt as though she was being torn into little pieces. She still loved her father, but it was very hard to like the man he'd turned into. Neither did she want to spend any time with him. Guilt stabbed at her. Ma had asked her to look after Pa, but how could she if he wouldn't let her? Anger bubbled up inside. How could he have allowed that dreadful woman treat her mother's treasured bedspread with such disrespect?

Bethany wheeled the bicycle to the end of the unmade roads and mounted. She pedalled harder and harder, the wind whistling through her hair, blowing the smell and memory of her father's cottage away. By the time she reached Priory Hall, she was gasping for breath but exhilarated by the ride.

"Oh, Bethany, love, how was it?" Mrs Stewart asked, her face almost as red as Bethany's.

"Fine, thanks. It was as I'd expected. I might as well not have bothered." Bethany tried to keep the bitterness from her voice.

"But you did. And that's the important thing." Mrs Stewart nodded. "You wouldn't be a dear and fetch some more coal for the fire, would you? I'm all at sixes and sevens. So is the mistress. You'll never guess what…" she carried on immediately before Bethany could answer. "We're having a party tomorrow. Quite out of the blue. Mrs Richardson is just making a list of things to do."

"That's not like Mrs Richardson. She usually plans everything in advance."

"You're right. But it wasn't her, it was that chap, Hugh. You know the RAF pilot? The one with the out-of-control hands?"

Bethany groaned.

"Well, he's got himself engaged and he's asked if he can bring the lucky woman here so the family can meet her. And then, he invited several other people and before Mrs Richardson knew it, she's planning a party. He's sending over some food coupons, thankfully. But even so…"

"Don't worry, Mrs Stewart, I'll help. It'll be like old times."


Bethany spent most of the day playing with Faye and Mark in the nursery, keeping them out of the adults' way.

Mrs Stewart was busy in the kitchen while Mr and Mrs Richardson went into town for last-minute items, organised flowers and readied themselves for the guests.

Bethany dressed in her maid's black dress with its white collar and stared at her reflection in the mirror. It was the opposite of her factory uniform of white jacket and trousers, and it felt as though it was something she hadn't worn for years. Would she ever wear the white uniform again?

Well, at least the party would be a distraction and although she wouldn't be a guest, it would be a jolly evening with people celebrating. She wondered if Dr Howard would be there since he was a friend of the captain, but Mrs Stewart had said most of the people would be from RAF Hornchurch with several more from London – friends of Joan, the captain's fiancée.

How lovely it would have been to see Dr Howard again.

Don't be so foolish. He probably wouldn't even acknowledge you.

Well, she didn't expect him to spend any time talking to her, of course, but he might have had some news about her suspension.

*He told you he'd let you know immediately if he had news.*

That was true. And yet, she still wished she could see his face. He'd been the only person who'd believed in her. The only person who'd tried to help her – on two occasions.

He's a doctor. He's kind to everyone.

Bethany pushed the image of his face from her mind. The thought of seeing him filled her with something that felt like longing. But it couldn't be. It was foolish to long for something that would never be hers. She must concentrate. How would she feel if she were to drop a tray of glasses? No, she must do her best to repay the Richardsons and Mrs Stewart for their generosity.

In the kitchen, Bethany put on a starched white apron. She smoothed it down, and, after carrying two plates of sandwiches into the drawing room, she waited in the hall, ready to open the door for the first guests.

Captain Barnes-Crosier arrived first, accompanied by his fiancée. As Bethany led them into the drawing room, she remembered how the captain had behaved towards her the last time she'd seen him. This time, he only had eyes for 'his Joanie'.

Joan Lennox appeared to be a confident, strong woman who

wouldn't put up with any nonsense. Tall, and as glamorous as a film star, she held the captain's arm, placing her other manicured hand on his sleeve as if she didn't intend to let him out of her sight. She'd staked her claim, and Captain Barnes-Crosier appeared to be delighted, often laying his hand upon hers. He was like a young boy with an exciting secret he was bursting to tell.

Bethany kept them in view while she pretended to check the food. How marvellous it would be to have someone who loved you so much they couldn't even bear to let go of your arm. That sort of thing only happened in Hollywood films. She shivered as she remembered Mavis. She'd thought she had that sort of relationship with Harry.

"… of course, he'll be back on duty on Friday," Miss Lennox said to Mrs Richardson. She tilted her head on one side and studied her husband-to-be. A shadow passed across her face.

Bethany looked away. So, there was a price to pay for their happiness. How did Miss Lennox cope each time her fiancé took off in his plane? The anxiety must be overwhelming.

It was best not to fall in love in the first place. Yes, Bethany had the right idea. It was tempting to yearn for someone special, but a life on her own would be safe and steady. Surely that was the most important thing? She wouldn't be tricked like Mavis, and she wouldn't live under the shadow of loss like Miss Lennox.

More guests arrived and, in the drawing room, the excited voices grew in volume, accompanied by music and the chink of glasses.

Bethany moved amongst the guests as if she was invisible. Nobody noticed her unless they wanted a drink or something to eat. That is, except Mr and Mrs Richardson, who nodded at her from time to time as if to thank her.

As she left the drawing room with an empty plate, heading back to the kitchen to refill it with sandwiches, the doorbell rang again.

Leaving the plate on the hall table, she wiped her hands on her apron and opened the door.

For a second, she didn't recognise the man, not expecting to know any of the guests who so far had all been RAF personnel. She breathed in sharply when she saw it was Dr Howard, not dressed in his white overall but in a smart suit.

He glanced her up and down with a surprised expression. "Good evening, Bethany. Does this mean you've taken up your old job again?"

She looked down at her black dress and apron. "Oh no, sir, I'm just helping out tonight. It's the least I can do." Her voice tailed off. She didn't want to make it sound as though she considered she was doing the Richardsons a favour.

Stepping back, she took his coat and led him to the drawing room, where he soon was swallowed up by the joyful guests. As she hung up his coat, she couldn't resist lifting it to her face and breathing in his scent. Spicy, lemony – a heavenly mixture. Yet a smell of which she didn't believe she'd ever tire. How did he manage to avoid the clinical odour of the medical room where he worked?

As she picked up the empty sandwich plate to take it into the kitchen, she realised her hands were shaking. It was the shock of seeing Dr Howard, she told herself.

Shock? It had hardly been a shock. Surprising, yes. He'd come a long way to celebrate his friend's engagement.

But shock? Or were you disturbed, perhaps, by his presence?

It was nonsense. He was no one to her. Just a man who'd shown her kindness. She wasn't disturbed by him. She absolutely wasn't.

He'd made her feel like she mattered.

Like Harry made Mavis feel she mattered?

That wasn't the same at all! Harry was a Nazi spy. He had no right pretending to take an interest in her.

And Dr Howard is the brother of the man who owns the factory where you work. His interest in you is as great as in any other of the workers in that factory. You are nobody special.

"Is everything all right, love?" Mrs Stewart asked, her head on one side. "Has someone upset you?"

Bethany relaxed her face, realising it had been screwed up as if she was deeply troubled.

"Everything is fine, thank you, Mrs Stewart."

The cook tipped her head forward and peered at Bethany over the top of her glasses.

"That Captain Barnes-What's-His-Name hasn't been at you again, has he?"

"Oh no, nothing like that. He seems quite smitten with his fiancée."

"And so he should be. Now, can you take some of these in and put them on the table?" she said, holding out more sandwiches. "D'you think we need any more?"

"I don't think so. There were still quite a few left."

"Good," said Mrs Stewart, wiping strands of hair off her forehead with the back of her hand. "I'm getting too old for this. Still, it's nice to have the house full of laughter. Just like old times."

# Chapter Ten

♥

The following morning, Bethany rose early. As she went down the stairs, she could hear Mrs Stewart already in the kitchen.

"Morning, love. Did you sleep well? Not that we got much sleep after clearing up. Still, I think we did the captain and his bride-to-be proud. Did you hear them singing as they left?"

Bethany smiled. It had been hard not to hear Captain Barnes-Crosier's baritone voice booming out into the Essex night sky.

"Mrs Richardson asked for breakfast to be served formally today, for the family and two guests," said Mrs Stewart, filling up the kettle.

As Bethany set the table in the breakfast room, she wondered who the guests were. Not the captain and his fiancée. He'd sung until he'd got into a car and the door had closed, although his muffled voice had reached Bethany even then. But the car had accelerated down the gravel drive and the horn had tooted twice before, with a screech, the car had pulled out onto the road.

Mrs Stewart had said, 'two guests', so presumably, it would be one of the couples who'd come the previous evening.

Her stomach sank. Dr Howard must have left the previous evening. She'd have liked to see him before he went. Just to have laid eyes on his face once more. She'd deliberately kept on the opposite side of the room to wherever he'd been and had kept her eyes down, so she didn't make eye contact. Not that she thought he'd be embarrassed by her presence – he'd simply ignore her – but she didn't want him to think she was trying to attract his attention.

Foolish. He won't give you a second thought.

"I'll need to go into town later to pick up a few supplies," Mrs Stewart said, "I understand he's staying for a few days."

"He?"

"That lovely Dr Howard. Apparently, he's on leave. Such a fine man. I can't think why he's friends with that RAF chap. They're nothing like each other."

Bethany bit the inside of her mouth to stop her lips from curling up. He would be here in the same house. Not that she'd have anything to do with him, of course. He was a real guest – not like her – but even the thought of seeing his face, watching him steeple his fingers as he considered something, and then gazing at her, like she was so important...

Oh, stop it. He won't be looking at you like you're important.

But she knew if she continued in her role as maid, she would see him. It would be helpful to Mrs Richardson and Mrs Stewart. And anyway, what else did she have to do?

But who was the second guest?

Later, when everyone had gathered for breakfast, Bethany carried the tea in and put the tray on the sideboard.

"Ah, Bethany," said Mrs Richardson, "I wonder if you'd like to join us."

Join them? Whatever did Mrs Richardson mean?

"When the family eats in the kitchen, you eat with us, but I want you to feel like a guest now. I know this is a slightly strange situation, but you're no longer employed here. So, we think you should join us for breakfast just like our other guest. And it's time you called me Joanna. No more of the Mrs Richardson nonsense."

"And I'm Ben," said Mr Richardson.

"And I'm Faye and he's Mark," said Faye seriously, pointing at her brother. She bridled when everyone laughed.

"And I'm Matthew," said Dr Howard.

Bethany simply stared. "I'm n... not sure."

"It's perfectly proper, Bethany. Come, sit down." Joanna smiled encouragingly. "Of course, if you feel too awkward, I understand. Believe me, I have memories of sitting down to meals in this house with my in-laws, feeling very out of place. But you know Ben and me well, and, of course, the children. Matthew has been telling us about the outrageous way in which you've been treated, and I understand you know him, so please, do me the honour of feeling at home."

Bethany reluctantly sat down. It was such a kind gesture and yet, she felt self-conscious – afraid to move or say the wrong thing.

She'd lost her appetite but nibbled some toast and drank some tea, not wanting to say anything in case she showed herself up.

However, by the end of breakfast, she'd begun to relax. Everyone had been so kind and accepting. As she, Joanna and Faye carried the dishes to the kitchen, a loud hammering on the front door echoed through the house, accompanied by a man shouting at them to open up.

Ben hurried to the door, followed by Matthew. He opened it, and Bethany froze, a scream dying in her throat.

It was her father. His fists raised in mid-blow.

"Where is she?" His words were slurred, and beer fumes drifted into the hall. "What have you done with my daughter?" He swore and stumbled forward, recovered his balance and stumbled again.

"I want my daughter..." He collapsed on the threshold.

For a second, no one moved. The first person to spring into action was Matthew. He knelt beside the dishevelled figure of her father and began to examine him, checking his breathing, feeling for his pulse and speaking to him gently.

"I don't think he's seriously hurt," he said, looking up at the others. "Just drunk. Perhaps we can get him home and he can sleep it off?"

Hot tears of shame filled Bethany's eyes, and she realised she was repeating over and over. "Oh no, oh no, please, no, oh no." She crouched down beside Matthew and stared at her father. His eyes were shut, and he muttered nonsense under his breath.

How could he?

She felt heavy, as if a great weight was pressing her down.

This morning, she'd almost begun to believe she might be accepted by this wonderful, generous family and now Pa had ruined everything.

They could see what her father was, and they now looked at her with pity. It was kindly meant but it marked her out as different. Unfortunate. Disgraceful.

Joanna told Faye to take Mark and the plates she was carrying into the kitchen and stay with Mrs Stewart until she called them. She crouched next to Bethany and said quietly, "Whatever you need, just ask. We'll do our best to help." She patted Bethany's shoulder.

Bethany simply hung her head.

Her father, drunk and abusive, had attacked the Richardsons' front door with his fists and had now collapsed in the hall.

The shame. She wanted to close her eyes to remove the image. To wipe away this memory, but it would be imprinted on her mind forever.

"Perhaps before we move him, he might take some coffee?" Matthew asked her.

She nodded, so mortified she couldn't speak. She stood up and walked to the kitchen to make some strong coffee for her drunk father.

Bethany propped her father up on one side with Matthew on the other in the back of Ben's car. He'd come to his senses slightly, and had alternated between rambling and crying during the journey back to his cottage.

Bethany tried to hold his hand, but he shook her off angrily. She sat rigid, staring out of the window at the hedgerows, her eyes filled with tears of shame and sadness.

The Richardsons had been good enough to welcome her into the family and all she'd brought them was trouble.

Thankfully, the front door hadn't been damaged, but the day had been disrupted and it had been an unpleasant shock for innocent Faye and Mark.

Now they were undertaking an unplanned journey in the car using up scarce petrol, the disagreeable tang of unwashed humanity in their nostrils. Bethany was appalled and humiliated.

Next to her, Pa, in such a terrible state – unshaven, his clothes unwashed, his hair long and unkempt. And still, there was probably worse to come when they arrived at his cottage.

The last time Bethany had visited, Pauline and her dog had been there. The entire cottage had been dirty and had smelled.

What would Ben and Matthew think of her father's home? And what would they think of her?

You're not responsible for your father.

He's a grown man and makes his own decisions.

She knew that, and she guessed Ben and Matthew wouldn't believe she was responsible either, yet neither of them would now be driving towards a cottage, which was likely to disgust them if it hadn't been for her.

The best thing would be if she moved back into Pa's cottage, cleaned it thoroughly and looked after her father. Perhaps that's what she should have done in the first place. She had no right planning to make a new life for herself in London and turning her back on her father.

No, she must stay and make amends. It was likely to be a full-time job, but she'd surely be allowed to remain home and not be sent for war work once the authorities knew how disturbed her father was.

It might save Mr Howard the effort of dismissing her, if that was what he intended to do. No one would care if she'd been wrongly accused. She could hide her shame in Plotlands where no one would know what had happened, and she wouldn't bring disgrace to the people who'd been kindest to her.

Ben eased the car along the grassy avenue, negotiating most of the potholes, and Bethany pointed out the cottage. She withdrew further inside herself. The more distance she put between her feelings and those around her, the less she would hurt.

Ben stopped the car and helped Matthew half-lift the mumbling, sobbing man out of the back. Bethany rushed ahead up the path, praying that when she opened the door, the cottage would be as she'd left it all those weeks ago when she had gone to Elmford: shabby, but clean and fresh smelling.

She pushed open the scratched, peeling door and closed her eyes, hoping for a miracle. The stink of rotting food hit her, and she felt angry, momentarily, for having allowed herself to believe the silly notion the cottage would be tidy. Bethany opened her eyes and saw it was worse than when she'd been a few days before. Now, flies circled the room, presumably drawn by the smell of decay.

She clenched her teeth and with head lowered, Bethany led Matthew and Ben, holding her father between them, towards his bedroom.

She called out nervously, "Hello?" In case Pauline and particularly her fierce dog were there, but no one replied.

While the two men took Pa into his room, Bethany quickly ran to the bedroom that had once been hers. It too, was filthy, and judging by the dog hairs, the quilt Ma had made her had been used by Pauline's dog as a bed.

Bethany closed the door firmly. She'd have to clean that thoroughly before she slept in there. Perhaps a night in the chair in front of the fire would be a better option? She braced herself and went to the kitchen, opening the door and releasing more flies into the sitting room.

Bethany leaned against the door frame, closed her eyes and fought back the waves of despair. It was worse than she'd imagined.

Well, there was no point delaying. The mess wouldn't clean itself. She took the bucket and went back out into the avenue to the standpipe and filled it. It was going to require countless buckets of hot, soapy water and plenty of elbow grease before the place would be presentable again.

As she entered the cottage, trying not to slop the water everywhere, she mentally listed all the things she'd have to do before it would be habitable.

Before they'd left, Matthew had telephoned Dr Franks, Pa's family doctor, and had spoken to him. He'd told Matthew Pa had recently been diagnosed with diabetes.

"Your father probably hadn't eaten for some time, so it may have contributed to his confusion."

If the remnants of food that were left in the kitchen were any guidance, Bethany assumed he hadn't eaten for a long time.

She'd have to go to the shops soon, although not until she'd cleaned the kitchen. Kind Joanna had given Bethany some food – a loaf, some ham and cheese as well as a slice of Mrs Stewart's apple pie. At least she wouldn't starve while she cleaned the cottage. Luckily, there was still coal, and Bethany began to heat the water in the copper. As she picked up the bucket again to fetch more water, Matthew came into the kitchen.

"Your father's stable, but his own doctor will be calling soon." He paused as he noticed the chaos of the kitchen. "Well, this is…" he stopped, and she could see the distaste on his face. His upturned palms showed his disbelief and horror at such a mess.

"I'll clean it," she said briskly. "I'm boiling water now. I'll have it clean in no time and I'll look after him. If I can keep him off the drink and make sure he eats, we'll be fine—"

Matthew gasped and held up his hand for her to stop, his eyes wide in dismay. "No, Bethany, you can't stay here, not in this mess. It'll take hours and hours to clean. You may not need to, anyway. Dr Franks has explored the possibility of your father going into hospital. I didn't want to worry you earlier, but his heartbeat is irregular. Your father needs further testing and professional medical care. He'll be looked after in hospital, and you won't be in any danger. I'm sure he doesn't mean it, but he doesn't know what he's doing to himself or anyone else. He's confused and he'll receive proper care in hospital."

She stared at him, unable to take his words in. Pa in hospital?

"Now, I gather from the fragments your father was saying in the car, he fought in the Great War."

Bethany nodded. She couldn't speak. Pa would hate it in hospital. But then, Matthew knew best.

"Your father deserves to be looked after with dignity and care. That can be done in a special hospital. It's for the best."

Bethany felt as though the shell she'd constructed around herself for protection and to maintain the illusion she was in control had cracked. She'd tried to convince herself nothing could hurt her further, and she'd cut herself off from her feelings. Become numb. Ignored the rest of the world and hoped it forgot about her. Now as Matthew looked at her with such gentleness, that shell shattered into tiny pieces, and again, she cried. Her head throbbed, her eyes ached and her heart broke.

Matthew crossed the grimy kitchen in two strides and enveloped her in his arms. It felt so good, she let him hold her. She placed her hands against his chest and cried into his sweet-smelling coat, dreading the moment he'd draw away.

*Please, don't let go of me.*

Just a second or two more of his comfort.

Bethany needed this now. He was the most compassionate man she'd ever met. He'd push her away in a moment or two. She knew that, so before he did, she'd step away first, and save him embarrassment.

But just for now, she'd cling to him.

# Chapter Eleven

Dr Franks arrived with two nurses to take Pa to a hospital in London where he'd receive treatment and care.

Bethany wanted to go with them. She could see her father was confused; his eyes wide and staring; his gaze roving across the sea of faces, back and forth, as if looking for someone familiar. Yet, when she tried to take his hand and explain, he pushed her away.

"Don't pretend you care, Sarah," he said accusingly.

Sarah? Did he think she was Ma? Bethany felt as though her heart was being torn in two.

"You left me. I looked everywhere for you. I needed you but weren't there. So don't pretend to care now. It's too late." He turned his face away from her, but she'd seen the tears in his eyes.

Matthew put his arm around Bethany's shoulders and gently drew her away. "Come back to Priory Hall now, Bethany; there's nothing more you can do."

She allowed herself to be led away. She had no more tears; inside was an echoing emptiness.

Her brother had set sail once again without her having seen him and was at the mercy of the German U-Boats in the Atlantic; her mother and younger brother had died in tragic circumstances and her father didn't recognise her. A family torn apart by war and circumstances.

"If you like," Ben said as they got back into the car, "we'll all come over tomorrow and clean up the cottage so it's spick and span for him when he comes home."

Bethany's throat tightened until she thought she'd choke. Even now these wonderful people were helping her, despite all the trouble she'd brought to them. Thoughtful Ben was now suggesting her father might one day be well enough to come home. Bethany doubted it.

She'd seen Matthew's and Dr Franks's expressions as they'd quietly discussed her father. They'd spoken too softly for her to make out their words and even if she'd been able to hear, she probably wouldn't have understood them, but she could tell by the two doctors' faces her father was not well.

When they arrived back at Priory Hall, Ben quickly explained the situation to Joanna who turned to Bethany.

"Oh, my dear, what a terrible experience. I'll draw you a bath. Have a long soak and take your time. Believe me, I understand what it's like to live with a father who was affected by the Great War."

To Bethany's surprise, Joanna said her father had also come home from the trenches in Northern France a disturbed man, and that she and her mother had tried their best to care for him. Bethany allowed herself to be led upstairs and did as Joanna told her, lying in the warm water, feeling her rigid muscles relax as she stared sightlessly at the bathroom ceiling.

One day, perhaps she'd be able to do something for the Richardsons and repay them. But she doubted it.

The following day, Mrs Stewart walked Faye to school, taking Mark with them. After they'd left Faye, she carried on with the young boy to the shops at Laindon.

Joanna, Ben, Matthew, and Bethany went to the ramshackle cottage, taking with them all the cleaning tools Mrs Stewart had been able to find.

To Bethany's surprise, everyone was in high spirits. She wondered whether Joanna's mood would change when she saw the mess that awaited them.

She was puzzled when Ben took a longer route than the one he'd taken the previous day, and drove along a different avenue. He stopped in front of one of the largest bungalows on Plotlands and Bethany was surprised to discover it belonged to Ben and Joanna.

"That was the cottage we lived in when we were first married," Joanna said.

Bethany hadn't realised they'd once lived not far from her Pa's home. So, they weren't merely landowners who lived in a grand house and were able to afford servants. A few years before, they'd been Plotlanders like her and her family. She wondered if that was why Ben had deliberately taken that route – to show her they weren't so different. It would have been typical of him if he had.

The cleaning took all day and as Joanna said when they'd finished, "It probably needs another going over. But for the time being, it'll do."

The rotten, maggot-ridden food had been thrown away, and the whole place had been aired, swept, dusted and washed. Joanna had bought bundles of dried herbs, and they'd left them all over the house to add a little freshness.

When they'd finished, Bethany took the key from under the loose stone in the front garden and locked the door. She didn't know where Pauline was, but if it had occurred to her that she and her dog could move back in, she'd find that was not an option.

Bethany put the key in her pocket and noticed that someone had leaned the gate up against the front wall.

"I could send one of my farmhands over to fix it," Ben had offered earlier, but Bethany thanked him and said no. Other than Pauline, who might try to get into the cottage, no one else would visit. The gate wouldn't be missed.

"Pa can fix that when he comes home," she said, her voice catching on the word 'home'.

They all agreed wholeheartedly, and Bethany knew that each one of them had worked out it was unlikely her father would ever return. Nevertheless, they all kept up the pretence.

When they got back to Priory Hall, Mrs Stewart, with help from Mark and Faye, had prepared dinner, and the family and their two guests sat in the large kitchen and ate together.

Ben announced he'd be working with his Land Girls the following day and Bethany suspected that was something he should've been doing on that day rather than cleaning a cottage. If that was so, however, Ben was too polite to say so.

"And I'm taking Mark to town to see if I can get him some new shoes. He's growing so fast. We'll walk Faye to school then carry on," said Joanna.

"Can I have new shoes, please?" Faye asked, her face full of hope.

"No, darling, you've had new shoes recently. I'm afraid the coupons won't run to more just because you want to keep up with your brother."

Faye pouted.

"And I understand Matthew hasn't yet sampled the delights of Southend," Joanna said. "I was wondering, Bethany, dear, if Matthew borrowed the car, whether you could both drive down there. You once said your mother used to take you there and you know it well. Perhaps it'll take your mind off things."

Bethany almost choked. Spending the entire day with Matthew.

What a punishment for him after all his hard work cleaning a cottage. And what a waste of his spare time.

She looked at him, expecting to see a horrified expression, or at least a blank face that masked his attempts to politely excuse himself. To her surprise, however, he looked like a young boy who'd been offered a treat he couldn't wait to claim.

"That would be marvellous," he said, then added, "if you don't mind, Bethany."

"I'd be happy to show you around Southend." Her heart was pounding so hard, she wondered if anyone else could hear it.

A whole day by the seaside. Well, not exactly the seaside. Southend-on-Sea was at the mouth of the River Thames, but it was close enough. A day to forget what had been going on. And better than that, an entire day with Matthew.

It would storm – torrential rain that wouldn't stop all day in Southend. Or there'd be a bombing raid. The security check points wouldn't allow them through. The car would break down. More likely, Matthew would have changed his mind about their trip to the coast. During the night, Bethany went through all the possibilities that would prevent her from spending the day with Matthew in Southend. Before she'd opened her eyes, she strained to listen for the pitter-patter of rain on the roof. There was none.

She got out of bed and padded quietly to the window, pulling back the blackout curtains. Stars still spangled in the sky and in the east, the heavy black was fading to dark blue. It would be light soon.

Bethany got ready, cautioning herself against getting too excited at a day out and the thought of spending time with Matthew on her own. It wouldn't matter to him as much as it mattered to her. Of course, it wouldn't mean anything to him at all. Just a mild diversion while his hosts were busy.

Expect nothing, she told herself. No, that wasn't true. She should probably expect the worst.

If Mrs Stewart noticed the permanent smile on Bethany's face that morning, she said nothing. Neither did she remark on the tune Bethany suddenly realised she was humming. However, it was obvious from Mrs Stewart's satisfied smile when she thought Bethany wasn't watching – like someone who's been sworn to secrecy and who's bursting to tell their good news – that she'd picked up on Bethany's excitement.

By the time Ben had rushed off to the cottages where his Land Girls lived and Joanna had taken a reluctant Faye and even more reluctant Mark out, the sky was bright blue. The air was still and cold. Later, when the sun was higher, it promised to be a fine day.

No storm so far.

And as yet, no air raid warning sirens or bomb explosions, either nearby or further off.

Perhaps the car wouldn't start.

"Ready?" Matthew asked her with a sparkle in his sapphire eyes and the car keys dangling from his fingers.

She was more than ready and rushed after him before he changed his mind.

"I have some very good news for you," he said as they walked towards the car. "I've just finished talking to Robert and he confirmed you're no longer suspended."

Bethany gasped with relief. "Thank you so much." Far from being the disaster she'd feared, this had the makings of an excellent day.

Matthew opened the door for her and let her into the car. Once in the driver's seat, he continued, "Robert said MI5 had gained a lot of information from Zimmerman. Apparently, he'd noticed you and your friend at a dance and realised from your yellow hands you most likely worked on munitions. He soon made up his mind he was going to target your friend. And he added he'd had very little to do with you after that. So, you're in the clear."

It felt as though the air had been squeezed out of her. Relief that she'd been cleared and sorrow at how Mavis had been used.

"So, I ought to be on my way back to Elmford?" she asked, not wanting to hear the answer. How disappointing. But if so, why had they both got into the car as if they were going out?

"Certainly not. I told Robert you were on leave and that, in my opinion, you needed a few days to fully recuperate. So, you're safe until Sunday. Then we both return."

"Does your brother know we're together—" She blushed. "I... I mean, does he know we're staying in the same house?" 'Together' implied so much more than she'd intended.

Matthew started the ignition. "No, I told Robert I was taking a few days to go to Hugh's engagement party. I assume he thinks I'm staying in Hornchurch. I don't suppose he's given it another thought. Dr Dawkins is standing in for me, so there's medical cover in the factory."

"But I'm better now. Perhaps I ought to go back early. Do my bit for the war effort..." she tailed off, not wanting to persuade him but aware of her duty.

"Hmm." He tapped the steering wheel with his index finger as if considering. Then in a mock pompous voice, he said, "I'm the doctor and in my considered opinion, you require more time to recover." He returned to his usual voice and added, "I know there's a war on,

Bethany, but we're all human. Everyone needs a break so they can return refreshed. I must admit, I need to remind myself of that bit of wisdom. I was in danger of burning out myself. But you'll only be away for a few days. The war won't be won or lost by Sunday and when we get back, I'm sure we'll both be more effective for our little holiday. So," He assumed his pompous voice again, "I prescribe a day in Southend for both of us."

The car had started first time and Matthew changed gear and drove down the drive.

Bethany watched his hands on the steering wheel as he eased the car onto the road. They were strong, capable hands. She'd experienced their gentleness during her medical check-ups at Elmford ROF, and their tenderness when he'd held her and offered comfort. A warm glow crept through her and she forced herself to look out of the window away from him.

By contrast, her hands were rough, ragged-nailed and yellow-tinged. Thank goodness she was wearing gloves. Nevertheless, she curled her fingers to make fists and held them rigidly in her lap.

If he thought about it, he'd know her hands were yellow, so there was no point in hiding them. But why should he think about them at all? They were of no account to him.

However, to Bethany, especially on this day when she'd been thrown together with Matthew, her hands demonstrated her position in life. A former maid who was now a munitions factory worker. At least now she didn't have a shadow over her record, although she couldn't shake the feeling that it was still there.

Bethany clenched her fists tighter. How she wanted to be free of those memories that held her like an anchor.

Why couldn't she simply forget everything and pretend she was a woman out with a handsome man?

"Is my driving frightening you that much, Bethany?"

She turned her head slightly and caught the corners of his mouth twitch upwards.

"I'm not frightened," she said quickly.

Too quickly to sound convincing.

"Then why are you so tense? I've seen springs that are less tightly coiled than you."

She laughed.

"I know," he said. "It's because Hugh taught me to drive, isn't it? You've spotted his 'Put-your-foot-to-the-floor-and-hope-for-the-best' method of teaching." He was grinning broadly.

"Did he really teach you to drive?" Perhaps she could steer the conversation away from her. How could she confess she felt totally out of her depth with him? That suggested she liked him more than she should and implied she was conceited enough to believe he'd care.

"Yes, Hugh started driving his father's car when he was about twelve. He was tall but it took blocks of wood strapped to his feet so he could reach the pedals. I think the chauffeur was in on it. But even if he hadn't helped, Hugh would have found a way. Then, later, he taught me. He's a good teacher, but I'm not as fearless or reckless as him... I didn't think I was anyway."

"You drive very well. I suppose I'm not used to being driven in a car." That was nonsense. He'd know she travelled by train and bus. Was there really much difference? When she travelled on public transport, someone else was in charge of the controls. It was a ridiculous excuse.

"Or is your unease nothing to do with my driving and something to do with your hands?" he asked. "When I mentioned Zimmerman targeting your friend because he'd spotted the colour of her hands, I saw you flinch and squeeze your fists tightly."

She sighed. "I didn't think I was that obvious." Her cheeks flared with embarrassment.

"Oh, Bethany, why are you ashamed? May I suggest you consider your hands badges of honour and courage? Because that's exactly what they are. You put your health and life on the line every day. That's something to be proud of."

During the rest of the journey, he told her humorous stories about his life at university with Hugh and the foolish and sometimes dangerous situations his friend had dragged him into.

By the time Matthew eased the car onto the Western Esplanade, Bethany's gloved hands were no longer bunched into fists. They rested loosely in her lap and her stomach ached from laughter.

# Chapter Twelve

♥

The last time Bethany had been to Southend, she'd gone with Ma on the train. It had been a sultry summer day and her mother, who was seven months pregnant, had said she needed some air. A change of scene. A fresh sea breeze. And so they'd walked to Laindon and caught the train to the coast.

Ma had talked about her hopes for Bethany and for the new child. "One day, Stevie will come home, your Pa will be well and we'll be a happy family again."

Bethany wondered if she'd really believed that.

Matthew opened her car door and offered her his arm. She immediately regretted not stepping forward and taking it. Instead, she stared, not used to men treating her with such care and politeness – wondering if he'd forgotten who she really was.

He lowered his arm, and his face clouded over.

"I hope you don't think I overstepped the mark," he said. "I just thought with this brisk wind, you might get blown away." Then he laughed as he shielded his eyes with his hand and turned his head, pretending he was watching something take off, soar overhead and land in the water.

How did he always manage to smooth over the embarrassing moments she created? She owed him an explanation.

"I'm not used to being treated with such kindness or politeness. Please forgive me."

He held out his arm again. "Perhaps I took you by surprise. My fault. I'll try again. Bethany, would you care to hold my arm?"

"Yes, please." This time, she was determined to take the opportunity to be close to him.

"Now we've anchored you down and you won't end up in the water or on that wicked barbed wire on the beach, which way shall we go?"

She slipped her hand beneath his arm and indicated the pier. It was closed to the public, having been taken over by the Royal Navy the previous year, but it was still a magnificent sight, stretching over a mile into the sea.

The tide was high, with only small areas of beach still dry. Certainly not enough to walk along, even if the beaches had been open. Since the last time she'd been, they'd been covered in scaffolding and draped with barbed wire. Matthew and Bethany stood for a few moments watching the boats bobbing on the water. Despite the blue sky, the Thames was choppy, grey and uninviting. It was lucky the tide was high or there'd simply have been large areas of shiny mud and ugly sea defences.

What must he think of this place? Surely he'd seen better seaside towns than Southend? And surely he'd been out for the day with more suitable women? Was he already regretting his decision to come?

He breathed in deeply, closing his eyes for several seconds. "Isn't it good to take in lungfuls of fresh air? I miss this in Elmford." His brows drew together as he looked at her. "But you don't look very impressed. Please say if you want to go back to Laindon. We'll leave whenever you like."

"Oh no! I don't want to go back. I... I..." Why not tell him how she felt? At least he'd understand.

"It's just that... I'm sure you're used to better places than this. And better company. I wouldn't want to embarrass you."

"Embarrass me? Why? Are you going to burst into song? Fling yourself in the water? Turn cartwheels?" His eyes opened wide as if alarmed by the prospect.

She giggled. "No, nothing like that. But I work in your brother's factory. You're a doctor. I wouldn't want to show you up."

"Hmm. I see. Well, it doesn't matter to me. And I don't suppose anyone else will even know. I didn't bring my stethoscope today, so no one will have any idea what I do. And you're rather fetchingly dressed, no white trousers, jacket or turban today. We're more likely to draw people's attention because neither of us is in uniform. Particularly me. People will assume I'm an able-bodied man not doing his bit. But if it bothers you, how about we pretend to be other people?"

She'd assumed he was going to say that if it bothered her, they needn't hold arms and she bitterly regretted her words.

She frowned at him. "Other people? How do we do that?"

He considered for a moment. "Well, we choose new names and new identities. No!" he said, his eyes alight with excitement. "Even better, we choose names for each other. Yes, I'll start. You can be Geraldine." He bit his lower lip. "But Geraldine what? Jones? Smith? No, too boring."

A seagull flew low overhead and dived towards the tiny strip of beach.

"I know," Matthew said. "Geraldine Seagull." Placing his hands on her shoulders, he leaned back and pretended to study her face, then nodded with satisfaction. "Yes, perfect. Now, it's up to you to invent your identity. And, to name me, of course."

Bethany shook her head. This was madness. But such fun.

She tapped her lip as she considered. "Your name is... Peregrine."

"Right," he said slowly as if getting used to the name. "Peregrine. And my surname?"

Bethany glanced about, looking for inspiration. "Esplanade," she said. "Peregrine Esplanade."

Warmth spread through her as she saw his reaction to her silly name. She'd made him laugh. Real laughter, not simply politeness.

"Well, Peregrine, shall we continue?" Bethany said. Why not join in with the game? He'd made it clear he didn't mind being with her. Perhaps this wasn't going to be such a difficult day after all.

"Indeed, Geraldine, we shall. And you can tell me all about yourself."

"Why did you choose Geraldine?" she asked, not sure she wanted to know. Was Geraldine his girl? She hadn't considered he might have someone special. But surely, he wouldn't have given her that name if it belonged to a girl who was special to him.

"Geraldine Baker was my first love." He gave an exaggerated sigh and held his hand over his chest, pretending to be sad. "I was nine and she was eight. Unfortunately, it didn't last long."

"What happened?"

"It soon became clear it wasn't to be. My heart was broken. One day, she insisted I pose for her while she painted me. I'd rather have played in the garden, but it gave me an opportunity to study her, so I agreed. She took ages – probably all of ten minutes – but that's an age to a boy who wants to run about and kick a ball. And when she showed me the finished picture, I saw she'd spent most of her time painting the garden in the background. She'd even painted a large dog from her imagination. But the painting of me could only have taken a few seconds. I think it's fair to say she had no idea about human bodies. I had stick arms and legs and a large round head. But I suppose at that age, I wouldn't have been able to do better. On the other hand, I certainly wouldn't have insisted someone sit still while I produced a picture that didn't look anything like I was painting."

"Didn't you forgive her?"

"I probably would have done in time. But that's not why we broke up. That was because she never forgave me. All my fault, of course. Once she'd shown me her picture, I snatched it from her and ran away, then I folded it into a plane and aimed it at her. It missed. But she was so angry – rightfully so, because I'd behaved very badly – she shouted and stamped her foot. I instantly fell out of love with her."

"And do I remind you of Geraldine?" Bethany held her breath. She wished she hadn't asked.

"Yes, and no. After she'd stamped her foot, she chased me and pushed me into the lake. No less than I deserved. But the reason she reminds me of you is that she had spirit. So do you. And for some reason, it was the first name to pop into my head. So, that's why I chose Geraldine. Now, why did you choose Peregrine? Your first love? Or even your current love?"

Bethany shook her head. "No, not a first love. I've never had one. But when I was younger, I was rather keen on a neighbour's homing pigeon. He was called Peregrine."

Matthew laughed. "I'm not sure who should be most insulted – you, me or the homing pigeon. Anyway, Geraldine, all this laughing has made me thirsty. Can I persuade you to accompany me to a café for tea?"

"Thank you, Peregrine. Tea would be delightful."

Matthew suggested one of the cafés along the Esplanade and they were greeted at the door by a tall, thin woman who peered at them down her nose.

"Not in uniform?" she asked, looking around pointedly at the customers in the café, most of whom were in khaki.

Matthew leaned forward and held out the badge on the lapel of his coat. He indicated Bethany's too.

"ROF, front line duty," she read. "What does that mean? You're not one o' them conchies, are you? Because if you are, you ain't welcome 'ere."

A man joined the tall woman. "What's up, Mags? These two being difficult?"

"I ain't sure. What d'you make of that?" She nodded at Matthew's badge.

"Let 'em in," said the man. "Don't yer recognise that badge? Our Trevor's girl's got one."

"What? You mean, Dolly?"

The man nodded and added to Matthew, "Our son's girl, Dolly, works at Woolwich. It's a great job you people do, providing you-know-what to our boys." He tapped the side of his nose and nodded his approval.

"Oh," the woman said, smiling, "ROF, Royal Ordn—"

"Hush, woman!" said the man, looking about. "Walls have ears, you know."

After that, the woman led them to a table by the window. "The cake will be on the house to make up for the earlier misunderstanding. Our son, Trevor, is out in East Africa. If it weren't for you in the..." she paused and looked about, then leaning towards them whispered, "in them factories, our boys'd be in big trouble."

"That was lucky the man recognised our badges," Bethany whispered when the woman had gone.

Matthew nodded. "Although you have more right to be here than me. We might both work in a filling factory but it's you, and the others you work with, who do the dangerous work. I'm reasonably safe in my room. None of the hazardous chemicals you handle daily and none of the risk of having my hands blown off."

"Yes, but you keep us healthy," Bethany said.

He shook his head slowly, sadness in his eyes. "Sometimes I think I'm fighting a losing battle on your behalf. I can't keep you safe and I'm not in any danger myself."

"That's war," Bethany said. She wanted to reach out and smooth away the furrows between his brows. None of it was his fault.

As if determined to raise the mood, Matthew reminded her they hadn't made up identities for themselves to go with their new names.

By the time the woman returned with their tea and cake, they were laughing with possible personalities to fit their names.

Matthew, as Peregrine Esplanade, had decided he was a Naval submarine captain who, in peacetime, lived with his parrot in a seaside cottage. When the war was over, he'd travel to the South Seas and find a deserted island.

Bethany, as Geraldine Seagull, couldn't decide what her role should be.

"Nurse," Matthew said decisively. "I think you'd make a wonderful nurse. You're kind and practical, and you don't panic easily. Yes, you'd be a perfect nurse."

Bethany searched his face for signs he was joking, but he appeared to be serious. He thought she was kind and practical?

*He's talking about a fictional character, Geraldine. Not you.*

Well, of course. And yet, Geraldine didn't exist, and he'd seemed so definite in his views. They must have been based on something.

After tea, they strolled along the Esplanade and Bethany pointed in the direction of Leigh-on-Sea where there was a fleet of cockle ships.

"A few months ago, many of them went across to Dunkirk to rescue our troops with lots of other boats," she said. "So brave. And sadly, some didn't come back."

They walked as far as the Kursaal Pleasure Park and Bethany told Matthew about the rides she'd been on when Ma had taken her and Stevie many years before.

The park had closed at the beginning of the war and Bethany stared at it silently, wondering if it would ever open again. Before the war, Southend had attracted people to its amusements. It had been a place with a holiday feeling. But now, there was no escaping the war with so many uniformed people milling about, the barbed wire and the anti-tank coastal defences.

"It'll all be over one day," Matthew said, guessing her thoughts. "The war, I mean. We're putting so much effort into winning; how could it be otherwise?"

Bethany nodded, although she didn't voice her fears. In Matthew's world, effort meant results. In hers, it often didn't matter how much effort you put into something, frustration, and often, failure followed.

But it was pointless expressing something so negative and lowering the mood. Most of their time in Southend had been fun.

"This bracing sea air has given me an appetite, Geraldine. Shall we find a place for lunch?" Matthew assumed the voice he'd chosen to speak in when he was Peregrine.

Bethany put on her 'Geraldine' voice too. "Perfect, Peregrine. May I suggest the local speciality?"

"Please do."

They found a fish and chip restaurant overlooking one of the beaches. Since they'd arrived, the tide had started to go out, leaving a few boats that were close to the shore tipping to one side as their hulls rested on the mud. They looked forgotten and forlorn.

When the waitress brought their food, Bethany secretly glanced at her wristwatch, willing it to show they still had hours before they needed to get back to Laindon. What was it they said about time and tide? Both stopped for no man and both were slipping away. As she looked up, she noticed Matthew's eyes drop to his watch. Did he want time to go faster? The slight frown didn't tell her anything.

But he certainly hadn't been behaving as though he was keen to get away. Quite the opposite. He appeared to be enjoying himself, although she couldn't believe he was dreading their time together coming to an end as much as her.

He'd come up with some funny ideas for his character, and she'd amazed herself with inventing some amusing things for Geraldine, too. He'd laughed at her idea for Geraldine's plans to run away to join the circus as soon as war was over, and she could tell he wasn't simply being polite.

As a child, Bethany had loved making up stories in her head, but during the last few years, she hadn't needed to use her imagination. She'd been too busy trying to make sense of reality and to deal with its problems. The harder life had become at home, the more she'd lost the art of slipping away into make-believe.

But while they'd been in Southend, Matthew had reminded her of her imagination and had lifted her out of the real world.

After lunch, they sat on a bench overlooking the water. The tide had receded a surprising distance, leaving more boats stranded and revealing tangles of barbed wire. How strange that as you watched, there was no hint the tide was going out. Each wave that washed up on the beach appeared to be in the same place as the one before, and yet without anything appearing to change, minute by minute, the water retreated. Slow and silent. Constant. Like time passing.

And it was passing too quickly. It had been a wonderful day with none of the awkward silences she'd feared. Instead, they'd talked the entire time, sharing their past lives and hopes for the future.

They'd both avoided the present. There'd been no mention of Elmford ROF and the incident with Mavis and Zimmerman, or Bethany's father. Other than her time as a maid in Priory Hall, the Richardsons and their home hadn't been mentioned. Despite it being somewhere safe for Bethany now, Priory Hall was currently a reminder of things she'd rather not have thought about.

Matthew obviously understood this. And yet there was so much else to talk about, and it was only when the sun momentarily darkened, Bethany looked up to see clouds moving swiftly towards them. They must think about going home.

By the time they'd passed through a military checkpoint and got back to the car, the tide was far out, leaving large expanses of shiny mud. Similarly, the magic of the day was ebbing away. By the time they reached Priory Hall, Geraldine Seagull and Peregrine Esplanade would merely be funny memories.

Bethany had one hand beneath Matthew's arm, but she squeezed the other into a fist, angry with herself. She'd had a marvellous day. It was more than she deserved or had a right to expect. How dare she risk spoiling it now by being disappointed?

Tuck it into your memory. It will be something wonderful to look back on in the days... weeks... months ahead... perhaps forever.

Despite only clenching one fist, Matthew had felt the movement which had obviously gone through her body. He stopped and looked at her.

"Is everything all right, Geraldine? I felt you go tense, like you'd had a shock."

In the same voice she'd been using for Geraldine – a slightly posh accent – she said, "I'm perfectly fine, thank you, Peregrine."

He laughed, and she assumed he thought he'd been mistaken.

How could she tell him this had been one of the happiest days of her life? Certainly the happiest day for several years.

What would he have said? She had no idea, but she could imagine the look of pity in his eyes. It would be kindly meant, but she would feel small and pathetic. He might even think she was fishing for another day out.

Tomorrow, it was unlikely both Ben and Joanna would be busy as they had been today. Matthew would pass the day with them.

That wouldn't be so bad because it would allow Bethany to spend more time with Mrs Stewart. Kind Mrs Stewart. But even that prospect didn't make up for the thought that tomorrow she and Matthew would once again, be different people living in the worlds in which they really belonged.

Matthew helped her into the car, and as she looked back at the mud, she saw the water was now in the far distance. Relentless. Unstoppable. You just had to ride it or remain motionless like the boats that had now been stranded.

But there was nothing you could do to change it.

# Chapter Thirteen

♥

At dinner that night, Matthew told Ben, Joanna and the children about the day; where he and Bethany had been, what they'd seen, and his impressions of the town.

Bethany had smiled in the appropriate places, but otherwise, she'd been her usual shy self.

He deliberately didn't mention Geraldine or Peregrine. They were too private – part of a world he'd created with Bethany. She was more confident now than she had been when he'd first arrived, but even so, she was still very quiet and obviously feeling rather uncomfortable.

They were gathered around the large table in the kitchen rather than formally in the dining room – that had been Joanna's idea. Matthew knew she hadn't been born into the social circles in which she now mixed and would have known how much more welcoming eating in the kitchen would be for Bethany, rather than the room where she'd once served the family and guests.

Nevertheless, Bethany's earlier sparkle and wit had gone. When Joanna spoke to her, she replied politely, but Matthew could see she didn't feel at home.

It was as though she'd given up. The self-confidence and belief she'd displayed earlier had disappeared. They couldn't have completely vanished, but perhaps they were fragile buds that needed hothousing to allow them to grow. The more he saw of her, the more he wanted to ensure she had the right conditions to flourish. He would not give up on this woman. Never before had he met anyone like her. She deserved more from life than she'd had so far.

She was pretty, but not beautiful like some of the women he'd known – particularly those his father had pushed him towards. Bethany had something those other women hadn't possessed. It wasn't just good looks, although her features were branded into his memory. The way she tilted her head when something amused her, the way her eyes flashed when she said something mischievous. The spark of fire he saw every so often, which life appeared determined to quench.

She was like a diamond someone had dropped into a pile of pebbles, and he longed to pick her up and allow her to shine and sparkle. She didn't need polishing. She didn't need an expensive setting. She could glitter on her own, if someone would only give her a chance.

Matthew longed to be the one to give her that chance.

"I think it's more than just the gasket leaking," Ben said, bringing Matthew back to the present. "Do you know much about engines, Matt?"

"No, sorry, Ben. I'm fine with the intricate workings of the human body, but engines are beyond me, I'm afraid."

"Oh well," said Ben. "One of my Land Girls is a good mechanic but even she doesn't know why it's leaking. I'll probably see if Sam from the garage can come over and take a look at it for me. It's a nuisance though."

"I could stay home from school tomorrow and have a look for you, Daddy," Faye said with hope in her eyes.

"Sorry, Faye, but school comes first, I'm sure Daddy will sort it out," Joanna said ruffling the young girl's hair. "Tomorrow, I'll be at the church hall in town with the WI ladies. Mark is staying with Mrs Stewart. He causes havoc at the WI. Most of the ladies adore him but we don't get much done. What are you two doing?" She turned to Bethany and Matthew.

"Well, since you and Ben are busy, I wonder if I can persuade Bethany to show me around the local delights. Laindon's such an unusual area and I thought I might see if Dr Franks isn't too busy for a few words. Assuming this war ever comes to an end, I'm thinking about what I'll do. I thought Dr Franks might be able to offer me some advice."

And with those few words, Bethany's eyes began to shine.

"Yes, of course. I'd be glad to show you around. But please don't hold me responsible for Laindon because, really, it's such a small town, there's very little of interest."

He saw she was sitting straighter, although he doubted anyone else would notice. His words appeared to have given her permission to belong to the group. Or perhaps it was the accumulation of offers to join, and she'd suddenly realised she truly was wanted.

Ben and Joanna were quick to respond, and by the time they parted for bed, it was as if they were all equals. The atmosphere had been lively, and Matthew couldn't wait for the morning when he'd spend another day with her.

She deserved a chance. But it wasn't simply that, he acknowledged. He wanted to spend time with her. Couldn't wait for the morning when he'd see her again. He doubted he'd sleep well knowing he had to wait for hours until he could speak to her again, when she was only a short walk from his bedroom.

So tantalisingly close. But he mustn't consider the proximity. He must resist the urge to knock at her door in the night. It was the last thing he'd do. He knew she'd be shocked and he wouldn't want to frighten her. No, he'd stay in his room. But his dreams wouldn't be so easy to keep in check.

Matthew got up early, washed, shaved and dressed warmly. There had been a light frost overnight, and the garden was coated in white.

He went down to the kitchen, hoping to catch Bethany alone, and as he entered, his heart jumped. She was there, ready for the day, dressed in trousers and a pullover. Then he realised Mrs Stewart was by the sink, washing up. She called out a cheery 'hello' and, after wiping her soapy hands, she said she was going to fetch the eggs. Grabbing her coat and a basket, she left, leaving Bethany setting the table for breakfast.

"Good morning, Geraldine," Matthew said in his Peregrine voice.

"And a jolly fine morning to you, Peregrine," she said with a smile that made his stomach flip.

"Shall I make you a cuppa?" he asked, anticipating her reaction.

"Oh, no!"

"Why, Geraldine!" Matthew grinned at her mischievously. "How your voice has changed." He pretended to look pained. "Don't you think a submarine commander can make tea?"

She assumed her Geraldine voice. "I thought you were a submarine captain yesterday. Were you promoted overnight?"

"That's beside the point, Geraldine. We were discussing my tea-making abilities, which, I may add, are second to none. So, shall I make you a cuppa?"

"Thank you, Peregrine, that would be very nice." Bethany slipped back into her own voice. "I understand if you'd rather not have the grand tour of Laindon, by the way, Matthew. There really isn't a great deal here."

"Hmm," he said, pretending to consider. "It's tempting to spend my day looking at an oily tractor engine or, indeed, going to the WI. But on reflection, I'd much prefer to see Laindon with you. And seriously, I really would like a few words with Dr Franks or at least to arrange a time to chat to him."

"Are you thinking of becoming a family doctor like Dr Franks one day?"

"I'm really not sure what I want to do. I just thought I'd explore my options."

"Options," she said in a faraway voice. "So far, I've done what I had to do or what I thought I ought to do. It's hard to believe I'll ever have options."

"I think women will have more choice about what they do after the war's over. Elmford Factory wouldn't run without the women. I can't see all of them going back to their old lives. Some will get married, and it'll be as if they'd never worked in a factory. But others will want something else. Perhaps you'll meet someone who'll sweep you off your feet and settle down happily."

He searched her face for signs of approval of this idea. The thought of her marrying made him feel sick. She deserved a better life than the one her mother had led. Or was it the thought of her being with another man that made his stomach churn? After all, she might find someone who'd love and cherish her, not treat her as her mother had been treated.

"No," she said firmly. "Not marriage. I want to be independent. I don't want to answer to anyone."

He told her about his father's wishes for him to marry to benefit the family, and how he'd frustrated them. He was about to say he didn't intend to marry anyone either, but to his surprise, he realised that for the first time, the thought of spending the rest of his life with one woman was appealing.

You barely know this woman.

He knew that and yet, no one before had touched him so deeply. It was early days. Far too soon to think about spending the rest of his life with her but he was desperate to find out where his feelings for her would lead.

"When I've saved enough to move to London and found a job as a shorthand typist. That's when my life will start," Bethany said with such conviction, he had to look away. It would be pointless him falling for her if she was determined to spend her life alone.

"Why are you so keen on being a shorthand typist, Bethany? Not that there's anything wrong with that, but there must be lots of things you might do."

She stared at him. "That's true," she said slowly. "I wanted to be a shorthand typist because that's what Joanna was when she met Ben. I didn't want to work in a shop and I thought I could make a good life for myself working in an office."

"I bet you could do anything that took your fancy," he said. Well, if she was determined to be alone, she might as well set her sights high.

"I'm not sure you're right. I doubt I could be a submarine commander."

"Hmm, that's true. Although, as one myself, I could probably put in a good word for you."

They were still laughing when Mrs Stewart returned with a few eggs in the bottom of a basket. "That blasted Flossie isn't laying at the moment. If she doesn't watch out, she'll be in the pot before you can say chicken stew."

Matthew and Bethany had both laughed.

"It wasn't that funny," said Mrs Stewart.

But somehow it had appeared to be.

After breakfast, Matthew helped Mrs Stewart and Bethany wash up.

Mrs Stewart had objected but after Matthew had pointed out Bethany was helping and as he was a guest too, he ought to do his bit, she relented. And it gave her more chance to keep an eye on Mark who'd already escaped once into the frosty garden.

Faye had put up a good case as to why she ought to go with her mother to the WI so she could do her bit for the war effort, but Joanna was adamant she was going to school. Faye pouted, but finally put her outdoor clothes and shoes on, and left for school with her mother. Ben, dressed in oily dungarees, had already gone, shouting over his shoulder he'd left the bicycles out for them.

Bethany followed Matthew outside to where two bicycles were leaning against the wall.

She looked at him in surprise.

"You don't think I can ride a bicycle, do you?" he asked, feigning disappointment.

"Well, I..."

"Just because I'm a doctor doesn't mean I didn't learn all the things a young boy would learn. Watch this..." he said, getting hold of the bike the wrong way round and pretending to mount backwards.

What was it about this young woman that brought back the lightness to him, the humour that had been missing for so long? He thought back to the evening he'd returned to Brent House and had worried about his permanently low mood. Now, he only had to look at Bethany for his heart to soar.

Between gasps of laughter, she said, "Is that how they ride bicycles in submarines?"

They wobbled down the gravel drive, giggling like schoolchildren.

Matthew couldn't remember ever having been so happy.

# Chapter Fourteen

♥

Bethany decided to take Matthew to Dr Franks's surgery first. That would be the most important part of the day. There really wasn't much to show Matthew in Laindon, so it was best he spent most of his time considering his future and getting advice.

Dr Franks's nurse said he was free and would be happy to talk to Matthew about his practice, so Bethany wandered along the High Road, window shopping.

When she arrived at the dress shop, she stopped and looked at the garments in the window. Before, when she'd worked as a maid, she'd given her mother all her wages each week, although Ma had always slipped her sixpence pocket money.

Now Bethany had savings. She also had enough clothing coupons to buy a new blouse.

But should she? The habit of saving was hard to overcome, yet it was so tempting to have something new for that evening. The previous evening, Joanna had spoken about the film showing at the local cinema. Rebecca, with Laurence Olivier and Joan Fontaine, was on and Matthew had asked Bethany if she'd like to see it later that evening.

When she'd been living at Elmford ROF and had gone out with Mavis for the evening, they'd often swapped clothes so they didn't need to wear the same outfits.

But now she wanted to feel special.

Not that Matthew had ever appeared to notice her dowdy clothes. Perhaps all the more reason to make an effort for him.

You're wasting your time. And your money. Whatever is going on will be over by Sunday when you both return to Elmford.

Of course, it would be over. Bethany knew that. If all she'd have left were memories, then it was important these few days be special.

And anyway, she was only thinking about buying a blouse, not a house or a car or something she couldn't afford. She'd be able to wear the blouse again.

Yes, she'd convinced herself. She'd do it.

Bethany hurried into the shop before she changed her mind and after trying on several, she chose the prettiest – and the most expensive. With the blouse wrapped carefully, she put it in the bicycle basket and cycled back to Dr Franks's surgery.

A few minutes later, Matthew came out, his face alight. He'd obviously found his talk useful.

"Where are we going next?" he asked, getting onto his bicycle.

"I suggest we walk," she said. "If we cycle, we'll have been up and down the High Road in no time."

They walked slowly along, wheeling their bicycles, and Matthew told her what Dr Franks had said.

"So, do you want a country practice?" Bethany asked.

Matthew paused for a second. "One day, perhaps. But not yet. I'm glad I talked to him, though. It made me see I want something a little more challenging. When I first qualified, I worked in the London Hospital. It was really busy, but I enjoyed it, and now I'm sure I'd like to try something like that again. There were plenty of opportunities to learn about exotic and foreign diseases with so many immigrants in the area. I'd like to do something like that first and then to travel. I'd like to see the other side of the world. The only country I've ever been to outside of Britain is France."

"The furthest I've ever been," said Bethany wistfully, "is London. Travel. Oh, how marvellous. That sounds so exciting."

One day, when the war was over, perhaps she might travel too. Pa was being looked after, and she didn't have to stay in England. She didn't have to do anything. With enough money behind her, she could do as she pleased.

"That's the Radion," Bethany said, pointing out the cinema with its name in large letters set high on the building above a diamond shape. "It's where Rebecca is showing."

A ripple of pleasure ran through her. Later that night, she'd go to the pictures with Matthew. The first time she'd been taken to see a film by anyone other than her mother.

Was it a date? Not in Matthew's eyes, Bethany was sure, but she could pretend it was if she chose to. No one would know.

They carried on until they'd walked the length of the High Road, deep in conversation about the future. After tea in Baxter's Tearooms, Bethany was beginning to wonder what she could suggest they do next.

"I'd like to see the Plotland area," Matthew said. "Dr Franks told me a little about the history and it sounds interesting. Perhaps you could show me the places you used to go when you were a little girl." He paused and his brows drew together. "If that's not too painful, of course."

"It's only the last few years when things became difficult," Bethany said, grateful for his sensitivity. "My childhood was reasonably happy. There was a large group of children around where I lived, and we used to head out on the days we weren't at school. We'd go out early in the morning and not return until nightfall. Everyone looked out for everyone else. Things have changed slightly because of the war with so many Londoners flooding into the area after being bombed out. But the Plotland area still has the same atmosphere of kindness and generosity."

Bethany suggested they leave their bicycles by a large bush at the edge of Plotlands before they went onto the unmade road. There was another bicycle there and several pairs of rubber boots by the bush. She explained this was where people left their boots on their way into town and picked them up again to walk on the muddy roads of Plotlands on their way home.

"The bicycles will be safe," she said, knowing her blouse would be safe in the basket too. "People look after each other's property here."

As they walked along the grass, she pointed out some of the older properties and explained how they'd once been simple wooden structures onto which extensions had been added.

"And this cottage," Bethany said, indicating a tidy, brick-built property, "wasn't there when I was young. The family who owned the plot used to have a railway carriage on it, and they lived in that. I always thought that was so exciting."

She pointed out other cottages, some brick-built, others wooden, but all different from its neighbours. Each was surrounded by a plot of land, on which were vegetable gardens, chicken coops, and even in a few, there were goats.

People called out friendly greetings to Bethany and nodded politely at Matthew.

"Got yourself a fella at last, Bethany?" one woman called as she passed them, trying not to spill water out of her bucket. "Good for you. He's an 'andsome one and no mistake."

Bethany thought she'd feel embarrassed showing Matthew such a ramshackle collection of buildings. Recently, she'd wondered whether the pilots that flew overhead – both German and British – thought the area looked like a ragged and torn patchwork quilt. But Matthew didn't appear to be horrified at all – quite the opposite. He found everything interesting, and she began to see the place through his eyes.

Why not? Plotlands was remarkable. It was full of wonderful, warm people. No one who lived in Plotlands had as much money as Matthew's family, but they were rich in other ways.

"So, where did you play when you were a little girl, if you were out all day?" Matthew asked.

"We'd go up the hill next to the old church, especially in the winter when it had snowed. All day long, we'd toboggan down the slope on anything that slid, then carry whatever we had to the top and go down again. And during the other months, we disappeared into the woods and picked blackberries, or climbed trees. Oh, and we caught tiddlers in the pond and kept them in jam jars. We had a swing on a large branch once, too."

"Is it still there?"

"I don't know. It's been years since I've been up there."

"Perhaps we could look for it?"

As they'd walked along the High Road earlier, they'd wheeled their bicycles, and he hadn't been able to offer her his arm as he'd done the previous day. Walking along the unmade roads, they'd each had to pick out a different route as they avoided muddy patches and ruts. However, as they approached the woods, the grass was more even, and Matthew held out his hand to her.

"Well, Geraldine, if you're taking me into the woods, I'm not letting you out of my sight just in case I get lost." He smiled and took her hand.

How she longed to slip her glove off to feel her palm against his, but she didn't dare. What would he think? Nevertheless, the warmth of his hand through her glove and the firmness of his fingers around hers thrilled her.

"Now, no dawdling," she said in her Geraldine voice, hoping he couldn't see her flushed cheeks. "I'm not sure what I'm going to be able to show a submarine commander in the woods that'll be of interest, but I'll do my best."

She led him to the woods where she'd once played as a child with no thought that one day the world would be at war again.

Most of the trees were bare, their branches a tangle above them, and brown paper-dry leaves rustled beneath their feet. The sun was at its height and blue sky could be seen through the confusion of boughs and branches overhead.

Matthew stopped in the middle of a clearing, and after throwing his head back to feel the sun on his face, he closed his eyes and sighed with satisfaction. "I love it here. You could almost forget there's a war on." His hand gripped hers tightly, and with the other, she wanted to reach up to lay it against his cheek. To allow the sun to bathe them and to enjoy this shared moment. She'd wandered these woods for years in snow and sun, but never had it appeared as magical as that moment with Matthew. He made everything special. As he drank in the woodland sounds and setting, she drank him in. His head thrown back, his face at peace and the feel of his hand in hers. These were details she would commit to memory.

"Yesterday at Southend there were constant reminders of the war, with uniforms, checkpoints, barbed wire. And even in the factory – as far as it is from the town – there's the constant beat of machines. There's no escaping the war. But this..." He raised his hands, one of which was still holding hers. "Just birdsong and the wind."

And the frantic beating of my heart, Bethany thought.

"How lucky you were as a child. I'd have loved something similar. Show me more, Geraldine."

Bethany took him to where the swing had been. It had taken many tries until the group of children had finally managed to fling a heavy rope over a sturdy bough to make a swing. The tree was still there but there was no evidence of the rope. It had gone, along with the echoes of their childish screams and laughter.

They were on their way to the pond where Bethany and her friends had gone fishing when, in an instant, the bird song stopped. Bethany and Matthew froze, aware of the change but unaware of the cause.

"Thunder?" Bethany whispered as a low rumble penetrated the woods.

Matthew shook his head. He didn't need to say anything. Bethany could now hear the drone of aeroplanes. The sound grew louder, and as they both looked up, they saw the first planes pass overhead, visible through a small gap in the knotted bare branches overhead.

The aeroplanes were flying low enough to make out the German markings and swastikas on the tail fins.

"We're safe," Matthew said taking Bethany into his arms and pulling her towards the trunk of the nearest tree. "Messerschmitts. But they can't see us. I believe they're heading west, probably to London. They wouldn't waste bombs on us." He pulled her tighter.

Still, the planes flew overhead, wave after wave. This heralded a massive bombardment.

Bethany was sure they were safe. Nevertheless, the hairs on the back of her neck prickled. Somewhere a few miles away, people were about to receive a deadly surprise. She buried her face in Matthew's chest until the last of the Luftwaffe planes had gone, and he continued to hold her, silently stroking her hair for several minutes after the whine of the engines receded.

"It will be over one day. This madness will end," he whispered into her hair, then laid his cheek against her head.

Will it? She wondered. Matthew was so sure, yet suppose he was wrong? She realised she was gasping for air as if it was in short supply. For many, this day would be their last. They wouldn't know it yet, but today people would die.

It could so easily be her. Until she'd met Matthew, life had been grey, but he'd brought light and colour... and opened up a world of possibilities. Before, she hadn't thought further than the end of the week. Now there was so much she wanted to do. She wanted to travel, she wanted more than she'd ever dreamt possible, and she wanted to kiss this man. It would be her first kiss. It was unlikely they'd be blown up – as Matthew had pointed out, a pilot wouldn't want to waste bombs on a wood – but this was war and it was still possible that her first kiss might also be her last.

Well, there was no one in the world she'd rather share that kiss with than Matthew. Of course, it would never happen again – and not because she might not survive. They'd enjoyed two days together, but it would soon be over. And anyway, they hadn't really spent two days together – they'd been playing parts. She was Geraldine and he was Peregrine. No one could blame them for anything they did because they didn't exist.

The blood pounded through Bethany's ears. Could he hear it? Would he be scandalised if he knew she wanted to kiss him?

Did she care?

He wouldn't be holding her so tightly and stroking her head so tenderly if he wasn't drawn to her, would he? Perhaps he wanted to kiss her, too.

She tilted her head and looked up. Her breath caught in her throat as she recognised longing in his eyes.

Dare she kiss him? If she didn't, she might always regret her lack of bravery. Do it. It's now or never.

She took off one glove and raising her hand, she stroked his cheek then, standing on tiptoe, she closed her eyes and touched her lips to his. It was electrifying. How could something so simple send pleasure coursing through her body?

His arms tightened around her, and he pressed his mouth against hers, gently just for a second, and then he broke away although she could feel his breath on her cheek. He hadn't pulled away completely.

Had he been shocked? Or had she caught him off guard? She opened her eyes and gazed deeply into his.

"Bethany," he whispered. He cupped her face in both hands, and gently kissed her lips again then broke away and rested his forehead against hers.

He'd breathed her name, but had it been with longing for her or regret that she'd been so bold?

"Don't worry, I won't embarrass you when we're back at work by kissing you again," she said. It was best to make that clear.

He smiled. "It's probably best not to kiss me anywhere near the factory."

She shrank away from him. He hadn't spoken unkindly but it was obvious her kiss hadn't been welcome. Or if it had, he was worried she might do it again.

"I'm sorry. I know I should have behaved properly—"

"I think you behaved perfectly," he said, kissing her temple, sending shivers of delight through her. "What I meant was that when we kissed, there were sparks. Lots of them. And as we both know sparks in a filling factory are forbidden. Perhaps we need to test it out again. Because when we get back to Elmford, it would be good if there were more kisses."

Was he serious? He was smiling gently, as if he meant it.

"More kisses?" she murmured.

"If you'd like to..." He slid his fingers into her hair and leaned in to place his lips on hers again, kissing her more hungrily.

She clung to him, wondering at his words.

He was wrong. There could never be more kisses after they returned on Sunday. There could never be more of anything.

Enjoy him now.

"You don't believe me, do you?" he asked.

"I can't see how..."

"We'll make it work, Bethany. We will. Trust me."

She trusted Matthew. It was the rest of the world she didn't trust.


Bethany admired her new blouse in the mirror. Her skirt was old, but it would have to do. She hadn't had enough coupons for a new one.

Mrs Stewart had prepared Bethany and Matthew an early supper, and Ben had told Matthew he could borrow the car that evening to drive them into Laindon to the Radion.

Bethany ran down the stairs, her shoes in her hand, ready to put on her outdoor clothes. This was going to be the end to a perfect day. She and Matthew had walked, hand in hand, through the woods, talking about their futures. But not their separate futures. They both wanted similar things and although they were both aware they'd only just met, there was the promise of something together. As yet, it was too fragile to name or to examine, but they both knew that given the opportunity, it could grow.

Warmth crept through her as she remembered Matthew's hands caressing her back, holding her to him and his lips against hers. The sensation of his body pressed close to hers. When they'd broken apart, she'd been breathless and longing for more, but he was concerned she knew that when he'd kissed her, it hadn't been Peregrine kissing Geraldine.

"We made those characters up and they were amusing at the time, but I want you to know that I, Matthew Howard, kissed you, Bethany Anderson... well, actually, I suppose more accurately, Bethany kissed Matthew." He smiled mischievously and pulled her to him, nuzzling her neck. "But I want you to know it wasn't a game. Not for me."

Every time Bethany relived that moment, she glowed inside. She had wondered if it had all been part of the charade, but he'd been clear – it had been real.

She tiptoed down the stairs. Matthew was in the hall, the telephone receiver to his ear. He was absorbed in the telephone call; his face had drained of colour and his jaw was rigid.

It obviously wasn't good news. Earlier, the German planes had blocked out the sun as they'd streamed overhead. Now, a shadow passed over her as dark and as menacing.

# Chapter Fifteen

"It's for you, Matthew," Joanna had said when she'd answered the telephone in the hall. "It's your brother, Robert."

Matthew had groaned and leapt up. Not now, he'd thought. He was about to take Bethany out and he didn't want to be late for the showing.

It was puzzling. He hadn't told Robert he was staying at Priory Hall, simply that he'd been going to Hugh's engagement party.

If Robert knew where he was, then he must've been in touch with Hugh. And if he'd taken that much trouble, there must be a serious problem. A bombing raid on the factory? That wouldn't have been in the newspaper. It would have been kept quiet.

"Hello? Robert?"

"Matthew, I want you to come home immediately." Robert spoke in his most pompous voice. The one he used when he wanted to make it plain he wouldn't be contradicted or disobeyed.

"Why what's happened? Has there been an accident at the factory?"

"Suffice it to say there's been a crisis. And you need to return to work immediately." Robert's voice had a sarcastic edge. it wasn't the sort of tone Matthew would have expected had there been a real disaster at the factory.

He needed to reason with his brother. This was madness. Robert was being melodramatic. "Look, Robert, I'm on leave until Sunday. I'll be back then. Can't it wait? I'll come to Brent House as soon as I'm in Elmford Mere."

Robert's words shot out of the receiver like bullets. "Get home now! You've got some explaining to do."

Matthew had had enough. How dare his brother speak to him like that? "Robert, I'm not coming now unless you can speak to me with civility and explain what's happening."

There was a pause. Robert's tone was icy. "Then let me spell it out to you, brother, dear. Quite frankly, I didn't know you had it in you. Carrying on an affair with the girl who was implicated with that German spy—"

"What? Robert, have you gone mad?" Matthew held his breath. Robert knew he was at Priory Hall. Did he also know Bethany was here? No, how was that possible? He must protect her at all costs.

But Robert hadn't finished. "A fling with that Anderson girl, straight after having had an affair with my wife."

"What? Have you been drinking, Robert? What madness is this?" Matthew's stomach started to unknot. Robert was drunk. That was it.

"I know the Anderson girl is at Priory Hall with you, Matthew. I have friends in MI5 and they carried out extra checks on her before she was given the all clear. She gave that address for the period of her suspension and it's been confirmed. It was also confirmed you were at Priory Hall, too."

"So what if I am? The Richardsons are my friends. Miss Anderson used to work for the family. It's just a coincidence. It means nothing and we're definitely not having an affair.

"A coincidence, is it?" Robert sneered.

"Yes, as a matter of fact it is."

"Well, you can claim what you like, but when I discovered you and the girl were both at Priory Hall, I asked my friend in MI5 for a little further information as to your whereabouts. Southend-on-Sea. Laindon. You and the girl have certainly been seeing the sights. Of course, you're at liberty to find some cheap tart, but it's a different matter when you have an affair with my wife. Julia tells me the child she's carrying is yours."

Matthew's mouth went dry. Julia had cited him as the father? Thoughts whirled around his head.

"That's ridiculous, Robert, absolutely ridiculous."

"Let me ask you this, brother, dear. Did you know Julia was pregnant?"

Matthew hesitated. "Well... I"

"So, you knew."

"I..."

"Julia is distraught, and I need you home for damage control. If we handle this correctly no one need know what you've done—"

"But I haven't done anything—"

"Shut up, Matthew. Get home now. As you well know, I can't father children so it's not mine. But if it's yours at least it has the family genes. It stands a chance of looking as though it's a Howard. All you need to do is keep quiet. Come home and don't cause any more scandal."

Matthew's mind went numb.

Robert took advantage of the moment's silence. "If you don't come home immediately, I'll ruin that girl of yours. I'll drag her name through the mud."

Robert was bluffing. Surely. He couldn't know how close Matthew and Bethany had become. But suppose he did?

"The clock is ticking, Matthew. I want you home here on the next train." Robert hung up.

Matthew stared at the receiver, then gently placed it back in its cradle. This couldn't be true. Julia had implicated him? She was selfish and wilful but surely even she wouldn't resort to such deceit.

Matthew loosened his tie and leaned against the wall. He was finding it hard to breathe.

What to do? What to do?

He had to leave immediately. Robert was capable of hurting Bethany. Above all, Matthew must protect her. She was innocent of all of this. As was he, of course. But it was his family and his mess. Yes, when he got to Brent House, he'd make everyone see sense. Julia would back down and tell the truth and then he'd make it up to Bethany.

He felt sick. Julia would stick to her story. She was a desperate woman, and she'd take Matthew down with her if necessary. This mess was not going away.

He looked up to see Bethany. She smiled hesitantly. How much had she heard? He thought back over his words. He hadn't said anything incriminating. She wouldn't know what he'd been accused of, nor that Robert had threatened to ruin her.

"Bethany," he said, a catch in his voice. "I have to go. I must go back to Elmford now."

She held out her hand as if to comfort him but allowed it to drop. She glanced at the drawing room door as if expecting Joanna or Ben to appear. He understood her reluctance to show their closeness. It was too young, too vulnerable.

"Has something dreadful happened?" she whispered.

"Nothing for you to worry about. I need time to sort out a family matter." He couldn't bear the pain reflected in her eyes.

"I'll give my apologies to Joanna and Ben and then I must pack. I'm sorry, Bethany..." he tailed off.

A tear trickled down her cheek.

He'd caused that.

"Thank you, Bethany; yesterday and today have been the happiest two days of my life."

He hadn't added, "And now it's over." But it felt as though he had.

Ben drove Matthew to the station after he'd explained there was a family crisis, and he was required in Elmford Mere immediately.

As Ben drove along the High Road, Matthew remembered walking along there that morning with Bethany. Determination coursed through him. He'd fight for her. He'd get home as quickly as he could. There must be a way out of this tangle. There must be a solution. You couldn't put so much effort into something for it to fail.

But the more he thought about it, the more he knew he was trapped. If he upset Robert in any way, his brother would ruin Bethany.

Matthew would not allow that to happen.

Robert and Julia were arguing when Matthew arrived at Brent House.

Nothing new there.

But this day would be like no other in Matthew's life. There would be a radical change unless he could do something.

"So," said Robert, his tone icy when Matthew entered the drawing room. "The Prodigal returns. I suppose you're proud of yourself, fathering a child and doing what your older brother couldn't?"

Matthew took a deep breath. He'd thought over what he must say on the journey home. Above all, he must remain calm.

"Robert, we're all adults. I'm sure this can be sorted out. Yes, I was aware Julia was pregnant. But I knew because she consulted me as a doctor. I swear to you, the child is not mine."

Julia screamed and thumped her fists on the table, her face scarlet with anger. "Oh, how can you say that, Matthew? After what we meant to each other. How could the child be another man's?"

Matthew's mouth fell open. Julia was obviously lying. Why couldn't Robert see? She was like a dreadful actress reading her lines badly. And yet Robert didn't appear to doubt her.

A chill ran down Matthew's spine. Perhaps his brother wanted to believe her.

"As I see it," said Robert, interlacing his fat fingers over his paunch, "we have no choice now. The die has been cast. We must think of the family's honour. Unfortunately, our parents know I can't father children, so you must claim the child as your own, Matthew. I will tell Father I've forgiven Julia and that since the child will carry Howard genes, when it's born, I'll claim it as my own. Father will settle the sum of money he'd promised on his first grandchild – because it will be his first grandchild, although not from the son he'd expected. A few family members and friends know I can't have children, we'll explain it to them and ask for their discretion. And all will be well. That is the only solution."

"You're forgetting one small detail." Despite his earlier resolve to remain calm, Matthew's voice was louder than he'd intended. "The child isn't mine and I resent anyone being told I've cheated on my own brother with a woman who is..." He paused before he said something he'd later regret. Insulting his sister-in-law wouldn't help.

Julia gasped; presumably aware the words Matthew had cut off were not complimentary.

"I'm afraid you don't have any choice, Matthew." Robert leaned forward, his eyes narrowed. "That is the story we will all stick to. If you should contradict me, I will carry out my threat towards that girl.

She won't be able to hold her head up ever again. Furthermore, a word from me and MI5 might take a greater interest in her. She might not appreciate a spell in prison. Honestly, I don't know why you're being so awkward. This won't be made public. The fewer people who know about our affairs the better. But Father needs to know the truth before he assumes the child isn't a Howard. And your girl need never know... Unless you defy me, of course."

"Girl? What girl?" Julia asked.

"Matthew has been amusing himself with one of my workers."

"And, once again, you've got your facts wrong," Matthew snapped.

Robert's eyebrows rose in disbelief. "It's of no account to me. Just play your part in this affair and you can do as you please. I don't care if you corroborate the story or not, but you will not deny it. Is that clear?"

Matthew turned away. He didn't trust himself to speak. So, a few people would believe he'd betrayed his brother and although he wasn't required to admit to it, he couldn't deny it. And if he did, Bethany would pay.

Matthew picked up his bag and left. There was unlikely to be a bus to the factory at this time. Well, he'd rather walk than stay under this roof of deceit and treachery a moment longer.

# Chapter Sixteen

Bethany wiped a small circle in the condensation on the inside of the train carriage window with her finger. Outside, raindrops trickled down the glass.

About time. Finally, there was weather that matched her mood.

After Matthew had left, the skies had been brilliant blue, like they'd been on the days when she'd been out with him.

How had the world not known Bethany's heart was breaking? How could the sun still have shone as if all was well?

Nobody cares about your heart.

That wasn't true. Joanna, Ben and Mrs Stewart had been kind. They'd all been upset on her behalf that Matthew had left without explanation. But their concern had made her feel even more foolish. The maid who'd had the nerve to think she was worthy of someone like Matthew.

He hadn't even been able to look her in the eyes. She guessed Matthew's brother had reminded him of his family obligations. Associating with a girl who worked in his factory and a former maid of Priory Hall wasn't appropriate for someone of his standing.

Matthew was so kind-hearted; he wouldn't have been able to find the words to explain that to her.

But he ought to have tried...

She would have understood. After all, it was all perfectly true. But he'd left with no explanation.

She wiped more condensation away and peered at the platform through the raindrops. It was nearly empty. A few couples still clung to each other under umbrellas, and dripping porters walked back to their room with empty trolleys. The guard waved his flag and blew his whistle. Doors slammed and with a blast of steam, the train slowly chugged out of the station.

Bethany closed her eyes. She wouldn't cry. That would achieve nothing, and she was determined to find some good amongst the bad. She would continue to save every penny and by the time the war was over – if indeed, it ever did come to an end – she'd be ready to begin her life.

When she got back to Elmford, she'd ask to be put on the most dangerous work and her wages would rise accordingly.

One day, she'd be independent. She wouldn't need to worry about anyone's opinions, including the Howard family.

She may not be good enough for them. But in her opinion, they weren't good enough for her.

Bethany opened her eyes and stared out of the window seeing only the raindrops running diagonally across the pane as the train gathered speed.


When she arrived at Kestrel Block, she discovered a new woman had been moved into her bedroom, replacing Mavis.

"Hello, I'm Violet Yates. But my friends call me Vi," the new auburn-haired woman said, holding out her chubby hand. "I'm so pleased to meet you."

"Bethany Anderson. Welcome, Vi." She shook the new woman's hand. Bethany wasn't in any mood to be sociable, but she would at least be polite. "Have you been working here long?" she asked, more for something to say than because she was interested.

"Six months. I was in Heron Block, but I've been moved here." She looked around the room. "My roommate got married and left. I don't like being on my own, so I asked to be moved. This is pretty much the same as the room I moved out of." Her brow furrowed. "I hope you don't mind me asking, but is this the room where Mavis Jenkins lived?"

"Why?" Bethany asked sharply.

"Oh, I just wondered. She was the one who went out with the German spy, wasn't she?" Vi leaned towards Bethany as if she expected her to whisper a secret, then without waiting for an answer, she added, "Do tell! What was he like? Did you ever meet him?"

"If you don't mind," Bethany said. "I've got a dreadful headache. I'm going straight to bed."

"Of course. By the way, don't mind me. I'm a dreadful gossip, but I'm sure we're going to be great friends. When you feel better, you can tell me all about what happened."

Despite Bethany's initial annoyance at her new roommate's bluntness, there was something about her that Bethany liked. At least she spoke her mind. That was refreshing. It was easy to know where you stood with people who were honest about their feelings.

During the next few weeks, it became clear how much Vi loved to gossip. Bethany found out more about the people working around her than she'd ever known before.

Despite being an expert on everyone's business, there was nothing spiteful about Vi. In fact, she'd probably have made a good newspaper reporter – she appeared to have the knack of finding out the tiniest of details. Bethany made up her mind to tell her about what had happened to Mavis. It was better Vi heard the truth from her rather than an inflated version of the story from someone who'd only heard the rumours. Mavis deserved that.

"Heinrich Zimmerman, or Harry Carpenter as we knew him, was handsome, charming and totally believable. Apparently, he targeted Mavis and she fell for him completely. I don't suppose she'll ever get over it."

"Another untrustworthy man," Vi said, her voice trailing off. "Believable and deceitful. That describes quite a few men, doesn't it?" A note of bitterness had crept into Vi's tone.

Bethany hadn't asked her to explain. She, Mavis and Vi weren't the only women to have ever been let down by a man.

Vi had lots of friends and went into town as often as she could get a pass, going to dances and to the pictures. Bethany had no desire to go into town. She didn't want to remind herself of times she'd spent in Elmford Mere with Mavis. Instead, Bethany stayed home and in her spare time, she studied.

As soon as she'd started her first shift after returning from leave, she'd volunteered to work in one of the most dangerous areas of the factory. Bethany was soon on the roster in the mixing shop, where highly sensitive explosives were mixed together, and she'd also volunteered to work in the detonator section – a job so hazardous she worked alone in a locked room. If anything went wrong, only her life would be at risk.

As she worked, she concentrated on keeping her hands steady and her mind sharp as she did the repetitive work of filling and pressing, then passing whatever she was making on to the next step in the line.

During the following few weeks, Vi repeatedly asked Bethany to go out with her group of friends into town or to the social events that were held on site. However, Bethany always refused. She either wanted to study, or more likely, was too tired. Being constantly alert during her shift was taking its toll. And she'd developed a rash on her lower stomach, which she was certain she'd managed to conceal, unless it started to spread. Her wages had increased significantly, and she was reluctant to consider earning less by asking to be moved while the rash was given time to heal.

She'd seen Matthew on several occasions in the distance, but when it had been time for her check-up, Dr Dawkins had been there to carry out the examination.

At her first check-up since she'd returned from Priory Hall, she'd assumed Matthew would examine her, as he had in the past. Not that she'd have known what to say to him. The disappointment, when she realised Dr Dawkins was on duty, weighed heavily. But as the check-up continued, she'd been relieved Matthew hadn't been there. It would have been too awkward for both of them. He'd made his feelings clear. If he'd wanted to explain his behaviour after they'd both returned to the factory, he'd known where she was. She wondered if he'd seen her name on the list of patients and had swapped shifts with Dr Dawkins.

And really, the outcome was as she'd expected. Any sort of relationship with a member of the Howard family would be out of the question for her. It had been Matthew who'd sworn, on that day they'd walked in the woods, that he'd find a way for them to be together.

"I'm rather concerned about you, Miss Anderson," Dr Dawkins said when he'd finished examining her. "According to your records, you've lost a lot of weight since your last check-up. "I'm going to recommend you're moved to lighter duties."

"Oh no, please, doctor. I'm fine, really I am. I rely on the higher wages."

"Miss Anderson, if you don't stop punishing yourself, you won't be alive to enjoy your wages." He put down his pen and took off his spectacles. "You appear to be an intelligent woman, so how about this? I shall recommend you're put forward for promotion to a more supervisory role. How would that be?"

"Oh, thank you, doctor. And can I keep working in the detonator section?"

Dr Dawkins frowned and shook his head. "I'll tell you what. Come back and see me next week and if you're still losing weight, I'm afraid I'm going to have to recommend you're moved."

Bethany nodded. She'd have to try to eat more during the next few days. That wouldn't be easy because she had no appetite, but at least she'd managed to conceal the rash on her stomach. So far.

And if she could earn more in a supervisory role, so much the better. At least she might be able to sleep more soundly. Recurring nightmares where she was locked in a room with a ticking bomb filled her nights.

But would she be accepted for promotion? It probably depended on who was in charge of making those decisions. If it was Mr Howard, would he allow it? She hadn't attempted to contact Matthew, so there was no reason for Mr Howard to remember her at all.

After thanking Dr Dawkins, Bethany returned to her room to find Vi getting ready to go out.

"You'll never guess what!" she said as soon as Bethany entered.

More gossip, thought Bethany. It was a mystery how Vi knew everyone's business.

"You know that handsome Dr Howard?"

Bethany took a sharp intake of breath. "Yes," she said trying to keep her voice calm. What had Vi uncovered now? Bethany turned away, hoping to hide her pink cheeks.

"Well, you'll never believe this." Vi finished pinning her hair up on the top of her head and then patted it in place. "I've heard he's been having an affair."

Bethany swung around to face Vi. Who'd been spreading such vicious rumours?

Unaware of Bethany's reaction, Vi pulled the top off her lipstick and concentrated on her reflection in the mirror.

"Yes. An affair. With his sister-in-law. Can you believe it?"

Bethany couldn't speak. Blood pounded in her ears. Could it be true? Vi was usually uncannily correct, but Matthew having an affair with his brother's wife? She stared at Vi, who'd applied a layer of crimson and was squeezing her lips together, then pouting at herself in the mirror.

"It gets worse." Her eyes were still on the reflection of the perfect bow of her mouth. "He's having a child with her. Well, what do you think of that? It's a scandal, isn't it?" She tucked a stray curl behind her ear, unaware Bethany had sunk onto her bed.

Could it be true? If it was, Bethany hadn't known Matthew at all. She finally managed to push the words out. "How do you know?"

Vi was only too keen to tell her. "Well, my friend, Doris, is the cousin of Mr Howard's mistress, Gladys. Apparently, Gladys is furious. She thought that when Mrs Howard's condition became known, Mr Howard would divorce his wife and marry her. He can't have children, so the baby can't be his. But although he's told Gladys repeatedly, he loathes his wife, apparently, he's standing by her. Even though she's had an affair with his brother. Can you believe it? You just can't tell with some people. And the rich seem worse than anyone.

I suppose they've got more time on their hands to play silly games. The rest of us are too busy working to have the chance to carry on like that." She gave her hair a final pat.

"Right, I'll be back later. Don't study too hard." She grabbed her coat and hat and, slipping on high-heeled shoes, she tip-tapped out of the room.

Bethany lay back on her bed and stared at the ceiling.

Could it be true?

Well, what difference did it make? Matthew would never be hers, so let the Howard family deal with their own problems. But still, her stomach churned with a sense of betrayal.

The following day, Bethany was taking a report across to the administrative building, walking on one of the asphalt walkways, when someone shouted. She turned around to see a procession of three women. The first was walking towards her, waving a red flag. About thirty yards behind her was a woman carrying a red box and yards behind her was another woman, also waving a red flag. Bethany stepped to one side, keeping well clear.

She'd often been the one carrying a similar red box containing detonators to the lab to be tested. If dropped, the resulting explosion would have seriously injured anyone in the area. It was so dangerous; it was forbidden to carry a box through a doorway in case the door swung back and hit it. Of course, the box wasn't particularly heavy or difficult to hold, but nerves caused sweaty palms and that could lead to a slip. She knew exactly how the woman carrying the detonators felt, and her heart pumped faster and her palms grew slippery, simply watching and empathising with her.

Bethany waited, watching the procession intently, glad that for once, she wasn't the person carrying the box.

"Bethany?" The quiet voice came from behind, making her jump. Her heart thrashed even harder in her chest. Having identified so completely with the woman who had reached the hatch in the side of the lab building and was placing the box there, Bethany mentally swapped places with her and in her imagination, she dropped the precious box.

She swung around, eyes wide and breath catching in her throat. For a split second, she imagined the explosion.

"Oh, Bethany, I'm so sorry. I didn't mean to alarm you." Matthew's brows drew together in dismay. His hand stretched out towards her, then he stopped and withdrew it.

"I... I just wanted a quick word with you. I've been talking to Dr Dawkins, and he's worried about you." He frowned as he peered at her face. "You've been steadily losing weight and Dr Dawkins tells me you've lost so much in such a short time. I'm going to recommend you have a break from work while you recuperate."

"Thank you, Dr Howard, but no. I'm perfectly happy continuing working." After giving her such a shock, her pulse was still racing, the blood pounding in her ears.

She could cope.

She would cope.

More dangerous work meant a higher salary. It was none of his business.

"Bethany..." He'd blanched as she'd addressed him as Dr Howard and his voice caught in his throat. "Please, I'd like to help you."

She forced her lips to smile. It wouldn't reach her eyes but what did that matter? "No need," she said. "I don't need help." She turned on her heel and, clutching her report with sweaty hands, she walked swiftly towards the administrative building.

She made it into the entrance hall where everything began to spin and then to slide in and out of focus. Halfway across the hall, she fainted.

# Chapter Seventeen

When Bethany awoke, she was in the Elmford Factory hospital. Nurse Evans smiled, placed her hand on Bethany's forehead, and nodded encouragingly.

"Welcome back, Miss Anderson. I'll just take your temperature and blood pressure. At least you're a better colour now. You were quite grey earlier." She noted the results on Bethany's medical record.

"Your blood pressure's a little bit low. But nothing to worry about. Now, my dear, when was the last time you ate?"

Bethany shook her head. She couldn't remember. It must have been that morning at breakfast time. She'd had porridge, hadn't she? Or had that been yesterday? No, toast. She'd had toast that morning. But the memory had a strange feel to it, as if her mind had merely filled in a blank with something reasonable. A false memory. The one vision that played through her mind was of a box of detonators slipping from her hands. Well, that obviously hadn't happened. That definitely wasn't a real memory. What was wrong with her?

Nurse Evans smoothed the bedclothes over Bethany. "Then, if you can't remember, I think we must feed you up. I suspect your blood sugar has dropped. Dr Dawkins is carrying out some tests now, but in the meantime, if you want to get well quickly, you need to eat."

Bethany glanced around the room. All the beds were neatly made, and the only other person in there with her was Nurse Evans. Good, she didn't want Matthew to see her like that. She'd assured him she felt fine.

Dr Dawkins came in and checked her eyes and tongue, then listened to her heart. He prescribed bedrest in the hospital until she picked up.

"As soon as you're well enough, Miss Anderson, you can go. But you've got a nasty rash on your stomach. You need time away from work. And despite my warnings, I don't think you've been eating properly. We need to feed you up before you're strong enough to resume your duties. What would've happened if you'd fainted at work? Blown yourself up and possibly others." He shook his head slowly.

Bethany nodded. She understood it wasn't a luxury to eat. It was vital for her safety and everyone around her. She'd certainly lost her appetite since she'd taken on more hazardous duties.

Had she been trying to punish herself? Well, if she had, it would stop now. She was determined to become strong again, and then she'd work twice as hard as anyone else until the war was over and she was free to do whatever she wanted.

During the next few days, she spent much time with Nurse Evans. The kindly woman looked more like a farmer's wife than a nurse, with round, ruddy cheeks and curls tucked into her starched, white cap. People came into the hospital with cuts and wounds which Nurse Evans patiently cleaned and bandaged. She smiled and gave her full attention to each patient, reassuring and calming their fears. She treated everyone with the same respect and concern.

When Bethany felt well enough to get out of bed, she offered to help the nurse, cleaning and doing menial tasks. She'd expected Nurse Evans to shoo her away as if insulted by the suggestion an untrained person might help. However, she was as generous as ever and while she was working, she explained to Bethany what she was doing and why.

Finally, Dr Dawkins said Bethany was ready to go back to work.

"You'd make a good nurse, my dear," Nurse Evans said as Bethany helped her strip and remake the bed she'd occupied for several days. For a second, Matthew's words came back to her. He'd assumed his Peregrine Esplanade voice and had suggested Geraldine Seagull would make a good nurse. At the memory of that wonderful day, it felt as though the breath had been squeezed out of her.

Matthew had been wrong about them being together, but it didn't mean he'd been wrong about everything, and anyway, the nurse appeared to agree.

Bethany tried to imagine herself working on a ward in a real hospital with many patients who had varying needs. Then she pictured herself sitting in an office tapping at a typewriter, perhaps a boss shouting at her from his office.

The two jobs didn't compare.

Perhaps she could be a nurse and help people like Nurse Evans had helped her. Perhaps Bethany could be anything she wanted to be – as Peregrine had once said.

Yes, she would look into it. There was no sign of the war ending, and she didn't have to do anything yet. She'd need permission to leave the Elmford Factory and that would be unlikely to be granted unless she went into something as valuable as her munitions work. But surely nursing would be considered as important.

Trained nurses had joined the Armed Forces in huge numbers and the civilian population who were suffering from the bombs as well as the usual infections and accidents, were not as well served as they had been during peacetime.

While she might be allowed to move from a munitions factory into nursing, it was most unlikely she'd be allowed to move from the factory into an office. The more Bethany thought about it, the more she wanted to start nursing training.

If Bethany didn't intend to pursue her idea of becoming a shorthand typist, there was no longer any reason to study so hard at her Pitman shorthand books. With surprise, she realised she was lonely. Surrounded by people. Sharing a room with a chatty, friendly girl. And yet she'd cut herself off.

And for what? Because her heart had been broken?

She should have known better. She should have stuck to her earlier plans of not letting anyone into her life and her affections. Had she done that, she wouldn't feel so wretched and betrayed.

It wouldn't have been so bad if Matthew hadn't said those words when they'd walked in the woods.

"Trust me."

Against her better judgement, she had trusted him, and he'd let her down.

Well, never again. However, that didn't mean she should cut herself off from everyone.

"Are you going to the ENSA concert this evening?" she asked Vi when they got up the following morning.

"Yes. Why?" Vi asked, looking at Bethany quizzically. "Wait! You're not thinking of coming, are you?" She held her hands up in mock surprise.

"Yes. I was, actually."

Vi's face lit up. "Oh, good, that'll be such fun. You're not studying tonight, then?"

"No, I thought I'd like to go out for a change."

"That's a wonderful idea. Come with me. I'm meeting some friends there. At least tonight it won't be ENSA standing for 'Every Night Something Awful' again. Monday's concert was simply dreadful. The pianist couldn't play. The singers were atrocious, and the comedian kept forgetting his jokes. But tonight's concert is going to be wonderful. Raymond Blandford's coming." Vi held her hands over her heart and pretended to swoon.

"Who's Raymond Blandford?"

"Oh, Bethany! Everyone's talking about him. He's a comedian, and he's absolutely hilarious. And he's such a dreamboat as well."

"Hilarious?" Bethany doubted she'd find it hilarious, but going to the concert would be a good start in re-joining the social scene.

She wasn't keen on the idea of going to any dances in town after her experience with Mavis and Zimmerman. But sometimes dances were held on the factory site, she could start going to them. She wouldn't accidentally run into any Nazi spies there. And if she didn't like the dances, there was plenty more entertainment.

Perhaps she could join a club? Why not? Sometimes there were courses as well. She could ask if there was a first aid course. That would be helpful if she ever became a nurse.

If she ever became a nurse. The words echoed in her mind. If they wouldn't free her from her obligations in the factory, then after the war, she'd do her best to become a nurse.

When I become a nurse.

That night she put on the blouse she'd bought to go to see the film, Rebecca, with Matthew. It had been several months since she'd packed it away and left Priory Hall. It would be a waste not to get some wear out of it.

"Oh, that's a pretty blouse," said Vi. "I love that colour green. It really sets your eyes off. You ought to wear it more often. You need a bit of colour on your cheeks, though. Have you got any rouge? You're still a bit peaky."

Bethany nodded. She'd managed to get hold of some rouge, lipstick and mascara when she and Mavis had gone out to the dances in town, but she hadn't bothered to use any make-up after that.

"Would you like me to do it for you?" Vi asked.

Why not? Make-up was so hard to come by, it would almost have been a crime not to.

"Hand it over. I'll make a superb job." Vi held out her hand impatiently.

Every time Vi went out, she spent ages at the mirror doing her face up, and she expertly applied lipstick, rouge and mascara to Bethany. Standing back to admire her handiwork, Vi clapped her hands together.

"What a change. You look like a film star."

"I don't think so." Bethany said, but even she had to admire Vi's work when she stared at herself in the mirror. And the rouge did relieve her of the hollow-cheeked, deadly pallor that had accompanied her since she'd collapsed.

Bethany smiled and was startled at her reflection. She hadn't looked like that since... well, ever.

"Come on, we don't want to miss the beginning of the concert. Let's get going."

The members of ENSA, or Entertainments National Service Association, had set up in the ROF Elmford workers' canteen and there was a crackle of excitement in the air.

"Raymond Blandford's just arrived." A woman rushed into the canteen. Her hands over her cheeks and eyes wide with excitement. "I've just seen him. He's so handsome."

Vi led Bethany towards a group of men and women who were

already seated in one of the rows.

"This is my roommate, Bethany," she said, then introduced each person in turn. Bethany's head swam with names, Catherine, Deirdre, Susan, Thomas, Peter... She looked back at the faces, but several people had already moved, and she had no idea which name belonged to which person.

One of the men – possibly Peter – pointed out the chair next to him and she gratefully sat. Vi had already walked off to talk to another group of people.

The man's smile was friendly. "I'm Peter, by the way. I don't suppose you've remembered everyone's name. Did you go to the show on Monday?"

Bethany said she hadn't.

"It was so awful; it was really quite good." He had a pleasant face. There was nothing remarkable about it, but when he smiled, his eyes crinkled with humour and friendliness.

Bethany wondered whether to get up and move. She didn't want male company, but it would have been rude. He was the only person who'd shown her any friendliness or politeness. The other women Vi had introduced were in a huddle whispering about something.

If Peter began to show any interest in her, she'd make it clear where she stood. That would only be fair. But really, why should he be interested in her?

"I understand Raymond Blandford's going to sing some of the old musical numbers tonight. He's supposed to be a good singer as well as a comedian. Before this dreadful war, my wife and I used to go into London regularly to the theatre. Do you like musicals?"

Bethany nodded. At least Peter had been clear about being married. What did that mean? Was he one of those men who thought it was all right to cheat on his wife? She'd find out.

"Where's your wife now?" Bethany asked.

"She's staying at her sister's in Wiltshire with our children. We've got two." His face glowed with pride. "Look," he said, fishing inside his jacket for his wallet. He took it out and Bethany saw it was fat with tiny photographs of his family, which he showed to Bethany.

"That's me and my missus, Lorraine, on holiday on the Isle of Wight. And that's Maisie, my eldest she's seven now and so clever. She's going to be stunning when she's older. She gets her looks from Lorraine, thank goodness. And that one is Peter Jnr. Everyone says he looks just like me." Peter laughed. "Poor little lad."

"You have a beautiful family," said Bethany.

"I know. I can't wait for this to be over to get back to them. I suppose I should be grateful I'm not too far away from them. I've got one leg longer than the other, so they wouldn't let me join the army. If they had, I could be anywhere in the world. So, I suppose I'm lucky. Hopefully, the war will be over before I miss much more of their childhood."

Still Bethany wasn't certain about Peter's motives. But surely a man who took so much pride in his family wasn't after another woman?

The lights dimmed, and after a gasp of delight from the audience, a fanfare echoed around the canteen, and the first act began.

By the intermission, Bethany realised she'd been completely lost in the show. Her mind had not strayed once to Matthew. The singing had been excellent, and during the last act, everyone had joined in. Her skin was still tingling at the sound of so many voices in harmony.

And there was still an hour and a half to go. Peter fetched them drinks and continued to talk about his family and how he longed to see them. He had leave coming the following week and his eyes shone as he talked about travelling to Wiltshire to see Lorraine and the children.

"Thank you for listening," he said. "It's so nice to be able to talk about my family. It makes me feel closer to them. But you must think me so rude. Please tell me about yourself. Are you married? Or have a sweetheart?"

"No. I don't have anyone special and I don't think I want to marry." Bethany was surprised she'd confided in a man she'd only just met.

"Well, if you don't mind me saying, you're a beautiful woman. Perhaps one day, someone will sweep you off your feet," he said. "Although I can understand you wanting to be your own mistress. Most of the women in this factory have never had the chance to earn so much money. And that's bought them freedom. I think once the war is over, women are going to find it hard to slip back into the old ways. Men are no longer the only breadwinners. They'll have to get used to it, although I can't see many men giving up without a fight."

Bethany told Peter about her idea of being a nurse. She hadn't confided that piece of news to anyone else either.

Nevertheless, she was still wary of men after Zimmerman and then Matthew. And yet, Peter appeared to be genuine. If he was, how lucky Lorraine and his two children were, Bethany thought.

There was another fanfare and the lights dimmed again ready for the second part. It was just as enjoyable as the first, and during the final act, Raymond Blandford led the entire cast in singing 'We'll Meet Again'.

Everyone in the audience leapt to their feet, linked arms and joined in, singing at the top of their voices until Bethany felt she was floating on waves of sound. Optimism surged through her as she was caught up in the spirit of togetherness and single purpose. They would continue to make the bombs, bullets and mines for the Armed Forces until the world was once again at peace.

Bethany still had goosebumps as she stood up to leave with Vi.

"If you'd like to meet up sometime, I'd be really happy," Peter said.

Then he blushed and with eyes wide in alarm, he stepped backwards. "Oh, I hope you didn't think I was asking you for a date or anything like that. I swear I didn't have anything romantic in mind. You know how much I love my family. I'm just looking for… for friendship."

"No, of course not."

"It's just the other chaps here only seem to have one thing in mind. There are so many women here, they don't want to hear about my family. And if I understand you correctly, you aren't interested in anyone romantically, anyway. Perhaps we could be friends and just talk? Lorraine's sister is a registered nurse. Next time I write, I'll ask her about the training if you like."

"That would be nice, Peter," Bethany said. "I'd really like that. Thank you. Life's been rather difficult lately, but I think I'm coming out the other side now and I would very much like to see you again… as a friend."

He smiled with relief and then turned and followed the other chap, Thomas, back to their accommodation block.

Vi linked arms with Bethany, she was biting her lower lip nervously.

"You realise Peter's married, don't you Bethany?"

"I do," said Bethany. "He showed me pictures of his family."

"Then?"

"I'm not looking for romance, Vi. But a friend would be good."

"Well, thank goodness for that, I wondered if you'd set your sights on him. Several women have tried but he really isn't interested. He's a remarkable man. I wish I could find someone like him."

"Yes," agreed Bethany. One remarkable man one amongst millions, she thought bitterly.

# Chapter Eighteen

Matthew shook hands with Raymond Blandford and the other members of the cast. Greeting the people from ENSA and then thanking them after the performance was usually Robert's job, but despite Matthew having only just arrived back from Wales, his brother had claimed he had a clash of engagements.

Matthew knew exactly where he was and who he was with. He'd taken his mistress, Gladys, to the 400 Club in Leicester Square. It was one of the most popular nightclubs in London and one frequented by Matthew's friend, Hugh Barnes-Crosier. It was he who'd told Matthew he often saw Robert and Gladys in the nightclub – and very little detective work had been needed for Matthew to work out when he'd had a 'clash of engagements'.

Matthew suspected when Robert discovered he'd missed Raymond Blandford, he'd be most upset. But that was his own fault. Robert had obviously taken advantage of Matthew having returned to Elmford to insist his brother cover for him while he took Gladys out.

During the last few months, Dr Dawkins had taken over Matthew's role in the factory while Matthew had travelled first to Scotland at one of the ROF explosives factories where they had been extending the medical facilities, then to Wales at another ROF factory.

He'd been called in as a consultant. Not that Matthew considered he was any more knowledgeable than anyone else. Obviously, Robert had been pulling strings, and someone in Whitehall had thought it was a good idea to have Matthew visit the other ROF factories to advise.

Matthew wondered how it benefitted his brother to have him visit other factories. Perhaps he gained prestige if a member of his company was called in to offer advice? Perhaps he simply wanted Matthew out of the way. It was hard to know.

Since Matthew had returned from Priory Hall on that dreadful night, Robert had displayed an even more callous streak. His spite was aimed particularly at Matthew. To an outsider, it might have appeared this was because he believed Matthew had fathered the child. However, Robert was no fool and he knew exactly what Julia was like. Matthew couldn't believe Robert really thought he'd been capable of conducting an affair with Julia. So why was he so vindictive? The only reason Matthew could come up with was that although Robert knew the child wasn't his brother's, he had to try to convince the world it was. And that, in Robert's eyes, might simply have underlined his inability, so far, to father a child.

Sadly, Bethany had got caught up in the nastiness. If Matthew hadn't cared about Bethany, he wouldn't have agreed to keep silent about the baby. That had told Robert everything he needed to give him the upper hand.

Matthew had been pleased to learn Bethany had applied to study nursing. He also knew her letter was sitting at the bottom of Robert's in-tray where it was likely to remain. While Bethany was safe in ROF Elmford, Matthew would have to do as his brother wanted or who knew what might happen to Bethany?

If Robert blackened Bethany's reputation, it would be excruciatingly embarrassing for her, but his threat of involving MI5 was far more serious. Matthew doubted he would actually involve the Security Forces for his own ends. But who knew what he was capable of? After all, wasn't he blackmailing his own brother?

"An excellent show. Thank you," Matthew said, shaking yet another hand. As he got to the end of the line, the cast members broke away, keen to remove their make-up, wigs and costumes. Eager to get away ready to travel to another factory for the next show.

Matthew was careful not to show it, but he was impatient to go back to his room and go to bed, although he doubted he would sleep.

Bethany was somewhere on this vast factory site – perhaps even in the audience. On the few occasions he'd been in Elmford during the last few weeks, he'd only caught sight of her once. Somebody had come out of one of the workshops as he'd been passing. He'd glanced in and caught sight of Bethany from the side. She'd been sitting at a bench, a large press in front of her; she'd reached up to the lever and then the door had swung shut.

He hadn't sought her out. That would have been unfair. And he'd made sure if he took a clinic, Bethany wasn't one of the patients on his list that day. He wouldn't have been able to look her in the eye.

Despite Robert's assurances, they'd keep the supposed paternity in the family, Robert's mistress had spread the news far and wide.

Whether Gladys believed Matthew was the father or not, was irrelevant, Robert hadn't left his wife for her, and she was livid. It appeared she merely wanted to lash out at him. That Matthew had been caught in the crossfire of Robert's chaotic love life was of no interest to anyone.

The only person who gave the impression she thought Robert's behaviour was unacceptable was his secretary, Miss Grant, and even she wouldn't dare voice her views. Subtle sniffs, tosses of her head and clicks of her tongue revealed her true feelings when she was alone with

Matthew. She also occasionally put documents she thought Matthew should see in a special in-tray she had for him in her office. That was how Matthew knew Robert was still paying for Gladys's London flat out of company money.

What did it matter to Matthew? He wasn't interested in Robert's life. Although he wished he could extricate his life from his brother's. Julia would be giving birth shortly.

It was Miss Grant who'd let Matthew know Bethany had applied for nursing and that her letter was lying ignored in Robert's in-tray.

If only the war would end. The production of armaments would significantly decrease and most of the workers would be laid off. Not a good prospect for Robert, but an excellent one for Bethany if she moved away. As soon as she was gone, Robert wouldn't have a hold over her or Matthew.

He'd be able to explain everything to her. It might be possible to start afresh.

The ENSA performers had left and after a woman had cornered him and insisted on showing him her rash, he suggested she make an appointment the following day in the medical room and he'd see her then.

He turned to leave the canteen and froze. Bethany was talking to a man. Matthew recognised him as one of the security men who carried out spot checks. A pleasant man, if he remembered rightly. The sort of man who would look after Bethany.

Matthew lowered his head and hurried away. No, there wouldn't be much sleep for him that night.

The following day, Matthew spent the morning with his patients, then at midday, decided to go to the canteen for lunch. As he entered, he saw Bethany with the security man she'd been talking to the previous evening.

He and Bethany were looking at something – possibly photographs. They laughed together, and if Bethany seemed slightly remote, the man did not. His enthusiasm shone through.

A bitter taste rose in Matthew's throat. She'd moved on. More fool him for believing he'd ever have the opportunity to explain the truth and to win her back.

You're too late.

Too late. The words echoed around his brain.

Bethany was an attractive woman. Of course, she was going to arouse interest in the men around her.

But what of her dream to be a nurse? Was she abandoning that?

And if she is? It's none of your business.

He knew that was true. His exasperation was due to her leaning in towards that man and laughing with him, not because he was disappointed she hadn't become a nurse.

And her desire to be independent? She was entitled to change her mind if she met someone she liked.

"Potato?" The lady behind the canteen counter was poised to drop a spoonful of grey sludge onto his plate.

Matthew shook his head. He couldn't speak. The tightness in his chest was squeezing all the life out of him.

Be happy for her. She deserves someone she can trust not to desert her without explanation. She deserves a steady man. A man who's not caught up in his family's disasters.

That was true, but still, Matthew wished with all his being that man could be him.

He gripped his tray tightly and sat at a table far from Bethany and her friend, with his back to her. If it hadn't been for Robert, Bethany would have transferred to a hospital by now. But his brother was preventing that by not approving her transfer. She deserved so much more.

And so did he. But what did it matter? Who cared? Perhaps that was how Matthew's life was supposed to turn out. His father had wanted to decide his wife and his career. Now his brother was using him to sort out his marital problems and unfaithful wife.

Perhaps he'd just been placed on earth for other people's convenience.

Matthew put his fork down. He couldn't eat knowing Bethany was behind him with another man. Each mouthful tasted of nothing.

At the end of the war, he'd immediately leave. He'd go as far as he could from his family and from his memories. To Australia. There were opportunities there. He'd lose himself in that vast continent and do as he pleased.

As he made his way back to the medical room, he had an idea. There was one thing he could do for Bethany. Turning abruptly, he walked swiftly towards the administration block.

Robert kept Bethany's application for transfer to a nursing course in his in-tray. Matthew knew where Robert kept his stamps. Particularly the 'approval' stamp. And, although the application would also require a signature, Matthew was eligible to sign it. He'd never signed anything on Robert's behalf before, but he was entitled to. And he intended to put that right into practice now. But suppose the application form wasn't in the in-tray? There was only one way to find out.

Matthew entered Robert's office and found the form. He stamped 'Approved' across it, then after signing it, he quickly wrote an accompanying letter on headed notepaper.

Matthew went into Miss Grant's office and handed her the sheets of paper. "Please send this urgently, Miss Grant. If a reply comes, I wonder if you could let me know rather than Mr Howard?"

The secretary glanced at them, then put them in an envelope.

Matthew slipped out of the office, his heart thumping. He began to regret his actions. Suppose Robert found out? Then Bethany would pay.

The door opened behind him, and Matthew swung around to see Miss Grant holding his letter. "Urgent, you said, Dr Howard? I'm going to post it now. As you requested, when the reply comes, I shall ensure I let you know. I'm sure Mr Howard will be too busy to be concerned with this matter." She raised one eyebrow and gave him a knowing look.

"Thank you, Miss Grant. I will be most grateful."

Did she know what he was doing? Her expression suggested she did.

"I'm privy to many conversations I wouldn't repeat outside of this office, Dr Howard. That would be an inexcusable breach of confidentiality. I know a great deal about both factory business and Howard family concerns. However, I have a keen sense of fairness and sometimes, I find it hard to bite my tongue. Sometimes I long to redress the balance... Good afternoon, sir." She looked at him intently for a second and then turning, she closed the office door.

This was going to work. Miss Grant was an ally. He'd be able to do that one last thing for Bethany and set her free. In the morning, he'd make an excuse to see her and silently bid her farewell.

He was tempted to tell Bethany why he'd left her at Priory Hall and to explain everything, but she wouldn't be safe until she was no longer employed at Elmford Factory and was far away. No, he couldn't tell her tomorrow. He had to trust Miss Grant was clever enough to help him without Robert finding out. Or that if Robert did find out, it would be too late for him to do anything about it.

Matthew wouldn't be able to change Bethany's opinion of him but at least he'd have sent her away from danger and given her a chance to make something of her life.


As soon as Bethany's shift began the following morning, Matthew sent a messenger requesting she be allowed to go to the medical office. He knew if he called for her early enough, the supervisor would arrange for someone else to do her job. On her return, she'd be given something less hazardous than working alone in that dreadful locked room assembling detonators – a job so dangerous that if something went wrong, only one person's life would be forfeit.

Bethany's life.

Of course, whatever job she was given would still carry a risk, and she would take a slight cut in wages, but he would ask Miss Grant to discreetly arrange the finance department make that up out of his own pocket.

And then, as soon as she was accepted into nursing school, she'd be free.

Free of Robert.

Free of the hazardous work.

And, he thought, with a sinking stomach, free of him.

He tapped his pen on the blotter. Where was she?

Finally, Nurse Evans came in. "Bethany Anderson to see you, doctor," she said and opened the door.

Bethany hurried in, out of breath; her face flushed. "I'm sorry doctor—" she broke off abruptly "Oh." She froze. "I'm sorry to disturb you, I thought Dr Dawkins had called me."

"It's me who called you, Bethany." The words almost died in his throat as he took in her appearance.

She'd lost so much weight, her neck appeared too thin to hold her head up. Her face was pale, tinged with yellow, and above the sharply defined cheekbones, sunken and purple-smudged eyes peered at him.

Now, fully taking in the changes that had taken place in her, he felt numb.

Had she heard the pain in his voice? Or could she read his expression? As if summoning her pride, she pulled her shoulders back and held her chin up.

"Is there a problem, Dr Howard?"

Matthew swallowed, fighting to get his emotions under control. In the most business-like voice he could manage, he said. "Not at all. I'm sorry, I didn't mean to alarm you. I just wanted to give you something." He indicated the chair next to his desk.

She sat, her knees tightly pressed together, staring at her hands lying in her lap.

"This is for you," he said, withdrawing an envelope from his folder. "It's permission for you to transfer to the London Hospital Nursing School."

She looked up at him, the suspicion in her sunken eyes replaced with excitement.

"I can go?" she whispered, as if hardly able to believe it.

"Yes, I telephoned the matron at the London Hospital yesterday and it's all sorted."

"The London?" Her jaw dropped open in surprise.

"Yes. I telephoned a few hospitals but the matron at the London can take you immediately. You can make arrangements to transfer as soon as you like. Although, if you need any other formal documentation, come to me. I'll deal with it. Please don't bother Mr Howard. And it's best not to tell anyone other than your closest friends."

"But I ought to thank Mr Howard for approving my transfer—"

"No!" Matthew's voice was sharper than he'd intended. "I'll convey your thanks to my brother, but as I said, it's best not to bother him. Best to keep this information between us."

Bethany's brows drew together. "If you say so." It was obvious she was puzzled by his words.

He could hardly explain it was because Robert would stop her going if he found out and, knowing his brother, he'd make her life difficult. There were hundreds of workers on the site; unless someone drew Robert's attention to Bethany's disappearance, he wouldn't suspect she'd gone. And then Matthew would arrange his own escape from Elmford and his family. But Matthew must not arouse her suspicions.

"Because if people realise it's that easy to transfer to nursing, then everyone will want to go. And then who'll make the bombs?" He smiled and hoped she'd accept that.

The ghost of a smile that he remembered so well flickered across her face, only to be replaced by the serious expression again. She nodded.

"Thank you, Dr Howard. That's such good news. And thank you for..." She looked down at her hands again. "For suggesting I go into nursing."

He wondered if she, too, was remembering the day they'd shared together when he'd first recommended that.

"Thank you." As Bethany got to her feet, she inhaled sharply and froze.

Matthew stood abruptly, his skin prickling. They waited silently, listening intently. A rumble of something like thunder had vibrated through his body and he knew she'd felt it too.

Not the usual grumble and grind of machinery. It had been something immense. Matthew's eyes flew to Bethany's. They were open in alarm.

The thunder roared on, then far off, whistles and screams pierced the air.

"No." Bethany gasped, her hand flying to her chest.

Matthew wanted to hold her tightly. They both knew there'd been an explosion – and not the sort that occasionally occurred in a workshop. This was huge. But Bethany was safe. Matthew must help the others who would have been caught up in what would surely be devastation.

He grabbed his medical bag and called out for Nurse Evans. Turning to Bethany, he said, "If your area is safe, go back to work." The words came automatically as he followed factory protocol. "And if the... trouble... was in your area, then go to the muster point." In an emergency, it was important no one panicked. That could lead to mass hysteria.

He'd said the right things, but what he really wanted to do was to grab Bethany's hand and to run as fast as he could with her away from the factory to keep her safe.

"I'm coming with you," Bethany said. "If I'm going to be a nurse, then I need to understand the sorts of conditions I might work under. And you may need help."

"No," Matthew said firmly, although he recognised the determination on her face and knew she wouldn't go back to work. Dr Dawkins would not be in until later and Nurse Evans hadn't responded to his call. Bethany would come whether he wanted her to or not.

It was as Bethany had feared, an explosion in the section where she should have been working that day. She recognised several of the women from her shift being hurriedly herded away from the building, white turbans and uniforms grimy and streaked with dust. Huge, terrified eyes in faces drained of colour.

Matthew ran towards them, but no one appeared to be blood-stained or wounded, and when the supervisor jabbed her finger repeatedly towards the oily smoke that billowed out of what had once been a workshop, Bethany's breath caught in her throat as Matthew ran towards it.

After her desperate dash, Bethany was gasping for air. She hadn't realised how weak she'd become during the last few weeks, and she wiped the tears away angrily. It was important to keep up with Matthew because she knew the layout of the building. She'd be able to guide him to the most likely places where someone might be found inside. That is, if she could catch him. It was strictly forbidden for her to run towards an accident. She ought to leave it to the rescue services, but she wasn't going to leave Matthew.

The walls of the gigantic, camouflaged building had been blown out as they'd been designed to do in an explosion. Exposed blackened beams at strange angles were lit by the fierce, orange flames licking upwards into the mist yet partially hidden by the dense, oily smoke. A flickering, roiling scene from hell.

It felt as if her throat was filled with bitter-tasting cotton wool. She gagged, bending double as she tried desperately to suck in air. Powerful streams of water arced through the maelstrom as men trained hoses on the flames trying to bring them under control. A high-pitched scream sliced through the roar and crackle of flames. Bethany looked up, eyes streaming as she watched Matthew dive into the smoke.

If he could do it, she could too. He'd be lost in there. He'd need her. And if something should happen to him, then she'd be by his side. She took in as much of the scorching, choking air as she could, and started to run towards where Matthew had disappeared.

Teeth-jarring. Bone-wrenching. Bethany's arm was caught in a strong grip and the force with which she'd propelled herself forward, swung her around. Another hand grabbed her other arm and jerked her away from where Matthew had disappeared.

"What do you think you're doing?" The fireman's voice was muffled by his breathing apparatus, but she heard his fury. The one who'd first grabbed her swore and pushed her away from the burning building. "Get to the canteen, you stupid woman. The whole lot's about to blow."

"Dr Howard's in there," Bethany yelled.

But whether the fireman heard her or not she didn't know. There was another explosion and machine parts rained down to her left.

"Oh Matthew," she wailed, freeing herself from the firemen's grip.

She was grabbed again. The two of them lifted her between them and carried her struggling towards the canteen.

"Dr Howard is in there! He's in there!" she shouted.

"And the two of us would be in there looking for him if it wasn't for you," the man yelled back.

Bethany stopped trying to wrench her arms away. "I'll go to the canteen. I promise," she screamed. "Please go and look for him."

They dropped her and she watched as they ran back to the grotesque remains of the building, where if it hadn't been for Matthew calling her to his office earlier, she would have been working. Where she'd undoubtedly have met her end. The building into which Matthew had disappeared.

Despite the scorching air on her skin, she felt chilled to the bone.

# Chapter Nineteen

September 1941. The London Hospital, Whitechapel, London.

"Stop staring at him."

Bethany jumped, unaware she'd been looking at the patient long enough for her fellow probationer nurse, Grace Chisholm, to notice.

"Nurse Chisholm? You have something to add? Perhaps you believe I've forgotten something?" Sister Fisher's voice was as sharp as a scalpel. Her eyes narrowed as she surveyed the nurses lined up in front of her.

"No, Sister Fisher. Sorry." Grace flushed scarlet.

Bethany, who was standing next to Grace, looked down, reluctant to draw Sister Fisher's attention. She felt for Grace who'd probably saved her from a telling off, and possibly from being tasked with the worst duties on the ward.

Grace had been in trouble with Sister Fisher before, and occasionally, Bethany had been told off and punished along with Grace, even though she'd done nothing. Bethany had gone from sharing a room in ROF Elmford with Vi Yates who knew everybody's business to sharing a room in the nurses' home with bossy Grace Chisholm who wanted to be involved in everybody's business.

But this time, thankfully, it appeared Bethany had escaped Sister Fisher's attention. As for the worst duties on the ward, Bethany and the other probationer nurses already did those. How could Sister Fisher find anything more boring or disagreeable than the tasks Bethany already performed each day?

Anyway, if Sister Fisher did somehow find something, Bethany would have performed it without complaint. One day, she would be a qualified nurse, and nothing was going to deter her.

Bethany glanced back at the patient she'd been staring at before Grace had told her not to – then quickly looked away. David Baines. A man who'd been caught inside a burning building. Smoke inhalation. Burns. Shock.

Bethany fancied her nostrils were filled with the choking, oily smoke after the explosion in the detonator area. She could almost feel the heat burning her cheeks and streaming eyes.

Blinking, she pushed the memories of that day away. She lowered her head and hoped her face hadn't betrayed the panic she'd experienced.

Since she'd become a probationer nurse at the London Hospital, she'd seen so many victims who'd been trapped in bombed buildings. Each one had a tragic story to tell of broken lives and loss. Fear and despair. At the bedside of each, Bethany offered up a silent prayer of thanks for the patient's survival – and for Matthew's.

Sister Fisher had begun her morning prayers and Bethany opened her eyes and glanced once more at the patient, David Baines. She'd assisted in cleaning his wounds and helping the nurse apply dressings after he'd been admitted. Was that what Matthew had looked like after the firemen on the Elmford site had rescued him and the woman he'd been lying over, protecting? And what did Matthew look like now? Mr Baines was in so much pain, he'd been given morphine.

If only she knew how Matthew was.

On that dreadful morning, she'd stumbled to the canteen, eyes stinging and streaming tears. Lungs full of smoke and her skin tight as if she'd been in the sun too long. She'd been taken to the medical room. By the time she'd been released, Matthew and the woman he'd rescued had been transferred to the local hospital – an indication of the seriousness of their condition. But at least they'd survived. Three women who'd been working in that building had died.

As usual, when there'd been an accident in the factory, workers in that department were sent to the canteen while clear-up operations took place and then, as soon as the area was fit for work, the workers resumed their jobs. No one asked what had happened. No information would have been given if they had. The workers simply got on with their individual tasks. It was better not to know what had happened because it would have brought home the dangers. And what point was there in dwelling on those? The bombs and bullets had to be made. It was better not to think about what had happened and to get on with the job.

The women who'd worked in Bethany's department were temporarily housed in another building, which was modified for their dangerous work while rebuilding was carried out on the burned-out shell of their original building. No mention was made of the explosion nor of the reopening of the building. It was as if life hadn't been disrupted at all.

Vi, however, had heard from her friend, Doris, who was cousin to Mr Howard's mistress about the three women who'd died and about Matthew and the woman he'd saved. Bethany still received letters from Vi regularly. She said that fortunately, a safety screen had been blown by the explosion in such a way it had shielded both Matthew and the woman, giving the firemen enough time to rescue them. Both had survived, although they'd suffered with smoke inhalation, burns and shock. Matthew had also been concussed.

Bethany remembered how he'd fussed over her when her father had pushed her over in case she'd been concussed. How in control he'd been. Now it was he who was the patient.

Vi told her Matthew hadn't returned to Elmford Factory – he'd been replaced permanently by Dr Dawkins. However, Vi hadn't mentioned where Matthew had gone.

Not that Bethany had asked her to find out. It was none of her business. She hadn't mentioned Matthew to any of her new nursing friends. Not even when she'd woken in the night after a particularly vivid nightmare that had been filled with oily, chemical-laden smoke and flames. She particularly hadn't told Grace, or she'd have received her roommate's unwelcome advice on how to deal with it. Grace had opinions on everything.

"Amen," Sister Fisher said crisply, informing the Almighty that morning prayers had concluded and a new day on the ward had begun. She reported on each patient, then announced breakfast should be served.

The registered and probationer nurses all knew their jobs for the day, and they hurried to serve breakfast and assist those who needed help to feed themselves. After tidying away, the morning tasks began.

Bed pans and sputum trays given out, collected and cleaned. Beds stripped, sheets changed and geometric corners folded. Patients washed, given their medication and dressings changed... As soon as Bethany finished one job, another was started. Often, as soon as she'd finished one task, Sister Fisher told her it wasn't done to her satisfaction and to do it again. Finally, at 8pm that evening, Bethany's shift was over.

"I'm going to Mary's room to get my ticket for the concert tomorrow. I'll be back in about twenty minutes," Grace said as she and Bethany left the ward for the evening. "Are you certain you don't want to come with us? I'm sure there are still some seats available."

"No, thanks. I've got some studying I need to do." While that was true, Bethany didn't like the sort of music Grace and Mary enjoyed. It was serious, mournful music that left Bethany feeling gloomy. There was too much misery around her each day to want to actively promote depressing thoughts.

"You study too much." Grace wagged a finger at Bethany. "Everyone needs to rest from time to time. Haven't you heard the saying, 'All work and no play makes Jack a dull boy'? It's true. You really need to take a break. Study tonight and then take the evening off tomorrow. A concert is just the thing."

Bethany smiled politely and shook her head. She was too tired to say more. And definitely too tired to argue. The smell of the cleaning fluid she'd been using earlier to clean the enamel trays stung her nostrils and as she wiped the moisture from her eyes, her vision swam.

A cup of tea and an early night sounded like a dream. She didn't want to study, although she thought she might write up some of the notes she'd taken at the last lecture she'd attended while she drank her tea. Her mind was numb.

The following day, she'd be off duty, but she'd still have to get up early to attend a lecture. Her next set of exams wouldn't be for months, but Bethany was determined not to fall behind. She'd do whatever it took.

Wiping the tears from eyes again with her handkerchief, she winced. Each step was like a red-hot hammer blow to the soles of her feet, and she couldn't wait to get her shoes off. Perhaps she'd soak them in a bowl of cool water while she wrote up the notes from her last lecture. Yes, that was a good idea because by the end of tomorrow, she'd have twice as many notes to write up.

At the bottom of the staircase, she turned into the main hospital corridor making her way towards the entrance. Once there, she'd turn left and go out of the building into the garden at the back. It was a short walk across the garden to the nurse's home and finally, her room.

As a shadow fell across her, she looked up. She'd strayed into someone's path in the corridor. With a muttered, 'I beg your pardon,' she stepped to one side, hoping it wasn't a strict sister, or even worse, a busy consultant.

"Bethany?" It was a man's voice. A voice so familiar. One that haunted her dreams – so tantalisingly close, yet always so far away.

Her heart stopped. Indeed, the world stopped. The drone of the conversation in the corridor and the echo of footsteps, the rattle of the trolley two porters were pushing ahead of her, far off, the hushed tones of someone sobbing – all abruptly ceased.

Bethany looked up. "Matthew?" The sound was low and strangled, as if someone else had spoken his name.

He reached out to touch her arm, then immediately thought better of it, tucking his hands beneath the armpits of his white coat.

How she wished he had touched her. Just for an instant. To reconnect. But of course, there would never be a connection between them.

No, on reflection, he'd been wise. It was better they merely acknowledge each other with a polite nod and move on. She began to step to one side to allow him to pass.

Matthew didn't move. "I wondered how long it would be before I ran into you, Bethany."

Of course, he knew she worked in the hospital. It had been he who'd managed to get her into the nursing college, but his comment implied he hadn't tried to track her down. His white coat told her he worked there too. Why would he have looked for her? He'd have been too busy.

To have searched for her would have suggested he wanted to see her rather than relying on chance to randomly throw them together in a ward or corridor.

She'd noted his words – 'I wondered how long it would be before I ran into you, Bethany.' He had merely 'wondered'. Not 'hoped'.

He'd simply occasionally reflected on the possibility of seeing her again.

Or perhaps it had only occurred to him once.

"I had no idea you worked here now." The words tripped over themselves in Bethany's haste to say something. She wanted to groan. Why hadn't she thought of something sensible to say? How could she possibly have known he was working there?

"I only arrived last night." He smiled as if pleased with himself. "I found out first thing this morning you're currently working on the men's surgical ward."

"You did?" He had looked for her?

Don't read anything into his apparent interest. It's not you he's bothered about.

No, of course it wasn't. Perhaps his brother had asked him to follow up on her progress, although why he should do that, Bethany couldn't imagine. She'd assumed the instant she'd handed in her pass at the security check point and taken one step outside the factory, she'd have been forgotten. And anyway, hadn't Matthew warned her not to thank his brother for approving her transfer? He'd been quite insistent. It was unlikely Mr Howard had given her a second's thought.

"Of course; I wanted to find out where you were, Bethany. I still... that is, I wondered how you were enjoying your new job. Do you have time for a cup of tea in the canteen? If you're not busy, that is..."

Had Matthew been interested in finding her for old time's sake?

Hardly. It wasn't as though they'd spent much time together. A few days, that was all.

Was it because, as yet, he didn't know anyone else in the hospital and he appreciated a friendly face?

Yes, much more likely. Not flattering to her. But the most believable explanation.

Busy? No, not busy. But so tired. And yet, the warmth that was growing inside as he looked at her eagerly, waiting for her answer, had calmed the ache in her feet and the stinging of her eyes and nose.

"Bethany? Are you too busy?" He ran his hand through his fringe and left it there for a second as he raised his eyebrows.

She jumped. "No, oh no. Not too busy. Tea would be lovely."

Yes, she would go. This would be the last time he'd take any notice of her. Soon, he'd make friends with other doctors – probably other nurses too – and he would barely acknowledge her across a ward or if they passed in a corridor.

She gasped involuntarily as she realised he was probably a father by now. But it would be interesting to find out what happened to him after the explosion.

Interesting. Yes.

Only 'interesting' because he was nothing to her. And she was nothing to him.

He held out his arm to her as he'd done on the day in Southend-on-Sea.

"Are you sure?" she whispered. "I'm just a probationer nurse."

He smiled at her and left his arm there waiting for hers, igniting the warmth inside her to full heat. "You're more than that to me," he said.


Matthew found a table in the corner of the canteen and fetched two cups of tea. "So, tell me what happened to you after you left Elmford." He leaned forward, his eyes on her face as if he was unaware of the conversations, the chink of crockery and the bustle around them.

She kept her account brief, simply outlining the major events. It was hard to believe he was interested in her and she had to keep reminding herself not to detain him too long. Not to bore him. And yet, once she'd brought him up to date, he had so many questions.

Did she like the ward she was working on? What was the sister in charge like? Was Bethany happy in the nursing home? Did she get on with her roommate?

"And you," she cut in finally, "what happened to you?" She couldn't let him go without finding out how he was.

He looked down and tapped his forefinger against his lower lip as a shadow appeared to pass over him.

"I'm sorry," she said aghast. "I shouldn't have asked." Were the memories too painful?

"It's perfectly fine. I've quizzed you, so it's only fair…" He looked up at the ceiling as if remembering. "The truth is, I don't remember much about my time in hospital. Morphine. Lots of sleep. Mind-numbing routine. You know what hospitals are like." He smiled at her, and her stomach sank at the thought of him in bed, like the patient she'd stared at earlier.

"Then, when I got better, I stayed in a hotel just outside Edinburgh for a few weeks, convalescing. I couldn't go back to my room in the factory accommodation because it had been taken by a new doctor. And the thought of going to my parents' house or staying with my brother… well, let's say those options didn't appeal. Family problems." He turned both hands palm upward and shook his head.

"I'm sorry to hear that." It was none of her business, but she wondered if he was referring to his baby.

It must surely have been born by now.

He carried on, "As soon as I was well, I transferred here. I'd already been replaced at Elmford, so I wasn't missed. Here I can do something positive for people. Really make a difference to my patients. Not just try to heal the symptoms caused by those dreadful chemicals so people could be exposed to them again."

Bethany replaced her empty cup in the saucer and started to rise. He'd told her what had happened to him. He'd be keen to leave her now.

"Do you have to go yet, Bethany?" He appeared to be genuinely disappointed.

"Well... no. I just thought you would have something better to do."

"No." He reached out towards her hand and then stopped, curling his fingers and pulling his hand back.

"Actually, Bethany, I had another reason for wanting to talk to you. I'd like to explain about that night I left Priory Hall."

"Please don't." She didn't want to know. His decision had obviously been prompted by his brother. Bethany had mused about the telephone conversation so many times during the last few months. Perhaps Mr Howard had reminded Matthew of his family commitments and obligations. Or perhaps he'd warned Matthew that Bethany had been under surveillance by the security services because of her unwitting involvement with Zimmerman. Maybe he'd just found out Matthew had been having an affair with his wife.

Well, it was none of her concern, but at the thought of Matthew with another woman, an icy band tightened around her chest.

"You deserve to know why I left so abruptly, Bethany."

"You owe me nothing, Matthew. I knew there could be nothing between us. It was a wonderful dream for a very special few days, but I didn't expect anything would carry on after that."

"Well, I did." A spark of anger flashed in Matthew's eyes. "I intended to take things forward as we'd planned."

"I don't understand," Bethany said, "you left without a word."

"Please." The word sounded more like a groan. "I realise what it must've looked like, especially in the light of... of certain revelations later. But I can explain."

Bethany sighed. What sort of explanation could there be? Would he lie to her? Please no. She couldn't bear that.

"When you say 'revelations', I assume you're referring to the baby you fathered with Mrs Howard?" She might as well let him know what she knew and get his explanation over quickly. Suddenly, the weightlessness she'd experienced since she'd bumped into him drained away. Her feet throbbed, her hands stung and tears pricked her eyes.

But rather than flushing with surprise, again, she saw that flash of anger in his eyes.

"I'd hoped you hadn't heard about that, but assumed you probably had. However, now you're safe here, I can tell you if you'll listen."

"Safe?" That was a strange choice of word and even stranger he'd place particular emphasis upon it.

"Yes, Bethany, safe. Not only from the effects of those dreadful toxic chemicals, but even more importantly, your reputation is safe from my brother."

"My reputation? But I was cleared of any involvement with that spy. The case was investigated. My suspension was lifted. Why would he have wanted to bring it all up again?"

"I'm not talking about that, Bethany."

"Dr Howard." A tall, white-haired man stopped by their table and shook hands with Matthew, turning his back on Bethany. "I'm so pleased to have you in the department. You're a welcome addition, let me tell you. We've recently lost two doctors to the Army. But your credentials are most impressive. Have you got time for a chat in my office now?"

Bethany stood and slipped out from behind the table. Matthew wouldn't want her around now he'd been invited to talk to a consultant.

"I'll come to your office directly, Mr Patterson," Matthew said as the consultant turned to go. "I'll be five minutes."

Matthew caught up with Bethany. "Please, can we meet somewhere quiet? There's so much I need to explain. When do you next have a day off?

"Sunday. But I planned to go to my father's cottage."

"Perhaps I could arrange to stay at Priory Hall. Ben and Joanna know the truth now. I can meet you at the cottage. Forgive me Bethany, I should've asked about your father."

Tears came to Bethany's eyes. "He's being looked after well, but he's aged in the last few months. Before he went into hospital, the anger masked the sadness, but now he's just a broken man. I've visited him a few times since I've been here and we're rebuilding our relationship." She squeezed her eyes tightly shut. So many men were still suffering from the last war. How many would there be in a similar state when this war was finally over?

"If you'll be in Laindon at the weekend and you care to visit me at my cottage on Sunday, then we can talk."

"I'll be there," Matthew said firmly.

She turned and hurried away, not wanting to hold him up. It was best not to keep consultants waiting. But when she looked back, Matthew was still there. He waved and mouthed 'Sunday' to her.

# Chapter Twenty

As soon as Matthew had finished talking to Mr Patterson, he rushed to the public telephone and called Priory Hall. He spoke to Joanna, who said she and Ben would be delighted to see Matthew and he was welcome to stay with them for as long as he wanted.

Joanna told him she'd been to the Anderson's cottage on several occasions with Bethany and had helped tidy up. Ben had arranged for someone to mend the roof and Joanna and the children had started to clear the tangle of brambles and weeds from the garden.

At least now, Bethany had a home. It didn't belong to her; it was still her father's, and if anything happened to him, it would belong to her brother. But at least while Bethany's father was in hospital and her brother at sea, the cottage was hers.

Matthew thanked Joanna and arranged to arrive late on Saturday evening. He hadn't specified a time to go to Bethany's cottage on Sunday, but he intended to be there early. There was a lot to explain, and he wanted to spend as much time with her as she'd allow.

He thanked Joanna once again and replaced the receiver, then slowly walked down the hospital corridor. This building felt like home. The tang of antiseptic and the echo of shoes on the floors were so familiar after having spent years training there as a medical student. It was so good to be back.

He wondered how Bethany felt about the place. She hadn't been there long enough to have formed an attachment, so presumably it still felt strange and new.

He hoped she'd come to love it like him. That day he'd telephoned all the nursing schools in London to find her a place, he'd wanted the best hospital for her. There was no point trying to set someone free, only to deliver them somewhere they'd be unhappy. The London Hospital was a prestigious place to work and had an excellent nursing school. Hopefully that was enough to make it the right place for Bethany.

It had also been the most convenient, being the largest hospital in the east of London, which meant it was closest to her home. He'd been desperate to think of everything to make her life easier and thankfully, they'd had a place available for her.

Matthew turned out of the grand entrance and ran lightly down the stone steps to Whitechapel Road. Relief buoyed him up as if he'd been lifted on a cushion of air.

He'd broken away from his family. Now, he was free to live his own life; he'd spent time with Bethany and seen she was well, although understandably, things were strained between them. But on Sunday, he'd have a chance to explain everything to her. There would be closure of the past. If he had his way, that would be an opening to a future with Bethany, but he'd understand if she didn't share his dream.

No, that wasn't true. He wouldn't understand at all. It would be a bitter blow, but at least she now stood a chance of being happy. Perhaps she was still seeing Peter Chorley. Matthew had found out who he was after he'd seen them together at the ENSA concert. Alarmingly, he'd discovered from the records that Chorley was married, and

Matthew had toyed with the idea of telling Bethany. But he could imagine the look on her face when he told her. He knew he shouldn't interfere.

Anyway, if not Chorley, Bethany might have met anyone since she'd come to London. Or perhaps she'd finally decided she didn't need anyone at all. She had a job, prospects and a cottage. Why would she need a man?

Matthew crossed over Whitechapel Road. His room was in one of the turnings off the main road. A scruffy, old property that remained unscathed at the end of the street that was still standing after what the press had dubbed the 'London Blitz'.

Bombs still dropped on the East End, but there had been no repeat of the intensity of the campaign the Luftwaffe had waged at the end of 1940 and the beginning of this year.

At the far end of the street, houses were boarded up and others had simply been reduced to piles of rubble.

"Is that you, Dr Howard?" Matthew's landlady called out from her room further along the hall. She always kept her door half-open so she knew who was entering and leaving her house.

"Good evening, Mrs Irving."

"A bit later than you told me this morning, doctor. Your tea's ready but if you plan to be late in future, I'd appreciate knowing in advance."

"My apologies, Mrs Irving. I ran into an old friend. It was quite unexpected."

Matthew grinned to himself. Unexpected? Not at all. He'd intended to loiter in the corridor outside her ward at the end of her shift, but he'd been held up by an emergency. In a panic, he'd walked back and forth along the main downstairs corridor, guessing she'd have to walk along that whether she was going to the front or the back of the main hospital building. And luck had been with him.

If it hadn't, the following day, he'd have found some excuse to visit her ward. No easy task because he now worked in the gynaecological department and the sister in charge of men's surgical would surely challenge him if he wandered onto her ward.

"I'll make a fresh cup of tea," Mrs Irving called from her room. "You'll be down immediately, will you?"

Matthew assured her he would and hurried upstairs to take off his coat and hat. His landlady didn't approve of tardiness, as she'd told him on several occasions, and he didn't want to upset her. His room was clean, and she was as generous as rationing would allow with her portions of food. In fact, she appeared to favour him above her other two lodgers. That was probably because Matthew had been recommended by Miss Grant, Robert's former secretary.

She'd retired a few weeks before, but while she'd been at Elmford, she'd kept in touch with Matthew. Apparently, Robert had underestimated his quiet, diligent secretary. He'd treated the uncomplaining and efficient, Miss Grant as if she'd been part of the furniture, forgetting she could overhear many of his conversations. And failing to see how resentful she was of his bad temper and rudeness.

She'd written to Matthew when he'd been recuperating in Scotland and informed him that Robert had never discovered Matthew had signed the forms to release Bethany. That was a great relief. Matthew had tried not to worry that his brother might still carry out his threat of tipping off his friends in MI5 that Bethany had known Zimmerman. But although Robert was spiteful, he'd got his way with Matthew and the child. There'd been no reason to cause Bethany more pain. Or so Matthew had hoped.

Miss Grant had explained to Matthew that when Robert had finally noticed Bethany's transfer application form had disappeared from his in-tray and had demanded to know where it was, she'd told him she'd disposed of it because Bethany had been wounded in that dreadful explosion and would no longer require a transfer.

"I may have implied Miss Anderson was one of the unfortunate women who passed away in that dreadful explosion," she'd written. "As you know, one worker is as good as another in Mr Howard's eyes. He didn't pursue the matter and he's never asked about Miss Anderson since."

The day Matthew had received the letter with that news had been a turning point in his recovery. God bless Miss Grant. Finally, he felt Bethany was safe.

It had been Miss Grant who'd written to tell him Julia had given birth to a boy. She made it clear from her wording she knew Matthew wasn't the father, and since she'd been present during many telephone conversations and arguments between Robert and Julia, Miss Grant was almost certainly aware of the situation.

She'd also included details of jobs in various hospitals for which she knew Matthew was qualified to apply, and those had jolted him out of the depression into which he'd slipped. Miss Grant was the only person who'd offered him any encouragement to follow his dream, and she'd demonstrated she believed he was capable.

As he'd laid the details of the various jobs on the table and considered each one, his skin had tingled with hope. Could he do this? Yes, of course he could. When had all his self-confidence drained away? Why hadn't he noticed?

It was as though he'd been dormant since the explosion. Miss Grant's kindness had allowed a butterfly to break out of the chrysalis.

Matthew washed his hands and, after drying them, went downstairs. Mrs Irving was waiting for him and looked up, the teapot poised over his cup.

"Lamb chops tonight, Dr Howard. I had to queue for ages at the butcher's, but I think you'll find they're worth it."

Matthew sat down opposite her at the table and thanked her.

Mrs Irving was a few years younger than her sister, Miss Grant, but although they had sharp, unforgiving features, they both had similar kind, grey eyes. What a shame for Robert he hadn't recognised the worth of his secretary.

But then his brother had always prized beauty above all things – and look where that had got him. A tempestuous marriage, a resentful mistress and a son who wasn't his.

"Excellent lamb chops, thank you, Mrs Irving," Matthew said and noted with pleasure how the landlady's grey eyes lit up.

He'd seen that look of gratitude on several women's faces since he'd been back at the London Hospital. Haunted expressions of worry had melted to relief as he'd taken time with his patients. So far, he'd been able to suggest treatment for all the women he'd seen and to offer birth control advice to women who'd already had one child – or sometimes more – each year since they'd been married.

It wouldn't always be like that, but at least he was finally making a difference to many despairing women with symptoms they didn't understand and therefore feared.

"I've got tapioca for afters," Mrs Irving said as she cleared his plate away. "My goodness, you look like the cat who's got the cream. Did you have a good day at work?"

"Oh, yes, thank you, Mrs Irving. I had an excellent day."

After Matthew finished work on Saturday evening, he hurried out of the hospital to Whitechapel station, his case clutched to his chest.

Please, don't let there be an air raid.

Nothing must stop him from getting to Laindon for the morning. If necessary, he was prepared to walk all through the night to be there to see Bethany.

He galloped down the station stairs towards the platform for the eastbound train. Excitement bubbling up inside him at the thought of seeing Bethany the next day.

If only he'd known earlier that Miss Grant had fooled Robert into believing Bethany had died in the explosion, he'd have felt much happier. While Matthew had been convalescing in Scotland, he'd written several letters to Bethany, which he'd never posted. He was worried he might lead Robert to her. Not that his brother needed a hold over her once the baby had been born. Their parents had welcomed the boy into the family and Robert had been keen to promote the idea he was the proud father. The further Matthew faded into the background, the better for Robert.

What had worried Matthew was if Robert ever discovered he'd tricked him. Would he have taken it out on Bethany? Who knew what his brother was capable of? Robert needed to feel he was the winner in everything, regardless of who he hurt. And he had influential friends. It would have been easy to have Bethany thrown out of nursing school and to ensure no other hospital would ever take her.

But Miss Grant had taken her time revealing her cleverness. Perhaps she'd wanted to make sure where Matthew's loyalties lay. But once he'd expressed his gratitude at protecting Bethany, Miss Grant had also revealed she had sensitive material in her possession about Robert. She'd made it clear she didn't intend to use it for her own ends, but should Matthew ever need it for any reason, she'd said she'd be glad to step forward to help. Exactly what evidence she had, Matthew didn't ask, but he trusted that if Robert ever tried to blackmail him again, the secretary would be able to provide enough material to persuade his brother to think twice.

Now he and Bethany were free. And thanks to Miss Grant, for the first time ever, Matthew had the winning card. He wouldn't play it unless necessary, but it meant he and Bethany were safe.

"Bethany and me," he whispered to himself as he ran for the train. Once safely inside, he repeated it over and over in his head in time with the rhythm of the carriage. If only saying their names together was enough to really bring them together.

# Chapter Twenty-One

Early on Saturday morning, Bethany let herself into her father's cottage. She breathed in deeply, testing the air for that fusty smell of decay that had lingered for so long. Beeswax and lavender now hung in the air, and with a satisfied nod, she allowed herself to believe she'd finally banished the last traces of unpleasant odour.

It had taken many hours with the windows wide open for the smells to disappear. While the cleaning breeze blew through, Bethany had scrubbed, cleaned and polished every surface and piece of furniture. She'd used vinegar and baking soda along with her precious ration of soap until everything was as clean as it could possibly be. Joanna had helped and had brought Bethany soap flakes when she could spare them.

How lucky Bethany was to have someone in her life like Joanna. Once an employer and now – not exactly a friend – perhaps more of an aunt-figure. Bethany would never consider herself equal to Joanna, even though she'd made it clear she would be happy for Bethany to do so. Joanna had once been in Bethany's shoes – well, not exactly in her shoes – but close enough to understand how Bethany felt. Still, it didn't matter how their relationship was described – former employer, aunt, friend – it was precious to Bethany.

She closed the door behind her and went into the kitchen to put the kettle on the stove. First, a cup of tea, then an inspection of the cottage. It must be as tidy as it could possibly be for when Matthew arrived the following day.

The last time he'd seen the cottage, it had been a disgrace and although she knew Matthew understood the squalor had been nothing to do with her, now she wanted to show him that wasn't how she'd been brought up. She owed her mother that.

It was going to be interesting to hear his explanation for leaving her without a word that night. Half of her clung to the hope his reasons would be believable. That they'd been genuine and unavoidable. And then, once he'd explained and she'd seen why he'd had no choice, he'd declare his love for her again.

The other half – and if there could be such a thing, the bigger half – thought the explanation would be unsatisfying and fanciful. If there had been good reasons for him to leave her, he should have at least explained what they'd been. She suspected Matthew's brother had reminded him of his family obligations and he'd been embarrassed to tell Bethany she was too low born for him.

What did he want now? To salve his conscience? Did he simply want closure from the past and a blessing from her? If that was what he wanted, then she'd give it to him. What did it matter to her?

She'd always known she'd end up on her own. It wasn't as though she wanted or needed anyone. People only brought pain. And anyway, she had enough people in her life at work – her patients.

True, as a probationer nurse, they weren't exactly her patients. She only did the most basic, dirty and repetitive work, not the real nursing.

And yet on the ward, she was touched by each one of those men. As she tidied their lockers and plumped up their pillows, many of the patients wanted to talk about their families or their lives. Their hopes for returning to normality. She could hardly miss the wretched figures of wives, sweethearts and mothers who kept vigil by beds waiting for their loved ones to wake up – to recover, so they could resume their lives together. Sister Fisher had already reprimanded Bethany for becoming 'too close to the patients'.

"You must treat each patient with as much care as if they were members of your family," Sister Fisher had told her. "But do not let them become family." She'd narrowed her eyes, fixing Bethany with her you-will-do-exactly-as-I-say stare. "Ignore my words at your peril."

Bethany had seen the sense in what the sister had said, but it was impossible to disengage from the trauma that unfolded around her each day, especially after there had been a bombing raid. She was relieved and happy as soon as somebody was well enough to be discharged, but depending on how long they'd been in the ward, it was still a wrench to see them go.

No, there was enough emotional turmoil in Bethany's life. There was no room for anything or anyone who might bring more.

A knock at the door brought her out of her reverie. It was still early. She hurried to open it. Joanna and the children were coming over but not until the afternoon.

Matthew?

Don't be so ridiculous.

He'd told her he'd be there on Sunday. Could it be the postman? It was many years since the postman had brought anything other than Bethany's letters to her father. Perhaps Stevie had written.

She opened the door to find Pauline standing on the doorstep holding a box of miscellaneous items.

"I don't suppose yer father's back?" Pauline lifted her chin as if to look confident, but Bethany noticed she didn't meet her gaze.

"No, I'm sorry. My father's still in hospital."

"Yes. Right. I thought so." Pauline cleared her throat noisily and looked at the contents of the box. "Well, p'raps yer'll send him my regards. At least he won't be lonely now. It's all right for him." She sniffed, then added, "and let him know I returned these." She thrust the box at Bethany.

Bethany took the grimy container. "Thank you, I will."

But Pauline hadn't finished. "And yer owe me five quid."

Ah, so that was it. Pauline was trying to get money out of her. Bethany kept her temper. That foul smell of wet dog she'd spent so long getting rid of was wafting out of the box and she longed to close the door on Pauline and take the items into the garden. There wouldn't be anything of value in the box. Returning the things had probably been an excuse for Pauline to ask for money. Bethany peered around the thin woman in the stained dress and threadbare coat for the huge wolf-like dog. Thankfully, Pauline must have left him at home.

"And why would I owe you five pounds?" Bethany asked politely. She would not be fooled into giving this woman money.

"Because yer dad borrowed it. And if he ain't coming back I want it afore I leave Plotlands."

"Leave?"

"That's what I said. I'm going down to Cornwall to live with my daughter."

When Pauline had first asked, Bethany assumed she simply wanted money to buy drink, and she'd been prepared to give her the bread and ham Mrs Stewart had packed for her lunch instead. But money? No, definitely not.

However, if her father had borrowed the money, then she certainly owed it to Pauline. Bethany hesitated.

"Didn't think yer'd believe me," Pauline said, her mouth set in a hard line. "I've not always been a drunk, I'll have you know. But sometimes life's too painful when you look at it up close. Sometimes yer need something to blunt it. S'pose yer think I'm going to drink the money away..."

Bethany didn't reply.

"Yeah, thought so. Yer dad always said you was the clever one."

Bethany inhaled sharply. "Pa said that?" She examined Pauline's weasel face for deceit but surprisingly, she didn't see any.

Instead, Pauline's brow furrowed in a pained expression, as if it was unthinkable anyone might doubt her words. "That's what I said. You was always his 'little girl'." Pauline's impersonation of her father's voice sounded ridiculous. Why was she saying such things?

Pauline continued, "Yer dad was proud of his children. He talked a lot about Billy and you."

"Stevie," Bethany corrected.

"Yeah, him as well. But he didn't talk about them much. It was always you he talked about. 'Wise beyond her years... The apple of my eye', he said. I put him straight. I told him you was nothing but a selfish baggage leaving him alone like that. Going off, getting yerself a fancy job, earning a fortune and leaving yer poor, lonely dad behind to fend for hisself. Wise? My godfathers! I told him yer was nothing but a conniving piece o' work. But he wouldn't listen. When he was sober, he always spoke up for you."

Bethany stared at her. Could that be true? How could she trust this woman? She wanted to. It wasn't as though Pauline was pretending to like Bethany. She'd made it plain she'd tried to persuade Pa his daughter was worthless. It would have been so easy to tell Bethany her father had thought so too.

"Look," Pauline said, "I can see you don't believe me. Yer dad said yer'd understand when yer found the package. I never found it. An' I looked everywhere after he'd gone. I got the jewellery box but it were empty." She nodded at the grimy container Bethany was holding.

Buried beneath a chipped cup, Bethany saw the corner of her mother's jewellery box.

"Package? What sort of package?" Bethany's mouth had gone dry.

"Dunno. A package. Something yer pa had hocked. I never saw it, although I looked. But it cost him five quid to get it back. And I ain't leaving till yer pay up." Pauline looked over her shoulder and for a second, Bethany wondered if she was going to summon the dog.

Pauline smiled, showing a darkened front tooth. "Oh, yer think I'm going to threaten yer, do yer? Vic died two weeks ago…" She took in a deep breath as if fighting back tears. "I just keep forgetting he's gone. But I'll stand here all day on yer doorstep if that's what it takes. I might even get the constable…"

"No need," Bethany said. There was something believable about Pauline's story. "I'll get your money but in return, I want your door key."

Pauline smirked. "Deal."

Bethany closed the door while she got the money. She didn't trust the woman and as soon as she could, she'd change the lock. Thankfully, she'd brought more money than she usually carried because she had to repay Ben for arranging the roof repairs.

She'd have to explain to Joanna she wouldn't have the full amount but Bethany knew she'd understand. Taking five one-pound notes from her purse, she went back to the door. Pauline was still there. She licked her lips as Bethany passed over the money, and as she tucked the notes in her pocket, she turned on her heel.

"Pauline!" Bethany called sharply. "I think we agreed you'd give me back my key." She held out her hand.

With a wry grin, Pauline fished in her pocket and dropped the key onto Bethany's palm. "Yer dad was right. You are the one with brains."

Bethany watched the woman go. She didn't glance back. A poor, sad woman who'd relied on her disturbed father and a wolf-like dog for company. Hopefully, she'd find happiness in Cornwall with her daughter.

Thoughts swirled in Bethany's brain. Pauline had said her father had been lonely. But Bethany had been there in the cottage with him, and he'd turned her out. He'd appeared to favour Pauline's company over his daughter's. Was it the companionship of a woman – any woman – he'd craved after her mother had died? Bethany wouldn't have been able to provide that. And what about the mysterious package? Had Pauline lied to get money out of Bethany? She doubted Pa had borrowed as much money as five pounds, but at least she wouldn't see Pauline again and there'd be no opportunity for her to ask for more.

So, if the package existed, where would it be? Bethany had cleaned every part of the cottage. Had her father hidden it beneath the floorboards in his bedroom, as she'd once hidden her savings under hers?

She hurried into his bedroom and raised the rug, checking the floorboards. Everything appeared to be sound. But he was a joiner. Had he made a hiding place so skilfully it wasn't immediately obvious? If there was a package, why would he have concealed it so cleverly she'd never find it? What would be the point of that?

She gasped. Had he hidden it in her hiding place, so she would find it? She ran into her bedroom and pulled back the rug to reveal the floorboards. Her heart beat painfully in her chest. Suppose it wasn't there? She couldn't think of anywhere else he might have concealed it, which would mean Pauline had made the whole thing up. She bit down on her lower lip. If there was any justice in the world, she'd find it, and then past hurts would be wiped away in an instant. The entire perspective of her relationship with her father would change.

But this is real life, not a fairy tale…

And if the space beneath the floorboards was empty, then she'd know Pauline had tricked her out of money and her father had been incapable of showing his love for her.

Bethany's breath came in short gasps. Until she looked under the floorboards and knew for certain, she could believe her father loved her despite his problems. Once she'd looked, she'd know the truth.

Her heart thudded faster as she knelt, staring at the floor, her paper knife poised. Squeezing her eyes tightly shut, she slipped the blade into the gap between the boards and twisted it. The plank lifted with a puff of dust and Bethany's hand flew to her mouth. There beneath her floor was her mother's scarf, wrapped around something small and tied with a ribbon.

With a trembling hand, Bethany reached into the recess, and her fingers tightened around the silky fabric. Tears slipped down her cheeks as she pulled out the small parcel. It was heavier and bulkier than she'd imagined it would be but when she laid it on her lap and unfastened the ribbon, all the pieces of jewellery her father had pawned were there.

Surely a message from him to her. Bethany replaced the floorboard and climbed onto her bed, then cradling the jewellery in their silk wrapper, she curled up and cried into her pillow.

# Chapter Twenty-Two

Ben was waiting for Matthew at Laindon Station in the car on Saturday evening. Faye and Mark had accompanied him, and they chattered excitedly about what had happened since Matthew had been there last.

"We went to Beffany's cottage this afternoon an' I got stung with a stinging nettle," Mark said, raising his knee so Matthew could see the faint red line. "Beffany gave me a dock leaf to—"

"Shhh! Silly," Faye said, her eyes huge as she looked at her father, then back at her brother. "You weren't supposed to mention... her."

"Who?"

"Bethany. You idiot."

"But we did go to her cottage," Mark said, his brows drawn together. "Why can't I...? Oh... Sorry, Daddy. I remember now..." he mumbled with his head lowered.

Ben shook his head in mock despair. "Well, let's hope the Germans don't invade Essex or my two children will have informed them of everything they need to know before they've even asked a question."

"Oh, Daddy! You can't compare Uncle Matthew to the Germans. No one likes them but we all like Uncle Matthew. And so does Bethany—" Faye slapped a hand over her mouth.

"How about a nice quiet board game when we get home?" Ben asked. "At least that way, everyone will have to concentrate and remain silent for a while."

Matthew smiled. How thoughtful Ben and Joanna were to have warned the children not to speak about Bethany. But his heart had leapt when Faye had said, 'And so does Bethany.' Childish chatter? Probably. Faye may have been remembering the last time he'd stayed at Priory Hall with Bethany. On the other hand, perhaps Bethany had said something about him that afternoon? His breath caught in his throat at the thought.

If only he hadn't told her he'd see her on Sunday. He was desperate to see her now, but it would be rude to barge in on her a day early and it would be impolite to Ben and Joanna.

He'd simply have to be patient.

# Chapter Twenty-Three

The following morning at breakfast, Ben offered Matthew his car so he could drive to Plotlands. Matthew thanked him but declined, saying he wanted to clear his head, and the fresh air and walk would do him good.

Matthew didn't mention he wanted to avoid giving Bethany any reminders of their different backgrounds. If he turned up in a car – even though it wasn't his – it would merely be a display of the money his family had, and hers didn't. No, he'd rather meet her on equal terms, although that now was impossible. Things were no longer as they'd once been and now Bethany had the advantage over him, although she wouldn't realise that until he explained everything.

Once he'd been wealthy – a good marriage prospect. Now, he'd turned his back on his family along with any inheritance that might one day come to him. But worse than his depleted bank balance, he had a confession to make – one that he wouldn't divulge if it was clear Bethany was no longer interested in him. If he thought he stood a chance, then he must tell her.

He might break her heart again, but she deserved to know.

After ten minutes, Matthew began to wonder if he should have accepted Ben's offer of the car. His suitcase was in one hand and a picnic basket Mrs Stewart had handed him as he left, in the other. He wondered what she had packed that could weigh so much. Joanna had thoughtfully suggested she prepare a lunch for Matthew and Bethany, although he doubted Joanna knew how much food the cook had included. Not that Joanna would have complained had she known.

He'd only expected to be carrying a suitcase on his walk to Plotlands. After he'd seen Bethany, he intended to go straight to London. If he failed to win her back, he wasn't sure he could bear to return to Priory Hall for another night. He wouldn't be able to hide his disappointment, and Joanna and Ben would know his visit hadn't gone as he'd hoped. It wasn't fair to take his misery to their dining table that evening. Anyway, he'd have to leave for London early Monday morning, so he might as well go on Sunday afternoon.

What if he was successful? He didn't dare believe in the possibility. But if he was, he knew the Richardsons would welcome him back at Priory Hall for another night.

The previous evening, Joanna had confessed to Matthew that Bethany had become very dear to her – the parallels in their lives giving her a special bond with the young woman.

"I wouldn't want to see Bethany hurt," Joanna had said. She pinned Matthew in his chair with a penetrating look.

"That's the last thing I want either," he'd replied and had met her gaze with candour.

She'd nodded imperceptibly across the dinner table, and he'd known she believed him. Not only that, but she'd be on his side and would help to get the pair back together again – assuming Bethany was willing, too. If not, he had no doubt Joanna would support her.

Matthew ignored the burning in his arm muscles and increased his speed. There was still a way to go to Bethany's cottage. Earlier, he'd been worried he might get lost. But his day out with Bethany, when she'd taken him on a tour of Plotlands and told him about her childhood, was still vivid in his memory.

With the cottages being so distinct, he found he knew exactly where he was. How different from the streets around Mrs Irving's house in Whitechapel, where rows of houses all appeared identical with only different coloured doors or curtains to differentiate them. Or, of course, the bombed-out shell of a house amongst others still standing like a game of skittles.

He drew level with the cottage with the green front door. The Wilsons? No, the Wilkinsons. Yes, he remembered that house and the two goats in the back garden. And there the animals were at the far end of the plot, sniffing at the hedge.

So, the next cottage would be the one with the ivy climbing up the walls and chimney.

And the one after that…

Yes, it was Bethany's.

Matthew was slightly out of breath and his heart pounding when he arrived at the garden gate. He knew it wasn't because he'd been walking fast.

He smiled as he took in the cottage. The front garden had been weeded and was now tidy, and as he pushed the gate, it swung freely, with no squeal of reluctance. He walked up the path and stood on the doorstep. Through the closed door, he could faintly hear Bethany humming a lively tune. He closed his eyes and pleasure tingled across his skin, his nerve endings thrilling with the sound and the image the cheerful melody conjured up.

She sounded happy. He could hear the smile in her voice.

The last time he'd known her to be content had been when they'd walked together, hand in hand through the woods.

But he hadn't been with her since then. Somebody else might now make her so happy she sang when she was alone.

Wouldn't Joanna have warned him? If she'd been aware of a man in Bethany's life, she'd probably have given him a clue. But perhaps even she didn't know. Bethany had a life in London that Joanna might know nothing about.

Matthew's hand hovered over the now clean, shiny knocker. What right did he have to disrupt her life again? If she was content now, then perhaps he ought to walk away and leave her.

Before he had time to consider, the front door opened. Bethany jumped at the unexpected sight of someone on her doorstep, but an instant later, after she'd recognised him, her face lit up. Then, almost immediately, a polite smile replaced her delight. It was the sort of smile you give to a visitor you weren't expecting, and really didn't want to welcome.

Had she thought he was someone else?

"I... I didn't realise you'd be here so soon," she said, and he could feel her embarrassment. "That is, I wasn't sure that..." she blushed.

"You weren't sure that?" he prompted.

Her face hardened. "I wasn't sure you'd come."

"Of course, I'd come, I said I would..." He winced. He had no right to appear offended at her words. With a sigh, he added, "Yes, I'm sorry. I can see how you might assume that, Bethany. But there were reasons I left so abruptly that evening and I wanted to explain today. I want you to know the truth."

Her face softened and she stood back to allow him in. She went out into the front garden and shook out a duster she'd been using – obviously why she'd opened the front door and caught him hesitating.

Following him in, she closed the front door.

Matthew looked about in amazement. She'd certainly worked hard in the cottage. The furniture was still shabby but now polished and clean, and the faint smell of fresh paint and lavender hung in the air. Nothing remained from the last time he'd been there.

Matthew complimented Bethany on her hard work.

"Of course, I'll replace some of the furniture when it's possible, but until then this will have to do," she said, her voice defensive.

"It's beautiful, Bethany."

She swung around to face him, her eyes narrowed, searching his face for sincerity.

"Beautiful? Surely you're used to nicer rooms than this?" she said tartly.

"Do you know Fulward Street?"

Bethany frowned as she considered. Then she nodded. "Do you mean the street opposite the hospital?"

"That's the one. Well, I currently live in one room in a house on Fulward Street. And I can assure you, compared to that, this room is beautiful."

"But you've known beautiful, luxurious rooms in the past, I'm sure."

"That was the past, Bethany. Luxury isn't part of my life now and isn't likely to be again for some time."

Her face registered surprise. "Would you like to sit down?" she asked politely, "I'll make tea." She turned to go into the kitchen.

"I could help... if you like," he said. "I can see you're busy here and you probably want to get on... Not that it looks like there's much left to do," he added quickly. "But if you need any help, I have the rest of the day free."

She tipped her head on one side as if considering. "Thank you." She led the way into the kitchen.

"I'll be brief," Matthew said. "I don't want to hold you up. I know you've heard the rumours – you mentioned my sister-in-law and the child when we met at work, but I want you to hear the truth. That night we should have gone to see the film, my brother phoned. He told me his wife was expecting and that the child was mine."

Matthew saw Bethany's hand tighten around the kettle's handle and she lowered her head slightly, concealing her expression.

Matthew continued. "It wasn't true. The child wasn't mine. Not that anyone would have believed it. But there are many reasons why that was an impossibility. First, and most importantly, I would never conduct an affair with a married woman, even if I'd liked her. And I can assure you, I do not like Julia. I'm sorry to say it but my sister-in-law is a hard, selfish woman. She told me when she first knew she was expecting and asked me if I could recommend someone who might help her out of her predicament. Obviously, I refused. I don't think she told Robert the child was mine in revenge, but it would probably have sweetened it."

"Oh, Matthew, I'm so sorry." The hard lines around Bethany's mouth softened.

"Unfortunately for me, Julia's story fulfilled many dreams. Several years after Robert's marriage, he came to me to ask if I could find out why Julia hadn't conceived. Since you're a nurse, I'll speak plainly because I know you'll understand. I carried out a simple test on a semen sample from Robert and discovered it was unlikely he'd ever father a child. At first, he didn't believe me, assuming it was Julia's fault, but eventually, he accepted it. I don't think he ever forgave me for being the one to give him bad news. Only a few people knew about his probable infertility, including our parents. When Julia became pregnant, it suited everyone, except me, to tell our parents the child was mine. It might not be Robert's but if it was mine, at least it was a Howard and therefore their grandchild." Matthew looked at Bethany searching for signs she believed him. But it was hard to read her expression. There was sympathy in her face. But sympathy for the sorry tale of a fellow human being, or of someone she cared about?

"And now?" she asked gently.

"And now, unbelievably, Robert is a doting father to his son. Julia got away with adultery and has taken to motherhood. My parents are thrilled at the new Howard heir. And the child? Well, time will tell. But at least he's growing up in luxury rather than in a broken home."

"And you? How are you?" She poured hot water into the teapot.

He shrugged. "Humiliated. No one, other than our parents and a few close friends, was supposed to find out the child's paternity. Sadly, Robert's mistress ensured it didn't remain a secret to shame Robert. Sadly, I was caught up in the mess. And so were you, of course."

"Me?" Bethany was so surprised; she almost dropped the teapot. "What did it have to do with me?"

"Nothing directly. Robert wanted me to keep quiet about the paternity. As soon as our parents got used to the child and accepted it, he thought he'd step in and pretend to forgive Julia. Then he'd claim the child as his own. But he had to be assured I wouldn't talk... And he did that by threatening to tell everyone you and I were having an affair and to ruin your reputation."

Bethany shakily put the teapot down. She looked at him with large, surprised eyes. "But I'm nobody to him."

"It didn't matter who you were. If he thought it necessary, he'd have used you. And I couldn't let that happen. So, that evening we were supposed to go to the cinema, I had to go to Elmford Mere and try to sort everything out."

"But how did your brother know about us? We were in Laindon.

No one in Elmford knew, unless you told them."

Matthew shook his head. "No, trust me, Robert is the last person I'd have told about us. However, as part of the inquiry after Zimmerman's escapade, you were investigated. Someone in MI5 checked you really were staying in Priory Hall while you were suspended. Unfortunately, he was one of Robert's friends and when he discovered you and I were both under the same roof, he told Robert. Wondering if he could use it to his advantage, Robert suggested the man tail us. He followed us to Southend and, for all I know, to the woods that day. It was enough for Robert to know how much I liked you. While you were at Elmford, he had me under his control."

Bethany had gone white.

"Here, sit down and I'll pour the tea. If you throw any more into the saucer, we'll have to make more." Matthew smiled at her.

A look of disbelief crossed her face. "But in the end, your brother allowed me to leave the factory. Why did he do that if he needed a hold over you?"

"Ah. Well, that may not be completely true." Matthew put the tea strainer on the other cup and began to pour tea through it. "Do you remember Miss Grant, Robert's secretary?"

Bethany nodded. "The quiet, stern-looking lady in the office next to your brother's?"

"Yes, exactly. For reasons of her own, she had a grudge against Robert. If it had been up to him, your application would be sitting in his in-tray even now. I signed the forms and Miss Grant arranged to have them sent without Robert's knowledge. Then I phoned Matron at the London Hospital, and she agreed to enrol you. I hoped once you'd gone, you'd be free. Unfortunately, the morning I told you, I got caught up in the explosion. But when you left, it was without Robert realising. And definitely without his permission."

"I wish I'd known." Bethany shook her head in disbelief. She stared at the teacup Matthew had pushed towards her.

"I wish you'd known too," Matthew said. "But after I was hospitalised, everything was rather hazy for some time. Even when I knew you were safe and I was well enough, I didn't dare contact you."

"But why? Surely your brother couldn't have done anything to us."

"I couldn't take the chance. Robert wouldn't have thought twice about accusing you of having an affair and ruining your reputation. But worse than that, he had the power to have you dismissed from nursing school – even to spread a rumour to one of his MI5 friends about Zimmerman. You could have been taken in for questioning. Possibly imprisoned. I don't know if he'd have stooped that low, but I wouldn't have put it past him. Robert always has to have what he wants."

"And now?" Bethany asked, horror registering in her eyes. "What's to stop him doing all those things to me now?"

Matthew grinned and shook his head. "It turns out that the quiet, stern-looking lady wasn't as innocent as she appeared. Miss Grant contacted me a little while ago. She told me she'd given Robert the impression you were one of the unfortunate victims of the explosion, so he forgot all about you. And now, if for any reason Robert should want to threaten me again, she has much evidence in her possession that he wouldn't want to come to light. I don't know the extent of it, but I know a few things. And trust me, Father would be most upset if he knew how much money Robert had siphoned off for his own use. Clubs, restaurants, his new mistress and the house he bought for her. If Robert ever discovers the truth and tries anything against you, I can assure you, he'll back off when he discovers what I know."

Matthew poured himself a cup and sat down at the table opposite her.

"So, you've come to tell me I have no need to worry? That's very kind of you." She frowned. "But I had no idea I was under any sort of threat, anyway."

"That's not the only reason I wanted to see you." Now was the time to tell her everything. And yet, he was still uncertain how she felt about him.

Tell her.

If she didn't want him then what difference would it make if she knew? And if there was a chance she still wanted him but his secret put her off, then he was better off learning that now.

"There's another thing you might or might not want to know. I can't think of another way to say this other than to be completely frank and open. So, please forgive me."

She nibbled her bottom lip, looking as though she didn't want any more revelations.

Tell her.

"There's another reason Julia's child couldn't possibly have been mine even if we'd had an affair. Shortly before I first visited Priory Hall with Hugh, it had occurred to me that if Robert was most likely infertile, there was a possibility I might be too. I took a sample and checked it under the microscope. It was similar to Robert's – decreased sperm count and poor motility. That suggests I'm infertile too."

"Oh, Matthew, I..." she paused, obviously not knowing how to finish.

But he wasn't worried for him. He'd got used to the idea. He was concerned how – or indeed, if – it affected her. She was looking at him with sympathy and her hands had fluttered, as if she wanted to reach out to him – but she hadn't. Then he noticed the ring on her finger. Not her engagement finger. But it was a ring that hadn't been there before.

"No matter," Matthew said briskly, swallowing down the disappointment, "it's just something I must accept. The only thing that's certain is that Julia's child is not mine. At least now Robert and Julia are parents, they're focusing on their child and aren't making each other miserable. I've walked away from my family and given up all right to my inheritance. That will go to the child. So, everyone can relax now. And that," He held his hands out palm upwards, "is the story of my extremely muddled and messy life."

She stared into her cup of tea. "I'm so sorry, Matthew; you didn't deserve any of that."

"Neither did you," he said, his voice catching. He'd inadvertently caused such trouble in her life.

"It wasn't your fault."

She picked up the cup and sipped the tea in silence.

So, that was that. Matthew's disappointment sank like a stone in his stomach. But what had he expected? Bethany to rush into his arms? Of course, she wouldn't.

The ring suggested she had someone special. She wouldn't suddenly announce she had a sweetheart after he'd just told her his news. Matthew had assumed if it was possible to rekindle their relationship, it would have been obvious. Bethany would have given some sign. He'd have known. But there was silence between them and a gulf so large they might have been sitting in different towns. Bethany with her ring, and him with his dignity in tatters.

He wondered whether to excuse himself and leave immediately, but he couldn't bring himself to leave. He'd never have the opportunity to spend time with her again, and he wanted to prolong it as long as was polite. Conversation. He needed to make light conversation. Don't make her long for him to leave because of this awkwardness.

"So," he said, trying to sound as matter-of-fact as he could. "Tell me about your training. How's it going?"

Her brow furrowed, presumably at the sudden change of tone, but she told him about how much she was enjoying her new life and about her very serious and bossy roommate. The enthusiasm shone from her eyes.

"I love nursing, even though it's hard, and Sister Fisher is so difficult to please."

"I've seen the way some senior nurses treat the probationers and I have nothing but respect for you all," Matthew said, his voice now completely under control, even if inside, his emotions were reeling.

Bethany looked at him and he looked down into his teacup, unable to hold her gaze. Surely, she'd see the panic inside at the thought they'd soon part and the only time he'd see her was when he ran into her from time to time in the hospital? She couldn't fail to see how much that would hurt...

"I rather think," Bethany said in Geraldine Seagull's voice, taking him completely by surprise, "that I have Peregrine Esplanade to thank for directing me towards nursing. So, thank you, Peregrine, from the bottom of my heart." There was a challenge in her gaze.

Dare he believe she'd assumed Geraldine's voice and used the name Peregrine, because she wanted him to know they still shared something secret? Or did it mean nothing? The ring told him it was just a game and meant nothing.

Well, he had nothing to lose. At least if he assumed the persona of Peregrine, they'd be more likely to part as friends rather than as the two awkward strangers they'd become.

Assuming his Peregrine voice, Matthew told her he had a surprise and fetched the picnic basket, pretending he'd made the apple pie himself and packed the basket, telling her silly stories about each item. Bethany joined in, pretending to question his cooking skills until they were giggling like school children.

While he laughed, inside, his heart was breaking. He dared not ask the one question whose answer he so desperately wanted to know.

Was there any hope for them?

He already knew the answer. Of course, there wasn't. If she hadn't been wearing a ring, and there had been a chance for them, he'd now ruined everything by telling her it was unlikely he'd ever father children. Why would she choose him? She wouldn't.

So, if this was the last occasion they'd be together, then he'd remember this time when they played at being Geraldine and Peregrine.

He'd blank out the future.

Everything was under control.

Then suddenly, it wasn't. Without thinking, he blurted out in his own voice, "Do you have someone, Bethany? I mean someone special? Someone you love?"

Stupid. Stupid. You've ruined everything.

He held his breath, appalled at his stupidity.

Bethany flinched at the change in his voice. Why had he sounded so demanding? So desperate? Why hadn't he asked Geraldine gently as if he was Peregrine?

Because he, Matthew, needed to know whether she, Bethany, had someone or not.

She sighed and shook her head. "No, I don't have anyone."

"But the ring?"

She looked down at her hand and smiled. "The ring is my mother's. It's very precious to me. Very precious indeed. Do you have someone?" Her voice was challenging. Well, why not? He'd just asked her.

"There's never been anyone for me, except you, Bethany, but I understand, you must have believed I'd deserted you. I understand you not feeling the same. But I can honestly say you are the only woman I've ever felt drawn towards. We didn't have long enough to fall in love, but if we had, I'd have been head-over-heels for you."

She stared at him. "What are you saying, Matthew? I thought for so long you didn't want me. I dared not hope you still felt the same. Are you telling me you want to pick up where we left off?"

"More than anything, but I understand if that isn't what you want after my revelation."

Bethany smiled. "I felt the same about you. If you think we can make a go of it, I'd like to try. And by the way, I've never been bothered about having children. Some people might find that rather unnatural, but the thought of childbirth horrifies me after what I witnessed years ago when my mother died."

Could this be true? Reaching across the table, he slid his hand over hers. He closed his eyes, and shivers travelled across his skin at the touch of his palm on the back of her hand. He tightened his grip and she stood, pulling him to his feet.

"If this is real," she said, "then show me."

He slipped his arms around her waist, and she locked hers behind his neck. Then he leaned towards her and placed his lips on her waiting mouth.

# Chapter Twenty-Four

Bethany broke away from Matthew and stared into his eyes. She hadn't expected this. And to think she'd believed he'd simply walked away, and all the time his brother had been manipulating him.

And now they were together again.

It was exciting... and unsettling. Bethany sensed Matthew felt it, too.

Was it too good to be true?

It was so hard to believe they could finally be together and get to know each other properly.

Matthew swallowed. "If you're having second thoughts, Bethany, please tell me now. I've spent a lifetime having something I wanted dangled in front of me, to have it whipped away at the last minute. If you have any doubts, please let's talk them through now and if we can't resolve them. Then..." He glanced at the suitcase by the door and sighed.

"I can't offer you security in the way I might once have done. And I probably can't give you children. But I believe I'll love and cherish you forever." Matthew stood; his head bowed as if waiting for rejection.

"I've never wanted a man to offer me security and I don't feel the need for children, so I won't miss those. I didn't realise until earlier when a neighbour called and allowed me a glimpse into a world I'd never noticed before how my life might turn out. Pauline talked about my father's loneliness. Her sadness. Living alone has benefits, but the happiest times of my life have been when I'm with you."

Bethany stepped forward, and linking her arms around his neck, laid her cheek against his chest. She heard his sharp intake of breath, as if she'd taken him by surprise. Matthew wrapped his arms around her tightly and pulled her close.

He whispered into her hair. "This feels so fragile, Bethany. I'm afraid I'll do something wrong and break it. I'd do anything rather than risk that."

She looked up and, with a smile, traced her forefinger around the outline of his lips.

He groaned with pleasure and closed his eyes. "Bethany, I don't think I can be so close to you and not want to kiss you."

"Then kiss me. I'm not as fragile as you think," she said, and tipped her face back ready for his lips.

A loud knock on the door made them jump apart, and they looked at each other in alarm.

Bethany checked her wristwatch and gasped. "It's Joanna. Where did the time go?" She ran her fingers through her hair and smoothed it back into place.

While she went to open the door, Matthew sat at the table, his half-empty teacup in front of him as if minutes before, he'd been drinking tea.

With a joyful shout, the children burst into the kitchen followed by a flustered Joanna, telling them to calm down. "Is everything all right?" she asked Matthew and turned to Bethany; her face wary as if she'd picked up on an atmosphere she didn't understand.

"Oh, yes, quite all right," Bethany said with a mischievous smile on her face.

"Perfectly," said Matthew with a hint of Peregrine in his voice.

Bethany burst into giggles.

"We've come to help you," Faye said. "What would you like us to do?"

Joanna placed a restraining hand like daughter's head. "No, darling, I said we were coming to see if Bethany wanted us to do anything, but it appears everything's under control. It is, isn't it?" she asked Bethany, her eyes wide as if trying to convey more than her words.

"Oh yes," Bethany said. "Perfectly under control, thank you."

"But we were going to dig in the garden," Mark said with a frown. "Can't we dig in the garden, Mummy?"

"No, not today, darling."

Joanna's gaze moved swiftly from Bethany's to Matthew's and back again. "Today isn't a good day for digging in the garden."

"But why, Mummy?" Mark scowled.

"Err, because today is the day…" Joanna paused as if trying to think of an excuse, then added, "today is the day we visit Billy and Grunt."

"Really?" Faye asked. "But, Mummy, you said we wouldn't have time to see them."

"Did I? Well, I think I might have been wrong. We actually have plenty of time."

"But we can't just leave Bethany and Uncle Matthew," Faye said. She added in a loud whisper, "We said we'd help, and you told me to always be true to my word."

"That's quite right, but in this case, we're not needed this afternoon. We'll come back another day. Now," she flashed an angry look and raised a finger to stop Faye's protest, "say goodbye to Uncle Matthew and Bethany."

"But Uncle Matthew will be back for dinner, won't he?" Faye asked. "You told me you start work on Monday, didn't you, Uncle Matthew?"

"Uncle Matthew may get called back to the hospital urgently," Joanna said, taking Faye's hand and leading her out of the kitchen.

"But how will the hospital let him know? Joanna hasn't got a telephone. We've got one. If Uncle Matthew comes back to stay with us…"

"Well, there are lots of new developments in modern medicine…" Joanna said, looking desperately at Matthew for help.

Faye frowned. "But how can—"

"Come on, Mummy!" Mark pulled Joanna's hand. "Can we go and see the goats now?"

"That's an excellent idea." Joanna's face showed relief as she smiled at Matthew and Bethany, then led the children to the front door.

"I'm so glad everything is… under control," she said, opening the door and shooing the children out.

Matthew and Bethany watched as they walked along the avenue towards the Wilkinsons' cottage, the children chattering excitedly.

Bethany put her arm around Matthew's waist and smiled up at him. "I understand you may have to return to the hospital immediately?"

Matthew returned her smile. "I don't need to be back until tomorrow morning. How about you?"

"The same." Bethany closed the door.

"So, are you going back tonight? We could go together." He kissed her forehead.

"That's true, we could. Or, we could stay here tonight and leave early in the morning."

He narrowed his eyes and stared at her. "Just to be clear, when you say, 'we', presumably, you mean you'll stay here and I'll go back to Priory Hall, then we'll travel in early tomorrow?"

"No, when I say, 'we could stay here tonight', I mean 'we'. Us." Bethany swallowed nervously. "Us, alone, together." Had she really said that? What had got into her?

"Are you certain? I'd like nothing more than to have you to myself all night, but I want you to be sure."

She hadn't expected to be sure, but yes, she realised with surprise, she was positive. "Didn't you say life dangled things in front of you, then snatched them away? Well, let's not give it a chance to take anything. We could play it safe, spend the night apart, and tomorrow, a bomb might drop on the hospital killing one of us, or both. At least we'd have spent one night together. At least if one of us remained, they'd have those memories."

"You're a very wise woman, Bethany Anderson." Matthew wrapped his arms around her.

Wise. Pauline had said Pa had described her as that. But thus far, she hadn't been wise. Merely careful. Risk-averse. Would that bring her happiness? Who knew? But surely the wise thing to do was to take this opportunity with Matthew.

"If I'm wise, I'm all the wiser for being with you, Dr Howard." She snuggled close to him, fitting her body against his. With her cheek against his chest, she could hear and feel the rapid thud of his heart.

"Now, where were we?" Matthew asked breathlessly.

"I think you were obsessing about breaking something fragile. I'm wondering if you ought to look at it differently. If you consider a muscle, it strengthens with exercise. If you don't use it in case you hurt it, it will simply weaken. We can either stand back in case we break this fragile thing, in which case, it might wither and die. Or we can just dive in and see where it leads." She kept her head tilted down, unable to look him in the eye. Would he think less of her? She'd made up her mind she was committed to him but was she moving too fast?

He placed his hand against her cheek and stroked it with his thumb. "I see. And what exactly do you mean by 'dive in'?"

She took a deep breath. "How about this for a start," she said, undoing one of the buttons on his shirt and sliding her fingers inside to draw circles on his chest.

Matthew groaned with pleasure and leaned to whisper in her ear. "And if I should do this...?" With his tongue, he traced the rim of her ear. She shivered as he undid the top buttons of her blouse, and continuing his downward journey, he placed feathery kisses down her neck to the bare skin he'd revealed. Bethany could barely breathe.

She threw her head back, drowning in pleasure as Matthew explored her body with his kisses. As every nerve on her body thrilled, she knew she'd made the right decision. He hadn't dived in, as she'd invited and taken what he wanted. No, Matthew was spending time getting to know her body and her desires.

She couldn't remember when, but shortly after they'd both half-undressed each other and her legs had almost buckled beneath her, she'd led him to her bedroom. There, they'd continued to excite each other, driving each other to the heights of passion until the early hours.


Bethany remained alert long after Matthew had fallen asleep, their fingers still entwined. Her body still thrummed with the magic. If she slept, would she wake up and discover it had been a dream?

But the warmth and smoothness of his skin against hers and the rise and fall of his chest reassured her their lovemaking had been real.

She knew she'd pay for her lack of sleep later. Sister Fisher would keep a vigilant eye on Bethany if she thought her nurse was tired.

"Tired nurses are sloppy nurses," she said when anyone dared to yawn.

But Bethany wasn't tired. She'd never felt more energised. Renewed. And loved.

But nonetheless, slightly worried. Would there be any awkwardness between them in the morning? Would Matthew hurry from the bed? Would he feel different?

Time would tell.

It was still dark but already the cockerel a few doors away was beckoning the dawn. Soon, she and Matthew would have to get ready and make their way to the station to catch the first train. Later, at Whitechapel, they'd go their separate ways. Matthew to his lodgings and Bethany to her room to drop off their bags and hurry to work.

They wouldn't have a chance to meet again until later that night but there would be no shared bed. So, until they both had time to come to her cottage again, this would be the last time she'd be able to run her fingers over his nakedness and the outline of his muscles. The last time she'd tingle as his strong hands caressed her. She intended to savour every moment of their togetherness, even if Matthew was asleep.

"Are you awake?" Matthew whispered through the dark, his words brushed her cheek like butterfly wings.

"Yes."

"Is it time to get up?"

"Not yet. But it will be soon."

He unlaced his hand from hers and with gentle fingertips, drew a sinuous line down her body. Her breath caught in her throat, and she made a small sound like a gasp.

"Then, if this is all the time we have left today, let's not waste it," he whispered into her hair.

"You were late back from Laindon this morning," Grace whispered to Bethany as they gathered on the ward.

"Nurse Chisholm! Once again, I find myself interrupted by one of your comments. I will not have anyone speak over me. This is my ward, and you abide by my rules. Is that clear?"

"Yes, Sister Fisher." Grace was horror-stricken.

"I shall be keeping a special eye on you and your probationer nurse friend, Anderson, who is looking remarkably pleased with herself today. Let's see who's looking pleased with themselves by the end of your shift. Now, if you have nothing further to add, Nurse Chisholm, shall we pray?"

Bethany lowered her head. She dared not look at Grace who'd once again got her into trouble. Still, never mind. Nothing would get her down today.

There had been no one in the train carriage that morning when she and Matthew had pulled out of Laindon. They'd held hands and even shared a kiss. And Matthew had talked about their future together.

He longed to travel to Australia to work and had suggested they go as a team. A doctor and a nurse. "A match made in heaven," he'd said.

"Of course, we'll wait until you're registered. Hopefully, by then, the war might be over."

He'd wait for her. And together, they'd go to a new continent and work.

"Amen," Sister Fisher declared, announcing a new day in the ward had begun. "Nurses Chisholm and Anderson, follow me. I have a special task for you."

Bethany dared not exchange glances with Grace. Wherever they were off to, the job they'd be given wouldn't be pleasant. Nevertheless, she wanted to skip, to sing, to shout out to everyone that she loved Matthew and one day, she'd be with him on the other side of the world.

But first, she must complete Matron's task, whatever that may be, and by the end of her shift, she'd be one day closer to Australia...

# Chapter Twenty-Five

♥

1946

Dr and Mrs Howard stood together on the deck of the Southern Star, ocean liner, arm in arm.

The crowds that had leaned against the rails waving to well-wishers on the quay were beginning to drift away once they could no longer see their loved ones.

No one had come to see Bethany and Matthew off. Bethany wondered if she might feel homesick knowing there wouldn't be anyone there to wave them off, but she'd been surprised instead, to feel a surge of optimism. Life in Australia was going to be different from anything she'd known before. She'd make friends in her new home; she'd have a new job and she had Matthew.

Stevie and his new wife, Jennifer, had waved them goodbye at Laindon Station, as had Joanna, Ben and their children. It wasn't as if she and Matthew wouldn't be missed. And when she'd left the London Hospital, her fellow nurses had bought her embroidered sheets and strict instructions always to make her bed using Sister Fisher's instructions.

Her brother and new sister-in-law would live in the cottage in Plotlands now Stevie had left the Navy. He had a job as a mechanic in the garage in Laindon and he'd told Bethany he'd visit Pa's grave regularly and update her as often as the mail would allow.

Their father had died several months after being taken into hospital. At first, Bethany had been distraught until she'd realised he had now attained the peace that had eluded him while he was alive.

"Sad?" Matthew asked, placing his finger beneath her chin, and tilting her face up towards his.

Bethany shook her head. "Quite the opposite, I'm so excited. But how about you?" Obviously, Matthew hadn't told his family he and Bethany were married, but he hadn't told them he was about to embark on a journey halfway around the world.

"If you mean, am I regretting not telling my family? No. I don't have any family... well, except you, of course." He bent and kissed the tip of her nose. "It's a shame Hugh couldn't come to see us off but quite understandable. With Joan about to bring baby number three into the world, he wanted to stay close to her."

Bethany had been wary of Hugh after her first encounter with him in Priory Hall, but she had to admit, he'd changed. He'd crash landed a few years back and had taken many months to be able to walk again with the aid of sticks. Joan had encouraged him to get up and start exercising when he'd wanted to give up. However, it had been the birth of his first child that had changed him the most. He was now an enthusiastic father to two girls and was hoping for a boy next.

Matthew bit his lower lip.

"What is it?" Bethany asked, recognising something was wrong.

"Nothing..." he paused. "It's just that both Robert and Hugh changed beyond recognition when their children were born. I was wondering if at some stage in the future, you would resent me—"

"No, never!" she said sharply. "It's you I want. And one day, if we both decide we'd like a baby, let's adopt. Let's give a child who's lost its parents a chance. We could provide the home we never had and together, I bet we could give a child a better childhood than either of us had."

"You're so wise, Mrs Howard. Have I ever told you?"

END

Dawn would be thrilled if you would consider leaving a review for this book on Amazon and Goodreads, thank you.

If you'd like to know more about her books, you can find out more from her newsletter on her website: dawnknox.com

**About the Author**

Dawn spent much of her childhood making up stories filled with romance, drama and excitement. She loved fairy tales, although if she cast herself as a character, she'd more likely have played the part of the Court Jester than the Princess. She didn't recognise it at the time, but she was searching for the emotional depth in the stories she read. It wasn't enough to be told the Prince loved the Princess, she wanted to know how he felt and to see him declare his love. She wanted to see the wedding. And so, she'd furnish her stories with those details.

Nowadays, she hopes to write books that will engage readers' passions. From poignant stories set during the First World War to the zany antics of the inhabitants of the fictitious town of Basilwade; and from historical romances, to the fantasy adventures of a group of anthropomorphic animals led by a chicken with delusions of grandeur, she explores the richness and depth of human emotion.

A book by Dawn will offer laughter or tears – or anything in between, but if she touches your soul, she'll consider her job well done.

If you'd like to keep in touch, please sign up to her newsletter on her blog and receive a welcome gift, containing an exclusive prequel to The Duchess of Sydney, three short humorous stories and two photo-stories from the Great War.

**Following Dawn:**

Blog: https;//dawnknox.com

Amazon Author Central: Dawn Knox https://mybook.to/Dawn Knox

Facebook: https://www.facebook.com/DawnKnoxWriter

X: https://twitter.com/SunriseCalls

Instagram: https://www.instagram.com/sunrisecalls/

YouTube: https://tinyurl.com/mtcpdyms

# Also by Dawn Knox

**A Cottage in Plotlands**
The Heart of Plotlands Saga – Book One
London's East End to the Essex countryside - will a Plotlands cottage bring Joanna happiness or heartache?
1930 – Eighteen-year-old Joanna Marshall arrives in Dunton Plotlands friendless and alone. When her dream to live independently is cruelly shattered, her neighbours step in. Plotlanders look after their own. But they can't help Joanna when she falls in love with Ben Richardson – a man who is her social superior... and her boss.
Can Joanna and Ben find a place where rigid social rules will allow them to love?
Order from Amazon: https://mybook.to/ACottageInPlotlands
Paperback: ISBN: 9798378843756   eBook: ASIN: B0C4Y9VZY9
Also, **A Canary Girl in Plotlands, A Reunion in Plotlands** and **A Rose in Plotlands**

**The Duchess of Sydney**
The Lady Amelia Saga – Book One
Betrayed by her family and convicted of a crime she did not com-

mit, Georgiana is sent halfway around the world to the penal colony of Sydney, New South Wales. Aboard the transport ship, the Lady Amelia, Lieutenant Francis Brooks, the ship's agent becomes her protector, taking her as his "sea-wife" – not because he has any interest in her but because he has been tasked with the duty.

Despite their mutual distrust, the attraction between them grows. But life has not played fair with Georgiana. She is bound by family secrets and lies. Will she ever be free again – free to be herself and free to love?

Order from Amazon: https://mybook.to/TheDuchessOfSydney

Paperback: ISBN: 9798814373588   eBook: ASIN: B09Z8LN4G9

Audiobook: ASIN: B0C86LG3Y4

Also, The Finding of Eden, The Other Place, The Dolphin's Kiss, The Pearl of Aphrodite and The Wooden Tokens

Printed in Great Britain
by Amazon